Published by Story Garden, Columbus. StoryGardenPublishing.com
ISBN: 9781735587585 (paperback)
ISBN: 9781735587578 (ebook)

Cover design by James T. Egan, BookflyDesign.com
Managing editor: Diane Callahan, QuotidianWriter.com
Developmental editor: Angela Traficante, LambdaEditing.com
Copy editor: Lia Fairchild, LiaFairchild.com

Sign up for notifications of upcoming releases by Jordan Riley Swan at JordanRileySwan.com

For A.J., the Chase to my Tyler – K. C. Norton

AN INVITATION

You are cordially invited to the
—UNWEDDING VOW—
a nine-book series
about one promise
made by ten strangers
who have vowed to never say their vows.

But love has a funny way of slipping through the cracks
of even the most jaded hearts,
as each member of the Unwedding Vow is about to discover.

PROLOGUE

This is why I'm never getting married, Tyler thought as he looked around the packed reception hall.

The noise, the busy crush of people all around, the forced smiles and pleasantries . . . It was all exhausting, and none of it was even aimed at Tyler. How much worse would it be if he were the one sitting at the table at the front of the room? Right now, Ethan Cartwright was next to his new bride, guzzling what was, by current count, a fourth glass of champagne; he looked surprisingly miserable for a man who was supposed to be celebrating the happiest day of his life.

"Have you talked to them yet?" asked the woman seated to Tyler's right. Her copper-colored bob just brushed her jawline, and she had a soft accent that stood out to Tyler's Midwestern-attuned ear. French, perhaps?

Tyler nodded nervously and took a sip of his water. "Mm-hmm." He tried to think of something else to add, but he barely knew the groom, and the bride, Kylie, was a distant cousin from his mother's side. If his mom hadn't insisted he represent their side of the family, he'd have stayed in his dorm and avoided his cousin's wedding at all costs. Apparently, though, this was the price he paid for being within driving distance and having his parents foot the bills for college. Nobody in his family could stand dealing with Kylie's side, and while his mom had insisted that *one* of them ought to be there, she'd announced that there wasn't enough cabernet in the world to entice her to Aspen for the event. Tyler had drawn the short straw and been sent as their representative.

Ironic, considering that his anxiety rendered him functionally mute at most events.

"She's a total bridezilla," the woman next to Tyler observed, crossing her pale arms and leaning back in her seat.

"Oh, um, is she?" Tyler fiddled with his napkin. From his limited interaction with his cousin, Tyler couldn't argue the point, but insulting a woman on her wedding day seemed . . . wrong.

"I'm Amy, by the way." She held out her hand, and Tyler wiped his sweating palm on the thigh of his rented suit before taking it. "And you are . . . ?"

"Oh, geez, sorry. I'm Tyler." He laughed, then wondered why he was laughing. He was a mess at the best of times, and there, surrounded by nine strangers at the reception table—plus the crowd spread across the oppressive, expensive-looking room—his nerves had only grown worse. Kylie's father was a movie agent of some sort, and there were a number of starlets clustered at tables closer to the front. He even thought he might have spotted Henry Cavill schmoozing by the bar, although a quick Google search had revealed him to be a stunt double.

Amy gave him a shrewd look. "And let me guess, Tyler. You're single?"

He felt himself wilt under her scrutiny. "Yeah."

"Oh!" she exclaimed. "That probably sounded super shi—uh, crappy of me. I just can't help noticing that this seems to be the rejects table. We're way at the back where nobody will have to deal with us. We're the cast-offs." She grinned at him and raised her champagne glass in a toast. "Here's to being the ones that bridezilla doesn't want in her wedding photos!"

"I'm guessing that you're not friends with Kylie, then," Tyler said.

Amy, who was in the middle of taking a sip, nearly choked. "Tyler, are you secretly funny?"

His best friend, Xavier, had warned him that women sometimes saw weddings as a chance to pick up single guys. Xavier's advice always had to be taken with more than a few grains of salt. None-theless, Tyler had steeled himself to be flirted with and to hopefully not make a complete idiot of himself on the off-chance that anyone did.

To his relief, Amy didn't reach over to lay a hand on his shoulder, or even scoot her chair closer to his the way women sometimes did when they wanted to get a guy's attention. Not that she was unattrac-tive—quite the opposite, in fact—but she seemed like she might be in her mid-thirties, and he was barely twenty-one. Plus, her attitude felt more friendly than flirty.

Amy twisted around in her seat to look up at the dais where the wedding party sat. "I barely know either of them, to be honest."

"Same," Tyler admitted.

"That's no surprise," added a velvet-voiced, dark-skinned man leaning in and joining the conversation across the round table. "How many people are here? Five hundred?"

"More," said a tanned, and rather beautiful, blond woman two seats to Tyler's left. She, at least, fit in with the rest of the crowd, aside from her clothes. They seemed affordable, unlike the upscale fashion of the other guests.

"Nobody has that many close friends," the man added. He adjusted his tie; now that Tyler looked closer, he realized it was covered in a star-and-planet pattern. "I haven't seen Ethan for years, and I only know him because his dad helped me out when I was a teen. I'm willing to bet it's the same with most of the other guests."

The man sitting directly next to Tyler smiled awkwardly. "I've never even *met* either of them. I worked with Kylie's father *once*, and that was more than five years ago."

Tyler turned his head to meet the man's eyes and froze. He was a little older, his figure a little stockier, and his black hair just a little thinner than it was in the posters Tyler had stuck to his bedroom walls in high school, but even so . . . *Oh my God. Is that Austin Jericho? No, it couldn't possibly be him . . . Why would the star of a science fiction cult classic be stuck back here with the rest of us cast-offs?*

"Let's take a poll." An older, gray-haired gentleman spoke up, raising his glass of wine and smiling sardonically. "Who's only here because someone expected them to bring a good gift?"

Nobody raised their hands.

"Are you someone of moderate fame who thought they might make an interesting business connection here?"

This struck Tyler as impolitely specific, and he peeked at the Austin Jericho lookalike to see how he was taking this pointed comment.

To Tyler's surprise, several of the other hands at the table went up, including that of the older man himself.

"Well, isn't that something?" the older man said. "You know, I think we might be at the most interesting table at this whole event. What do you all say to a little game I like to play when meeting new people? An occupational question-and-answer game?"

Tyler squirmed in his seat. Whatever the rest of these people were going to say, it would be ten times more fascinating than anything he could come up with.

The older man adjusted his wineglass. "Shall I go first to prime the pump, so to speak?" A general murmur of assent rose from the cluster of guests, and he folded his hands in front of him. His eyes sparkled as he looked around the table. "I've built my life around the principle that things become better with age."

"Wine," Amy said immediately. "You work in wine."

The man laughed. "That was quick! But you're correct. The bride's father is an excellent customer of mine—in fact, if you make use of the open bar, you'll be sampling some of my favorite vintages."

"The cabernet is amazing," said the gorgeous blond woman from earlier. She lifted her glass of ruby-red wine to demonstrate.

Tyler hadn't bothered to visit the open bar, knowing that being tipsy increased the likelihood of him embarrassing himself.

"I guess it can be my turn to play the job game," the blond woman continued, taking a sip of wine and tapping her fingers on the table-top. "Let me see . . . I love to do my favorite thing on camera."

"And I film her," said the dark-haired girl in glasses sitting beside her.

One of the other guys, Reed—who had loudly introduced himself to everyone when they'd first sat down—snorted. "That's one way of putting it."

The Black man in the starry tie sitting next to Reed steepled his fingers. "Is it something to do with a hobby?" he asked the blond woman.

She nodded.

"Ooh," Amy said suddenly. "Something that people don't expect?"

Another woman, this one in her forties, who had been as silent as Tyler until that moment, asked, "Something, perhaps, that people assume a woman can't do?" Tyler heard an edge in her voice.

The blond woman beamed. "Exactly."

"Are you a gamer?" asked a punk-rock-looking girl sitting beside Amy. Tyler squinted at her. Wasn't that Kylie's sister? He hadn't memorized his whole family tree, though, and he had more cousins than he could count. What was she doing at the cast-offs table? She should be up at the main ones. No, it couldn't be her.

"I would answer, but that would be cheating." Reed smirked. "I know who you are, Elizabeth. I'm just surprised no one has recog-nized your voice from your channel."

"Thank you for not giving too much away." Elizabeth's voice dripped with sarcasm as she shot Reed a disdainful glare. Tyler tried to stop himself from smiling. There was definitely a story there.

"How is your job being filmed if we're supposed to recognize your voice but not your face?" the punk-rock girl asked thoughtfully.

"Trucks." When Austin spoke, the word came out so softly Tyler wasn't sure he'd heard it. *Can I call him Austin? It feels like I should call him Mr. Jericho.* Who was Tyler kidding—he wasn't going to talk to Austin at all. He probably wouldn't even tell Xavier that he had sat next to a famous actor, because then Xavier would yell at him for not getting an autograph. "You have that truck YouTube channel," Austin elaborated.

"*Ding ding ding!*" Elizabeth exclaimed. Her friend chuckled.

"Oh my God, wait—are you The Pickup Chicks?" Amy gasped. "I'm obsessed!"

"Guilty." Elizabeth winked.

Amy squealed, and it took ten years off her in a moment. "I totally subscribe!"

"What do *you* do?" Elizabeth asked her.

Amy paused for a second, fiddling with the ivory tablecloth. She tossed her hair and raised an eyebrow as if what she was going to say was tawdry. "I'm surrounded by players all day."

Elizabeth pointed to Reed. "This one knows all about players, don't you, Reed? Do you recognize Amy here?" When he narrowed his eyes as if he were about to let loose a snarky response, Elizabeth turned her attention back to Amy. "Let me guess, you work in the gaming industry?"

"In a way." Amy reached for her champagne.

"Board games?" someone else asked.

"Warmer, but think old school."

"A-arcades?" Tyler ventured.

"We have a winner!" Amy cried, and the rest of the table applauded. Tyler sank lower into his seat, smiling shyly. It occurred to him that by guessing correctly, he'd probably just volunteered himself to go next.

But what am I supposed to say? I work in construction. Painting buildings. They're going to tell me I'm boring and laugh in my face! How was he supposed to make that sound interesting or fun? When they realized how dull he was, even the outcasts would shun him.

"I bring people's fantasies to life," Reed bragged with an eyebrow wiggle, taking over the next contestant slot.

Tyler sighed in relief, happy to have an extra few moments to work on his answer.

"Video game design?" Amy asked.

"Close but not quite. I specialize in miniatures . . . I can create anything I've imagined with computer-level precision." Reed grinned. "I've worked with LEGO, Hot Wheels, even Days of Wonder. Pretty cool, right?"

Elizabeth coughed loudly into her fist. It sounded like she had said *grown man who plays with toys for a living*, under her fake coughing attack.

"And you two are rivals?" Amy pointed between Reed and Elizabeth.

They scoffed in unison.

"Hardly," Reed said.

"I film useful, informative videos about my work," Elizabeth retorted. "I repair complex, functional machines. Which is definitely *not* the same as what he does."

"All you're really getting paid for is ad revenue," Reed grumbled.

"And all you're really getting paid for is making tiny models of things," Elizabeth replied. "How is that any better? At least my projects *work*."

There were only four people left, and Tyler was beginning to quietly panic. Austin had already passed, but only because most of the other guests recognized him. Tyler wouldn't be able to worm his way out that easily. Besides, everyone knew that only one person in a group got a free pass from the conversation, and if Tyler tried to skip now, he would just look like a weirdo. The girl who might have been Kylie's sister answered that she was in a band without even trying to make it a guessing game.

All eyes went to the Black gentleman next to Reed, as if they could sense he was going to go next. "Let's see." He rubbed his chin, making a big show of coming up with his hint. He delivered it in a booming voice that would've carried all the way to the back of the house if they'd been in a theater. "My name is Dalton Young, though I usually go by another name, and I manage a bunch of clowns."

"Restaurant owner," Reed said at once.

"Shopkeeper," Elizabeth countered.

"I think you're underselling him," the wine guy said thoughtfully. "CEO?"

"Not exactly."

"But you are a business owner," Amy pressed.

"Yes. And some people might say that my work is"—Dalton's lips quirked up ever so slightly, as if at some private joke—"a real juggling act."

He does something in show business, Tyler thought, but he wasn't brave enough to speak his guess aloud.

"It's obviously something corporate. No offense, but *boring*." Reed gave the man's job a thumbs-down. "I think we can agree that my job is more interesting than sales. I'm winning so far."

"Winning what?" Elizabeth demanded in exasperation. "According to whom?"

Tyler cringed on Dalton's behalf, but privately, he thought Reed had given up too easily, as Dalton's mannerisms were a little too theatrical for the average businessman. Besides, his suit didn't fit very well. It was most likely a rental. Wouldn't a full-time businessman own a suit of his own?

I bet he performs in a circus, Tyler thought, but he couldn't make himself follow through on the urge to speak. Besides, he was in the spotlight now. He wanted to get his turn over with.

"And you, Tyler?" Dalton asked. "Do you care to challenge the inimitable Reed's dominance in the job arena?"

"It's not a contest." Amy seemed to have picked up on Tyler's nerves.

"I'm, er, covered in colors all day," he blurted. Before the words were even out of his mouth, he'd thought of ten more interesting ways to phrase his clue, but of course, those words hadn't come to him when he still had time to form them. How come he only got smarter *after* his words were already out of his mouth?

"You paint buildings," Reed said. Without waiting for Tyler to respond, he carried on. "Don't get me wrong, you all have great jobs, but I think we can all agree that I won."

"You don't *win* a conversation," Elizabeth insisted. "That's not how they work, Reed."

Tyler turned to the only person who hadn't spoken yet: the forty-something woman in an unapologetically tweed-based ensemble sitting directly across the table from him. She seemed as bored with Reed's antics as Reed claimed to be with everyone else's jobs. The woman looked like a librarian or a schoolteacher, but he bet her job was something really unusual, and she was as tired of being put in a box as Elizabeth was of being put in hers.

He should speak up. Should point out that the woman hadn't taken her turn yet. Why did he always clam up when it came to speaking in public? On one hand, the worst that could happen was that Reed would give Tyler another thumbs-down for standing up to him.

On the other, Tyler still couldn't force himself to open his mouth.

"Let's put it to a vote," Reed said.

"Only you would turn a meet-and-greet into a popularity contest," Elizabeth groaned.

Tyler leaned toward Amy, who had been nice to him so far. "Um, what about her?" he whispered with a gesture across the table.

"Yeah," Amy said loudly, drawing everyone's attention. "She hasn't gone yet."

Reed turned to the last player of the impromptu employment game, looking only slightly apologetic. "Sorry, my bad. What do you do?"

The woman in tweed tucked a strand of her pin-straight hair behind one ear. "I study the interplay between celestial bodies and the relative expansion of the universe."

For the first time since the game had started, the whole table fell utterly silent, and the chatter of the other guests filtered through.

Elizabeth let out a sudden bark of laughter and slapped her palm on the table. "You're an astrologer!"

"Astrophysicist," she corrected immediately. "Astrologers are frauds."

"You're an honest-to-God rocket scientist!" Elizabeth howled, wiping tears from her cheeks. "Oh, that is *priceless*. Who's winning now, Reed?"

The look of utter stupefaction on Reed's face was enough to send the rest of the table into peals of laughter; even Tyler let himself chuckle audibly.

"Well, I don't actually work with rockets . . ." the astrophysicist began.

"You won the contest hands down," Amy said, dabbing her napkin against her blotchy cheeks. "Don't quibble over semantics."

"Excuse me," said a cold voice from just behind Tyler. The whole table turned to look, and he pulled his shoulders up to his ears, feeling like a kid who was about to be sent to time-out. The former Kylie Arnold, now Kylie Cartwright, was standing with her hands on her ivory-silk-clad hips, glaring at the table.

"Hello, darling, and congratulations," the winery owner said, clearly biting back another chuckle.

"Aww. *Thank you.*" Kylie opened her eyes wide and batted her eyelashes. She even put one hand to the front of her dress as if his words had touched her heart. "I'm so glad that you could all be here on *my special day*. It's super nice to see you all enjoying yourselves back here. But maybe, since it is *my day*, you could keep it down just a teensy-eensy bit? So that you don't distract from the main event?" She glared at the punk-rocker, who seemed to shrivel up beneath the force of her gaze. Tyler made a mental correction—she was definitely Kylie's little sister.

"Oh, my goodness, were people looking back here and not at you?" Amy covered her mouth. "I'm so sorry!"

Kylie swung to face her. She was clearly trying to determine whether or not Amy was teasing her, but when Amy's apologetic expression never faltered, the newlywed batted her eyelashes again. "Thank you all for being so understanding," she said.

As she walked away, Tyler guiltily adjusted his napkin.

"That right there?" Reed said, pointing at Kylie's retreating form. "That's why I'm never getting married."

"That and your personality," Elizabeth mumbled.

Reed rolled his eyes. "Are the guys in your life lining up to put a ring on it?"

"Oh, don't you think I'd make a good wife?" Elizabeth asked, widening her blue eyes in fake surprise. "But I've dedicated my whole life to making myself desirable to men! Nothing matters more to me than the male gaze." She pretended to gag. "Oh, God, I think I made myself sick just saying that."

"Not everybody's made for relationships," her quiet friend murmured. She seemed to be lost in her own head rather than trying to derail whatever longstanding argument had spawned this rivalry.

Tell me about it. Tyler's fingers, still plucking at the edge of his white cloth napkin, suddenly stilled. While he had no interest in marrying anyone like Kylie, that was because of her personality, not because he thought that all women were as passive-aggressive as his cousin. It would be nice to get married someday.

Except that if he wanted to get married, he would have to start by going on a date.

Which meant asking a girl out.

Which meant talking to a girl he liked without having a total melt-down or saying something unforgivably weird.

So, yeah, the quiet girl was right. Not everyone was built for relationships.

"That's fine by me," Elizabeth said, reaching for her glass of wine again. "My work is my husband."

"Amen," Amy added, although she suddenly looked more self-conscious than she had all night. "Who has time for that?"

"I don't particularly like the idea of putting so much energy into another person who might suddenly vanish without a word," Dalton said. His rich, performer's voice had a distinctly bitter edge. "But what about you, winemaker? You strike me as the sort of man who believes in true love."

"I do," the winemaker said. His smile had faded, and he looked older than he had before. More careworn. "I married the love of my life, but . . . she's gone. I won't be marrying again."

The table sobered up, and Amy looked over at the older man with true empathy on every inch of her face. "I'm so sorry."

"There's nothing to be done about it, is there?" he asked.

Tyler wished he could think of something to say, but when it came to death, he was at even more of a loss over what to say than he was the rest of the time.

Fortunately, Elizabeth didn't seem to have that problem. "Listen, you silver fox, you can't go breaking my heart like this—owning a winery and believing in true love? You sound perfect for me."

His smile softened. "I thought you were married to your work?"

"I like to keep my options open." Elizabeth grinned at him before turning her attention to their table's own private rocket scientist. "What about you, Madame Astrophysicist? How are the dating options in your field?"

"About the same as everyone else's." A muscle pulsed in the older woman's temple. "Theoretically fine, but in practice, men are condescending and pathologically incapable of thinking about anyone's needs but their own."

"Yikes," Elizabeth said with a chuckle. "Sounds like that one's fresh."

The astrophysicist nodded, her expression softening only slightly. "It's *possible* that I may have broken up too recently to view the subject of marriage objectively."

"It's not an issue of who's to blame," Kylie's sister said with all the gravitas of a woman twice her age. "Dating is a drag."

I wouldn't know, Tyler thought miserably.

"Dated a lot, have you?" Amy asked in amusement.

The younger woman pulled a face and shook her head. "Are you kidding? I'm going to be a rock star. Ain't nobody got time for that! You know what I'm talking about, right?" She looked halfway down the table to Austin, who recoiled. "Fame and marriage don't mix."

Austin's eyes widened, and Tyler tried to make himself say something to draw attention away from the cornered man. The actor was obviously trying to lie low—he was probably tired of strangers asking him for autographs and selfies.

"What?" Kylie's sister looked around at the members of the table, all of whom were focused on anything but the actor. The only exception was Reed, who was now examining Austin intently.

"Hang on, are you—" he began.

Elizabeth cut him off. "Well, since my wine source won't have me, I guess I'll have to run away with Austin. Unless you're not getting married, either?"

Austin's shoulders relaxed slightly. "Nope. Not planning on it."

"Then it's settled." Elizabeth lifted her nearly empty wineglass. "Since none of us ever plans to walk down the aisle, I think we should toast—"

"Hang on," Reed interrupted. "You're the one leaving someone out this time. What about you, Tyler?"

"Oh, uh." Tyler flattened himself back against his chair, as if by holding very still he could blend in and disappear. "Well . . . I mean, you already said that you were never going to get married, Reed, so I guess I won't either."

Everyone stared at him, and Tyler felt the heat rising in his cheeks. He'd only meant to go with the flow, not make what sounded like a pass at Reed, but the words were already out. That was the trouble with talking: you said things that weren't *quite* the things you meant, and then you either had to wallow in your own uncomfortable silence or trip over your own tongue in a vain attempt to clarify your original meaning.

"So, Tyler and Reed can get together, and the silver fox, Austin, and I can move into the house next door," Elizabeth said at last. "It sounds like the rest of you will have to fend for yourselves."

Tyler resisted the urge to run from the table. *I should take a vow of silence. Every time I open my mouth, I say the exact wrong thing.*

Elizabeth held up her wineglass again. "To Tyler, for being the second person at the table to leave Reed completely speechless."

"I'll drink to that." To Tyler's surprise, Reed grinned as he lifted his tumbler. Maybe the guy had a sense of humor in there somewhere after all. "And to the Unwedding Vow. May none of us ever find ourselves dragged down the aisle," Reed added.

Obediently, Tyler joined the toast. It sounded like most of the other guests had good reasons for not wanting to get married. Out of all of them, Tyler was the only one taking the vow out of necessity rather than choice.

He took a sip from his glass of water and set it back on the table with a thump. At least his commitment to the vow was a sure thing. He couldn't imagine the circumstances under which he'd be able to hold a girl's attention for two minutes, much less the rest of his life.

CHASE

Chase was sick to death of naked bodies. Or *nude human figures*, as her art professor would say, but that was just semantics.

As their final model of the semester walked into the art room, Chase no longer wondered what lay beneath his white bathrobe. She already knew, and she'd already seen it—heck, she'd already painted it a dozen times over the course of the semester. His face was cute enough, for sure. The legs poking out from beneath the terrycloth robe were shapely and covered with fine black hairs that would be difficult to capture on the canvas. The model's slippers whisked across the tile floor with every swaggering step as he made his way to the small dais. He stepped up to the simple folding chair in the center of the room and shrugged off the cotton robe, answering the unasked question.

Either it was colder in the room than it felt, or he was a "grower and not a shower."

Chase shook her head. *No need to look so cocky, buddy. We've seen it all before.*

Her eyes were already skimming the rest of his body, not in search of titillation but to determine the colors she'd be pulling from her palette. She'd purchased a new set of oil paints for this very occasion and was already tending toward burnished bronze as a base, then a storm gray with a splash of cerulean to capture the shadows and dimples of his torso.

"Now remember," Professor Roberts said gravely, "this piece counts for thirty percent of your grade. You'll have two hours a day for the next week to finish the project. You're welcome to work in oil, watercolor, or acrylic, and you aren't limited to using colors that are true to life. I want this to be a celebration of the human body. You aren't restricted to capturing what the eye can see; your job is to find the person beneath."

Chase had to resist the urge to roll her eyes.

It must be weird for the model, Chase thought, *to sit there in the buff and pose while the professor talks shop.* Judging by his expression, though, he didn't seem to care either way. Maybe he was a nudist.

Chase dug through her backpack to find the tin of oils, shoving aside charcoals, colored pencils, watercolors, a set of fine line markers she'd used in her cartooning class last semester, and the box of crayons she kept on hand just in case. With the added weight of the sketchbooks, her bag was already groaning at the seams. The previous bag had finally succumbed last semester when Chase tried valiantly to add a woodblock carving set into the mix.

Art in Living Form was Chase's least favorite class of the semester. In fact, it was probably her least favorite class of all time. She'd considered dropping it after the first week, but Professor Roberts was a great instructor, even if she did tend toward the romantic in her project briefings. There was something about staring at a stranger's butt for two hours a day that felt . . . well, honestly, dull. Chase preferred to sketch people as they went about their day, preferred images that could capture the personality of her subject. Nudes were more about depicting the body than the spirit of the person inhabiting it.

Despite her frustrations, she had a nearly perfect grade in the class. It wasn't only that she was a bit compulsive about mastering every challenge in front of her—although there was that too. Technically, she could skip this project and still pass the class, but it would cost

Chase more than her pride to do so. Her scholarship required a GPA of at least a 3.5. Low GPA, no scholarship. No scholarship, no art school. Chase wasn't gifted at math, but that equation was simple enough.

And so, she painted butts.

"You'll be turning your paintings in on Friday, and we'll be scheduling meetings to discuss them over the next few weeks. I want to make time for a one-on-one with each of you before finals. Does anyone have any questions about the project that aren't covered on the syllabus?" Professor Roberts looked around the room, and the model shifted in his chair. "Nobody? Well, please let me know if that changes, and remember that I'm always available for a private meeting if something comes up. Let's begin."

With a name like Zalinski, Chase's one-on-one meeting would almost certainly come at the bitter end, but she had resigned herself to that a long time ago. *It's not like you're going anywhere for spring break,* she told herself. *Now you're just* looking *for reasons to whine about this class.*

She adjusted her wood-stretched canvas and the angle of her paint-spattered easel before setting her phone in the drawer along with her fresh brushes and the tin of paint tubes. Now that she was really focused, she could see she'd need a few more colors than she'd first considered. A bright yellow would reflect the light on the model's collarbone, and his hair would need more than a flat black. *Should I add his curls with a blue undertone?* she mused. *Or maybe a purple—something unexpected that could still catch the contours?*

Chase was about to start opening her paints when her phone vibrated in the tray. She glanced at it, frowning. Why would Sarah call her during the school day? Maybe one of the boys had gotten his little hands on the phone again. It wouldn't be the first time. Other people got butt-dialed. She got nephew-dialed.

Ignoring the phone, Chase reached for the bronze paint. Some of the other students were sketching on their canvases in pencil first, but Chase preferred a little spontaneity in the process, to make up for the fact that nudes were getting so damn tedious.

The phone buzzed again, and Chase capped the paint. If it really was Sarah calling, it had to be an emergency.

"I'm sorry," she mumbled in the general direction of Professor Roberts, backing toward the hallway with her phone in hand. "I'll be right back."

"Thank God you're there!" wailed Sarah the moment Chase picked up. "I've been trying to call Mom, but she hasn't answered . . . You know how she is, but I can't wait much longer, and—"

"Sarah. Calm down." Chase took a steadying breath and willed her sister to do the same.

"Sorry," Sarah whimpered. "It hurts."

"What does? You okay?"

"I'm in the hospital."

Chase was beginning to quietly panic, but she forced herself to take steady breaths, even though the room suddenly felt airless. She didn't want to upset Sarah any further, especially if it was serious. "Tell me what you need."

"I have appendicitis, and they're about to take the damn thing out. Can you get ahold of Mom? Somebody needs to watch the boys."

At least it's only her appendix, Chase thought. *That isn't too dangerous, is it?* The word "hospital" had her imagining all sorts of vivid, gruesome possibilities. People had their appendixes out all the time, right?

"Where are the little monsters now?" Chase asked.

"With a neighbor. Michael's still deployed, and you don't have a car, so if Mom can't make it, I really don't know what I'm going to do." Sarah sniffled into the receiver. "Sorry, I'm . . . I don't know what I'll do if she . . ."

"I can get a ride up," Chase said. "That way you wouldn't have to put up with Mom being, you know, *Mom*."

"I don't know how long it could be. I might be in and out for the surgery, but I could be laid up for a week." Sarah's tone turned hopeful. "And the cost of the bus ticket . . ."

Chase shook her head as if her sister could see her. "That doesn't matter. I'm on my way."

Sarah hesitated. "What about school?"

She had a point, of course.

"I can do most of my work remotely," Chase assured her. "The only one I'm not sure about is this life modeling class. But that's not as important as my nephews."

There was a hum from the other end of the line, followed by some muffled conversation. Sarah's voice returned clearly a moment later. "They're taking me back now. It would be amazing if you could come, but if you can't, call Mom. I'll deal with her if it means that I have some help. Love you."

The line went dead, and Chase frowned at the phone. It would be great to see her sister, and she wouldn't wish an appendectomy *and* her mother on her worst enemy. It would be too much like one of those shows on the nature channel, with an injured gazelle limping away from an approaching lioness. Mom was all right in small doses, and when you could fight back, but not when you were down for the count. *Grow up, Chase. Think about your choices, Chase. Actions have consequences, Chase.* Nobody needed that kind of attitude when they'd just had a vestigial organ removed.

"Everything all right?" Professor Roberts asked, and Chase swung around.

"My sister's having emergency surgery." She held up the phone, as though that would explain things. "She lives in Boulder, like an hour from here, and I was hoping to go help her. She's got two boys, and her husband's in the Marines and currently deployed."

Roberts winced. "I just have the one rug rat, and it takes both of us to keep up with him. But what about your painting?"

Chase swallowed. "I was hoping I could get an extension . . .?"

"That doesn't seem fair to the other students," Roberts said, crossing her arms. "The syllabus is pretty clear about the deadline."

With another glance at her phone, Chase bit her lip. Perhaps she'd been a little too quick to volunteer her babysitting services. *Sorry, Sarah, but if I lose this scholarship, I'm done here. Good luck with Mom.*

"Although . . ." Roberts leaned toward her with a secretive smile. "Your work this semester has been exceptional. I've been secretly hoping that we might be able to submit your final project to one of the national exhibits in New York. It would look great on your résumé, and there's prize money involved. And the school *does* love to see its students succeed . . . Gives Dean Pollock something to put in the school's newsletter, you know."

"One of *my* paintings?" Chase asked, pointing at herself in shock. "They're really not—"

Roberts clicked her tongue. "They're spectacular! None of this imposter syndrome nonsense, if you please."

"It's not me, exactly. This is just, um . . ."

Roberts waited.

"It's kind of my least favorite class," Chase blurted. When Roberts frowned, she hurried on. "I don't mean you! I mean the subject matter."

"I wouldn't have been able to tell that from your paintings. Your work is so emotional." The professor's eyes twinkled. "Well, let's make a deal: you get a one-week extension on your painting, and you let me send in one of your *least* favorite paintings to the show."

Chase nodded eagerly. At least her professor hadn't failed her on the spot.

"I hate to ask," Chase said, "but Sarah could be laid up for at least a week, and I'll need time when I get back. Can I have two?"

"Really pushing the boundary of my good graces, huh?" Roberts lifted an eyebrow. Could eyebrows be foreboding? Hers were.

Chase gave a weak smile, hoping it would be charming enough to buy her the extra seven days.

"If I give you an extension, you can't be so much as an hour late with it."

"Cross my heart." Chase did that very thing as she spoke.

Roberts tapped one paint-stained finger against her cheek. "This means that your one-on-one will be postponed until after the break, but I doubt I'll make it through the T's by then anyway, so it's not like it will impact our timing. Fine, you can have the extra days."

"Thank you," Chase said, clasping her hands in front of her, her phone still clutched awkwardly between them. "I know it's a big ask, but my sister and I are really close."

"Do you want me to arrange for the model to sit for you that week? He only costs a hundred dollars an hour."

"*Only?*" Chase gasped, before she could stop herself. Two hours a day for five days? She'd have to sell a *useful* organ. "I mean . . . no, thanks, I think I'll figure something out on my own." She was already struggling with the math on how to pay for her bus ticket to Boulder, and the thought of coughing up a thousand dollars for a ten-hour modeling session was giving her the old anxiety of math facts drills.

"Fair enough. But I want you to use a live model, not a photo. If you use a flat medium like that, you'll only capture what the camera shows you. Tell your sister that I hope she feels better soon. And good luck with the boys." Roberts chuckled. "You're going to need it."

They went back into the classroom together, and Chase repacked her bag. Maybe she could find a classmate who would be willing to help be her model—it wasn't as if she had a lot of guy friends. Besides, the idea of asking one of the boys she knew to pose naked for her made her skin crawl. It would send the wrong impression.

I'll just post something in the dining hall, she decided, *and hope I don't turn into a freak magnet.*

With a grunt of effort, Chase hoisted the monstrous backpack onto her shoulders and left the classroom, along with the hundred-dollar-an-hour male model, behind.

TYLER

It was a terrible thing to be scared all the time. Frightened that he'd say the wrong thing and embarrass himself. Nervous that he'd draw too much attention, and people would begin to expect too much. Terrified that he'd be injured either physically or emotionally, left exposed for the world to judge.

Tyler Wilson would have liked to say it all stemmed from an emotional trauma in his youth. He wished he could point back to some unbelievably embarrassing moment and go, *"This! This right here is why I don't speak up, volunteer, or otherwise make waves."*

There was nothing in his past like that. His childhood had been uneventful and beautifully quiet. Tyler had no good reason for it, but he hated risks. When other kids climbed to the top of the jungle gym, walking on top of the monkey bars instead of swinging across them as they were designed for, Tyler could do nothing but watch them from across the playground and shake his head. He would've reprimanded them for their foolhardy behavior, but that would have taken too much courage. It was easier to watch from the ground and be thankful that nobody was making *him* do it.

Now in college, the same safeguards of youth stayed in play. Old habits dying hard and all of that. Which was why they were in the long line at the student cafeteria.

"Dude, why'd you pick this one?" Xavier groaned. "This guy always takes forever to ring people up. I could probably do it faster than him at this point. Look over there. That one's like half the size. Let's jump over to it." He pointed to the other cashier's line. The one with the *redhead*.

More importantly, the one with the *flirty* redhead.

Tyler adjusted his grip on his tray and shrugged. "It's not like we're in a rush."

Naturally, Xavier was right. The other line was moving fast. The flirty redhead was twice as efficient as the guy currently punching in numbers on the beat-up plastic cash register at the head of their line. Maybe three times more efficient, considering their guy was constantly having to look on a cheat sheet for the prices. But this line had one thing the other didn't: there was no chance of Tyler getting flirted with.

It happened every time without fail. As she checked Tyler out, she also "checked him out." It might have been flattering to most guys, but all it did was put him on edge. The moment her eyes landed on his face, he found himself praying that the cafeteria floor would open up and allow him to descend into the earth somewhere deep out of sight. Somewhere he wouldn't have to make *eye contact*. He wanted to buy his apple and leave, not feel like she was going to take a bite out of him. Even a little bit of attention made Tyler uneasy, and Xavier would have a field day with it if he caught her in the act.

"So," said Xavier grandly, "classes are wrapping up. Got any big plans for the break? You're going on that cruise, right?"

"No. My parents are going," Tyler muttered. "I'm . . . I'm busy."

Xavier snorted. "Surely the guy you work for won't stop giving you jobs if you're away for a couple days. It's not like you're leading a construction crew, anyway."

"It's not that."

The line moved one place forward, but Xavier was too busy squinting at Tyler to notice. "Not a big swimmer? I mean, you don't have to actually go in the water. Those ships have, like, a million things to do."

"Swimming's fine," said Tyler stiffly. "I like it just fine. In a pool. With filters and chlorine and lifeguards. But there are sharks in the open water, and besides, do you know how many people get sick on cruise ships? They're like breeding grounds for bacteria."

Xavier sighed, finally noticed the gap in front of him, and shuffled up in the line. "Then what's the plan?"

"I'm going to stay in the dorms for the week. I'm not exactly loaded, you know."

"I could spot you some cash," Xavier offered. "Of everyone I know, you're the most likely to actually pay it back." He paused for a moment and added, "Even if it does take a long time."

"And there's the problem with loans . . . you always have to pay them back."

"Well, don't think I'm going to start tossing twenties at you like some stripper. You ain't *that* good-looking." Xavier looked around again. The redhead's register had no line at all now. "This is stupid. Come on, we're going over there."

Tyler swallowed. "You first. I forgot my silverware. Get us a table, okay?"

Xavier trotted off, and Tyler wandered away from the slow line to grab a set of plastic utensils from the stainless-steel rack full of condiments and extras. He looked down at the apple and sandwich on his tray and realized neither needed the crappy plastic fork and spoon. Sighing, he grabbed a small bowl of pasta salad so he wouldn't look like a complete idiot.

He considered returning to the longer line, but then the teasing would become all about *that*. There was no winning. Instead, he dragged his heels over toward the flirty cashier, hoping his friend would have already finished checking out and moved on.

No such luck.

"You're a real whiz with numbers," Xavier said to the redhead, making that cheesy duck-face he always did when he was trying to hit on unsuspecting victims. "Maybe you want mine?"

Dear Lord, if thou art merciful, you will strike us both down with light-ning where we stand.

The cashier turned to Tyler. Judging by her expression, she was not impressed by Xavier's attempt at flirting. When she saw him, however, her face broke into a smile just for Tyler that shifted the pattern of freckles on her cheeks. As always, his eyes fell to his tray, though this time they paused in their descent exactly long enough to read her nametag. *Jenna.*

"Is this guy for real?" Jenna asked. A movement of her hands brought his eyes back up in time to see her point a thumb at Xavier. "He's got worse opening lines than a Reddit post."

Tyler grimaced. "I'm afraid so."

"I bet his Instagram is nothing but shirtless pics taken in the bathroom mirror." She smirked. Xavier shifted as if he were going to protest but then scoffed out a self-mocking laugh; she must have nailed him on first guess.

"Oh, I, uh . . . I don't really know." Tyler tried not to look at Xavier but couldn't help himself. His friend had taken a few more steps back and was watching the conversation intently. "I'm not really on social media."

"But you have a phone, right?" asked Jenna. "Everybody's got a phone."

"Of course." Tyler shoved his tray forward. The apple rolled around in a wobble before bouncing to a stop at the edge. "Can I, um, pay for these?"

Jenna rang him up with the liquid-smooth keystrokes of someone who had a thousand hours of practice, her eyebrows lifting when she saw the total. "What do you know . . . those are the last three digits of my phone number."

"Crazy," Tyler said, sliding his student ID in her direction.

She took his card but didn't swipe it. "What are the odds, right?"

"Like, one in a thousand," he replied. "The, er, the ID has a chip, but I think it can still be swiped."

"Almost seems like a sign." She tapped the corner of his card on her palm. "My horoscope said something like this was going to happen today. Didn't mention a tall and handsome stranger, though."

"It's a debit card, if that matters."

"Maybe I should write the other four digits of my number on the receipt, too, and fulfill the prophecy." She leaned closer to Tyler, giving him a cheeky wink while hooking her thumb toward Xavier again. "But promise you won't share it with that guy, okay?"

"Better not give it to me. To be on the safe side," Tyler squeaked. She wasn't swiping the card. Why wasn't she swiping the card? His lizard brain was screaming at him to snatch it out of her hand and bolt for the exit. If he did that, though, he might get in trouble for stealing, and then he'd have a record with the campus police. Were they real cops? Could a campus cop arrest you? Why wouldn't she swipe the stupid card?

"Aww, you're a shy one!" Jenna exclaimed. "That's adorable. What's your major? No doubt a quiet office-type thing."

Tyler squeezed his eyes shut and silently counted backward from ten. "Do you need me to pay cash instead?"

"Oh, right, d'oh!" Jenna tapped her head with her palm and swiped his card before handing it back over. "Let me know if you change your mind about my number. I'm here until five."

Tyler couldn't get away from her fast enough.

"Wait up." Xavier hurried after him. "So . . . that was interesting."

Tyler nodded but kept fast-walking to the table farthest from the half wall that separated the dining area from the food area. He flopped into a seat under the huge corkboard that ran along the back wall. It advertised jobs, research opportunities, internships, and an assortment of random dorm-related junk that people were trying to pawn off on their fellow students. Tyler stared at it as if enraptured, pretending to read, but mostly just giving himself an excuse to avoid eye contact.

Apparently, this wasn't going to work on Xavier. He dropped his tray opposite Tyler and settled his elbows on either side of it, putting his fingers together in a little steeple. "As I was saying, that was interesting."

"Hmm." Tyler shoved the corner of his turkey-and-Swiss-on-wheat into his mouth and chewed away.

His friend threw his hands into the air. "Oh, come on! What's wrong with you, man? She's cute. She's nice. She was straight-up *into you*. Why'd you run away?"

"I'm really hungry," Tyler mumbled through his mouthful of bread.

"That girl might be thirsty for you, but I don't think *she* thought far enough ahead to post her number on the board." Xavier chuckled. "Get your ass back out of that chair and go get it from her."

"She's not *thirsty*," said Tyler, appalled. "She just flirts."

"With you. She didn't want to give *me* the time of day."

"You cornered her at her job. She doesn't have to flirt back."

Xavier's lips pulled together in a grimace. Tyler was right and he knew it. "Couldn't help myself. She's good-looking, but you're right. I won't do that again," Xavier said, his tone softening. His friend wasn't normally a creep, but sometimes he overstepped and needed a reminder where the path was.

He went to pick up his own sandwich, a meatball sub monstrosity that wouldn't close all the way, when he seemed to think of something. "I don't want to make this too weird for you, but . . . are you gay?"

"Uh. No." Tyler blinked in surprise. "I mean, I don't think so. Are you going to ask me out next?"

"Ace, maybe?" Xavier rested his chin on his hand, staring at Tyler thoughtfully. "Because otherwise, I don't get it, and I don't want to be a jerk if that's what's going on. You remember Amanda? She's totally asexual, and I've always respected her, never have a bad thing to say, you know?"

"I don't know what you're talking about," Tyler said, peeling the plastic off of his silverware. "What does that have to do with me?" The sandwich was already gone, and he might as well eat the pasta salad. He *had* paid for it, even if he hadn't really wanted it in the first place.

"I'm talking about the fact that you never date. Like, ever."

"I've dated," said Tyler defensively. He stabbed at a coiled noodle in his pasta salad but didn't take a bite.

"Name one date you've ever been on. *One.*"

"Prom," Tyler immediately replied.

Xavier rolled his eyes. "Right. Sure. Becky Blackstone. Because you were *so* into her."

Tyler pulled his shoulders up to his ears like a turtle receding into its shell. "She was nice."

"Was she? Because if I remember, she told you she was going with you and what time to pick her up, and you just went along with it. Are you really calling that a date?"

Technically, there had been nothing wrong with Becky—except for the fact that she'd had literally no interest in Tyler. Not as a date, certainly not as a boyfriend, hell, not as a human being. A bunch of freshman girls had decided that they wanted to crash the upper-classmen prom and convinced single boys to take them. In Tyler's case, Becky had *ordered* him to take her.

"She singled you out because she knew you didn't have a date. Did she dance with you?"

"No," muttered Tyler, sinking down in his chair in the vague hope of disappearing beneath the tabletop. Becky had ditched him the moment they'd walked in the door, and he'd only caught brief glimpses of her for the rest of the night as she danced with about six other guys. She hadn't come back to him until the end of the night when she was ready to be driven home. He hadn't bothered to get out of his dad's pickup truck to walk her to the door. No way was there going to be a kiss on the stoop.

Which was fine. Tyler hadn't been particularly interested in Becky, either. As far as he was concerned, she was the perfect prom date. She hadn't expected anything from him, and taking her to prom had gotten some of his friends off his back for a while.

Judging by Xavier's expression, the statute of limitations had expired. "Are you really telling me that was your number one romantic experience?"

Tyler was forced to tip his hand. "It's the *only* one."

"Why?" asked Xavier. "I mean, if you don't like girls, that's one thing . . ."

"I do." Tyler let go of his fork and flopped back. "I have to erase my website history all the time. It's the real-world ones that are a problem."

"Have you never met someone you liked?" Xavier seemed incredulous. "High school was small, dude, but now you're swimming in a sea of college girls."

Tyler shrank back further still. If it had been anyone else, he would have run away, but Xavier was his best friend. His only friend, really. He might be brash and forward, but he actually cared about Tyler. This was his way of trying to help.

Even with Xavier, though, he had to be careful. What if Xavier decided he was too much of a weirdo and ditched him altogether?

"I get nervous," Tyler said at last.

Xavier considered this. "Kind of like how you get when we talk about traveling? Or going out? Or doing anything that might be perceived from *any* angle as a misdemeanor?"

"Yes." Tyler breathed a sigh of relief; Xavier was coming around. "Yes, exactly. What would be the point of trying to flirt? Either I'd hit on someone who thought I was a creep, or she'd be too into it and want to go too far, too fast."

Xavier laughed so loudly that Jenna could probably hear him from across the common area. "Tyler. Buddy. Is that *really* how you think dating works?"

"That's how it works for you," Tyler said.

Xavier was still chuckling. "I'd be offended if you weren't such a nerd. Maybe we need to start small. Maybe we need to work on your *risk* aversion before we work on your *girl* aversion."

They'd been so close to a reasonable understanding, but now Tyler could see this conversation was about to go off the rails. "We don't need to work on anything. I'm perfectly happy."

Xavier ignored him, twisting around to examine the job board. "Here!" he exclaimed, plucking a flyer off its pin and handing it to Tyler. "Why don't you start with that?"

Tyler looked down at the ad. "Nude modeling? Are you crazy?" He nearly flung it away in his hurry to get it out of his hands.

Xavier picked the paper up and read over it. "Why not? It's impulsive. It's interesting. It would be a great conversation-starter at parties."

"I don't go to parties," Tyler reminded him. "How is this starting small? You're asking me to show my . . . my *stuff* to a complete stranger."

"Starting small? Ha!" Xavier shook his head. "You gotta see that you played yourself with that line. Thanks for saving me the trouble. But seriously, why not?"

"No freakin' way."

"Yes way!" Xavier jabbed at the paper. "You're going to do it, or else . . ."

"Or else what? You're going to make fun of me for not stripping down for this Chase guy?" Tyler scoffed. "You make fun of me all the time. I think I can take whatever weak tea insults you pour on me over this."

Xavier looked Tyler in the eye, not blinking for an uncomfortably long time. *It's like he's trying to see into my soul*, thought Tyler with a shudder.

"Tyler, you're my buddy, and you know I love you—but it's time to do something outside of your comfort zone. You always have excuses for why you can't try new things. 'Can't go on the cruise. Have to work.' 'Can't get her number. She's only being friendly.'" Xavier took a breath and shook his head. "As much as I love being the fun half of this rad duo, it would be nice not to be the only one with wild stories to tell. You make a great audience and all, but maybe I'd like to hear a tale or two. So get out there and bring a wild story back with you, or I'll have to think about finding another raconteur."

"A what?"

"Somebody who tells stories really well. Someone who has *adventures*." Xavier widened his eyes significantly.

Tyler had felt signs of panic when Jenna flirted with him, but this was different. Xavier might be joking. But what if he wasn't? They'd been friends for most of Tyler's life, and while Xavier seemed to have no problem making friends among a certain social set, Tyler had stayed in his comfort zone. On the rare occasion that he went to parties, he usually sat in the corner with a cup of soda and waited while Xavier made the rounds. He didn't even *drink*.

What if he really was boring? What if Tyler was so boring that Xavier actually . . . left?

He's your only friend, the nasty little voice at the back of Tyler's head told him. *If he gets bored with you, you're going to be all alone.*

Tyler looked down at the paper, and with a sudden burst of anger, he crumpled it up in his fist. Xavier didn't get it.

"You're acting like we're breaking up," Xavier said. "All I'm asking is that you do something different. Something a little unexpected. Let some dude paint you, or get Jenna's number and go for a coffee—one coffee, Tyler. She's not going to climb you like a tree just because you stood still long enough."

Tyler stared down at the crumpled flyer still clenched in his fist.

"Do this one thing," Xavier said, "and if I ever bug you about playing it too safe again, just remind me of the time you let a guy paint your butt and I'll back off. I mean, paint a picture of your butt. He won't be *touching* your butt."

If only Tyler could destroy his frustrations as easily as that stupid flyer.

Gently, Xavier pried the crumpled paper out of Tyler's hands and flattened it out against the tabletop. "You owe it to yourself to take a risk or two, you know?"

Tyler wasn't sure he owed it to himself to take risks, but he *did* want to keep his friend. His *only* friend. If this was what it took, fine. He'd do it.

Without a word, Tyler pulled out his phone and began to draft an email.

"That's my guy," Xavier said, grinning.

CHASE

Chase's experiences with online dating had been dismal at best. Apps seemed to bring the weirdos out of the woodwork. Sure, she'd met all kinds of interesting and perfectly nice guys along the way, but people also used the relative anonymity of their profiles to exhibit genuinely creepy behavior that most sane humans kept under wraps.

That was nothing compared to the responses she'd gotten to her ad for a nude male model.

She'd already had to report two guys for sending unsolicited nudes to her university email—not full-body shots, either. Photos that were rather more *narrow* in scope. She'd also gotten a couple of randomly homophobic messages from people who thought she was a guy. Only one person who'd responded seemed like a relatively normal person, although his email had been minimal at best, barely three lines in total. If he actually showed up, she wasn't going to let him get away, time and quality of options being what they were. She needed the full week of modeling, and if this guy backed out, she would have to waste precious time finding someone else who wouldn't require her to carry pepper spray at all times.

Or worse, cough up a grand for the classroom model.

Chase already had paints laid out, easel assembled, and a fresh sheet draped over the podium for the derriere of her mystery man. She'd have felt weird putting her own naked butt on something that had been graced by who-knew-how-many other models, so she'd brought one from her dorm room. Now all she had to do was wait.

At two minutes to five, the classroom door echoed off a timid knock. Chase hurried over, yanking the door open. "Hey," she said. "You must be Tyler. Welcome. Come on in."

The guy on the other side looked nervous and more than a little taken aback by her abrupt greeting. Clutched in one fist was a very crumpled copy of her flyer, pushed hard to his chest, and after a moment, he held it out like it was a ticket for a circus show.

"Hi. Um, is Chase here? He didn't say anything about there being other people around . . ." Tyler's voice wobbled and cracked with nerves.

He's adorable, Chase thought. *Look, he's blushing.*

"I'm Chase," she said, holding out her hand. "Pleased to meet you."

Tyler blinked at it. "You're a girl." He actually took a step back as he spoke, his feet carrying him farther into the hallway behind him.

"Says so on my birth certificate and everything." She opened the door wider. "Don't worry, I'm not a biter. Get in here."

Tyler fidgeted nervously. He was definitely a flight risk. Before he could bolt, Chase took him gently by the arm, folding her hand in his elbow as if he were escorting her into a school dance, though she was having to almost push him at the same time.

"I *really* appreciate you showing up here." She gestured into the room with her free hand, indicating her easel. "This portrait is a huge part of my grade, and it means a lot that you're willing to help me. The only other people who responded were creeps and weirdos."

Tyler looked down at the place where their skin touched and did not reply. Instead of trying to run, he appeared to be rooted to the spot.

"I can't pay you in money, but I brought snacks," Chase continued, edging into the room and bringing Tyler with her. "A wealth of snacks. An *abundance* of snacks. And who doesn't like snacks? You'll be so happy you stayed."

"What all is involved?" Tyler asked warily. "The emails weren't entirely clear."

They had been, in Chase's opinion, and it wasn't like the scenario was terribly complicated—but he was so painfully, obviously shy. Some animalistic part of her was rising up and going into protection mode. Why were wallflowers always so attractive?

No problem, Chase reasoned. *I have enough confidence and personality for both of us.*

It was probably a good thing she hadn't told him she was a girl in the email, or he'd have backed out ahead of time.

"Really, all I need is for you to sit for a couple hours a day through the end of the week." She shrugged, trying to make the whole thing sound like it was an everyday event. She waited until the door was closed and well behind them before releasing his arm. "We'll do thirty-minute blocks with ten-minute breaks in between, for a total of about two hours a day. Don't worry, I won't have you doing any crazy poses."

"Do I have to be completely naked?" Tyler fidgeted with the strap of his bag, looking back at the door. "Can't I wear shorts or something?"

"It's a nude portrait," Chase said. The fast-talking hadn't worked, so now it was time to rip off the band-aid and hit him with the blunt truth.

"But can't you . . ." He gestured at his groin. "You know, imagine it? Or paint a fig leaf or something?"

"I totally understand. I'm not sure I could do this if someone asked me." Chase gave Tyler her most winning smile, the one she reserved for getting out of arguments with her mother or convincing her nephews to go to bed.

She could understand his trepidation, to some extent. Being in a room, even a semi-public one, with a fully nude guy she'd just met wasn't exactly easing her nerves. She did have a can of pepper spray near the paints, but it was little more than a pacifier. If she wanted

Tyler to leave, all she'd have to do was open the door and stand back.

"Look, this isn't exactly comfortable for me, either," Chase said, mostly to make Tyler feel like they were on equal footing. "What about this: let's find a pose that you're comfortable with. Will that make things go easier for you?"

"I doubt I'll be comfortable with anything," Tyler admitted. "But, um . . . I promised I'd do this, so let's get it over with." He squeezed his eyes shut. "What do I do?"

The classroom model had either brought a robe or been provided with one, so Professor Roberts had listed it as one of the things Chase would need to bring with her. Her own closet wasn't exactly full of men's clothes, so she had been forced to borrow one from her sister. It was Michael's, a big gray plaid affair with oversized pockets. Not the most formal thing in the world, but at least it was better than the one she used in the dorms. That one was bright pink and thigh-high, a joke gift from Sarah in freshman year. Tyler would probably not have found the humor in it. Not that his broad shoulders could have fit her robe, anyway.

Chase handed Michael's pilfered bathrobe to Tyler and pointed to a changing screen at the back of the room. "Just stack your clothes anywhere once you're done. When you come out here, we'll get you posed lickety-split."

After a moment's hesitation, Tyler sighed and took the robe, dumping his backpack by the podium.

He took a long time behind the pale-yellow room divider, so long that Chase wondered if he simply planned to spend the whole two hours back there, hiding behind the wobbly screen. When he reappeared, the gray robe was stretched over his frame and pulled tight around his middle. He kept it pulled closed with one shaking hand, as if he didn't trust the overly tight belt of matching wool to keep his modesty intact. Off-white socks rode just below his ankle.

Chase clicked her tongue. "Hate to say it, Tyler my guy, but you have to lose the socks too."

He paused and bent over, pulling off one and then the other. His bare feet padded back behind the screen for another minute. Was he folding them, or had the loss of the last article of clothing finally broken the little courage she was seeing in him?

Eventually, he reappeared.

"Ready?" she asked.

He squeaked.

Chase patted the seat. "Come on. Nothing to worry about."

Tyler shuffled closer and plopped onto the podium, staring down at his bare toes.

"Listen, Tyler, you don't have to do this," Chase said, although the voice in her head was screaming, *Don't give him an out! Roberts will never agree to give you another extension!* That was probably true, but if it really upset him this much, she shouldn't force him. "You're practically going to fall off the pedestal, you're shaking so bad."

Maybe it was the softness in her tone. Maybe it was the kindness of an out that wasn't going to emasculate him. Whatever the reason, he shook his head to her offer.

"It's like diving into a pool, right?" Tyler said shakily. "Or ripping off a band-aid. You do it all at once, and . . ."

He squeezed his eyes shut and yanked the robe off, tossing it to one side. Chase's eyes widened. He really had no reason to be embarrassed, from what she could see.

Her best bet was pretending he was still fully dressed and that nothing was out of the ordinary. *The opposite of the advice they give you when you're doing big presentations,* she thought wryly. *Imagine that your whole audience is wearing sweatpants and bulky turtlenecks . . .*

"Let's turn you this way," she said.

Tyler opened his eyes, hiding himself with his hands as he followed her instructions. He had to be naked, but there was no reason to leave him exposed like he had been, not if it made him that uncomfortable.

"You can sit to the side like this," she said, gesturing to one thigh until he draped it to one side. Chase was careful not to touch him. She'd probably get a better pose if she did, but she had been on the receiving end of too many Grabby-McGrabbers in her life to not respect his boundaries. "Yeah, that's great. And turn your head this way. I want to be able to see your profile, but it's probably better if you don't have to stare at me the whole time, right?" She gave him a comforting laugh.

"Yeah," Tyler muttered. "Thanks. Sorry I don't know what I'm supposed to do."

"You're actually being insanely accommodating. Is that comfortable?"

Tyler sat up straighter, lining up his chin with his left shoulder while turning his eyes toward her. "This is okay for me."

"Then it works for me too," she assured him.

Now that he was in position, Chase went back to her stool, adjusted her easel, and allowed herself to observe Tyler for the first time.

He sat with one shoulder facing the easel, almost as if he'd been sitting with his back to her and she'd just called his name. The top of his butt was visible over a rumple in the sheet, and she could see a bit of his chest and just enough of his flat stomach that his abs were exposed. His face was in three-quarters profile, his eyes wide with nerves.

I can't see his feet from the far side of the podium, she thought. *Poor guy —I could have let him keep the socks.*

If she'd been trying to sketch him, Chase would have focused on Tyler's upturned nose, his expressive eyes, and the nervous energy that radiated off of him as he sat with his back to her. She'd have framed the rough outline of his dirty-blond hair, which somehow managed to be both short and unruly.

Nudes were supposed to be different. She couldn't just catch the surface of things, the flurry of his shy movements and the nervous twitching of his hands. Chase had to look for the things taking place beneath, like the interplay of muscles under his farmer's tan, or the small scar over his left shoulder blade that had faded to a pink pucker of new tissue.

She let her gaze drift down to his shoulders and the tight, nervous curve of his spine. With the other model, she'd wanted to go more traditional, taking only the barest liberties with her color palette. Tyler already seemed more human to her than the paid guy had. Chase found herself wanting to highlight the planes and curves of his body with blues and greens and purples—cool colors, to soothe his nerves. He wasn't afraid, just self-conscious. Painfully so.

Her eyes dropped to his hands, and she smiled as she sifted through her paints. "What do you work in?"

"Huh?" Tyler jumped a little at the sound of her voice.

"You have paint on your hands." She would start with a peach base, she decided. Then a darker hue to show his farmer's tan, before she let herself experiment with the cool tones. "Do you prefer oils? Acrylics?"

He smiled, finally relaxing a little.

"Something funny?"

"Just thinking of a conversation I had at a wedding recently. And to answer your question, I work for a home remodeling company. I guess the answer is usually semi-gloss. But some clients prefer matte. Almost always latex, though."

Chase laughed, and Tyler's smile widened at her approval. *So he has a sense of humor, at least.*

"Should I wash my hands off?" Tyler asked and started to move off the pedestal.

Chase shook her head. "No. Absolutely not. I'll leave them in. It's kind of magical, in a weird way, to see them there. The paint will kind of . . . bleed into the painting, if that makes sense."

Tyler chuckled. "Not really."

He was definitely less anxious now, although he kept squirming.

"Can I ask you why you agreed to do this?" She snatched up the small pencil she barely used in the class, and her hand found the canvas, sketching out a blocky form of his general pose. Normally, pencils were a no-no for her, but this way she could at least get him back in roughly the same posture after their first break. "Doesn't seem like you are all that eager to be here. Not that I'm complaining, mind you. Just curious."

"It was . . . a dare, I guess," Tyler admitted. "I've been pushed out my comfort zone. Thrown out, more like."

"Hopefully, you don't bounce on landing." Chase built up the shoulders a little bit. Based on Tyler's physique, house remodeling was a good workout. "Who tossed you to the wolves?"

"My friend." Tyler looked back at her. "Or at least I thought he was."

"Trying to one-up each other, huh?" Chase teased.

"Um, not exactly. He's not the kind of guy who needs encouragement. He said that I needed to do something interesting. It was this or ask a girl for her number."

"So, let me get this straight," Chase mused, tapping the pencil against the edge of her other hand. "Your options were to either talk to a girl for, like, one minute, or get undressed for a complete stranger for roughly ten hours over the course of a week?"

"I hate hearing it put like that." Tyler blushed. "But yeah."

"She must have been scary as all get-out."

"She's actually cute." The admission seemed to pain him. "But I'm not great with girls, and I thought you were a dude, so . . ."

Chase set the pencil down and was about to uncap the tube of green paint when the door swung open, and a janitor backed through, whistling merrily while she pulled her cart along with her.

Tyler curled up into a ball, his mouth open in horror. Before the janitor could turn around, Chase was already moving. She sprinted the ten feet that separated her from Tyler and scooped up the large sheet hanging down the sides of the pedestal, tossing it around his shoulders in a makeshift toga.

"Excuse me," Chase said, striding purposefully over to the custodial worker, doing her best to keep the woman's eyes on her rather than on the podium where Tyler cowered. "I'm so sorry, but I'm using the room today. It's for a project. Professor Roberts gave me the key."

"I didn't realize," the woman said. She shot quick glance over Chase's shoulder and smiled ruefully. "I'm so sorry to interrupt . . . whatever I'm interrupting."

Chase sidestepped and passed the woman, getting the custodian to put her back to Tyler.

The woman seemed to be in no hurry to leave. "I'll just empty the trash cans, if you don't mind."

Tyler shook his head, eyes wide. Chase caught him glancing to where the robe hung, clearly planning his getaway.

Chase couldn't let that happen. "If you leave me the fresh bags, I'll take the old ones around to the dumpster when I'm done. It's no trouble."

The custodian shrugged. "Works for me." She dug around on the cart for a moment, and Chase nodded soothingly to Tyler. Once the bags were in her hand, Chase did a body-block on the door until she could close it at last. This time, she locked it behind her.

"Oh my God," Tyler gasped, still swaddled in the sheet like a shy babushka. "I never thought it was possible to die of embarrassment, but now I'm seriously wondering."

Chase smiled as she returned to her seat. "On the bright side, now you can tell your buddy that you were naked in a room with two women today."

Tyler choked out a laugh. "Yeah, that'll upgrade me to *raconteur* for sure."

"Huh?"

"Never mind."

"Listen, I know that this is weird for you." Chase looked down at her brushes. "But I can't tell you how much I appreciate it. My whole grade rides on this portrait, and even if this is my least favorite class, I need the A. If my grade drops, I'll lose my scholarship, and then . . ." She drew her finger across her throat with a grimace. "I'm out."

Tyler's head emerged from the sheet, although he still kept it wrapped around the rest of him. "Well, I guess I survived a random encounter with a stranger already. Might as well keep going, right?"

Chase rearranged herself, hoping that Tyler would follow her cues. After a moment, he shrugged the drop-cloth off and returned to his previous position.

"For what it's worth," Chase said, "you're braver than, like, half the guys I know."

Tyler swallowed, looking over at her again. He wasn't the best model, given that he was incapable of holding still for more than two seconds at a time, but he appeared to be a genuinely nice guy. "You think?"

"Absolutely."

"Did everyone in your class have to track down a model?"

Chase met his eyes for a split second, her brush frozen on the canvas. "Nah, only me. I'm picky about who I paint."

"You mean people who are absolutely terrified?" Tyler joked.

"Gotta get my kicks in somehow." Chase shook her hair out of her eyes. "Actually, it's because I missed class last week. My prof gave me an extension. My sister had emergency surgery, so I was in Boulder helping her out."

"Oh my God." Tyler looked shocked. "Is she okay?"

"It was pretty minor, actually, but she has two boys, so . . ."

"You're an aunt?" Tyler asked. "I've got two niblings of my own. They're fun, right? When I'm around them, I get to do all the cool parts of being a dad, and then when they start screaming I can hand them back."

"Tim and Justin basically never stop screaming, but they're pretty cute. And actually, they're good kids, they're just . . . *loud.* Anyway, that's why I had to figure out my own situation."

"Why painting?" Tyler asked. "In general, I mean."

Chase smiled. "It's what I'm good at. It's what I'm supposed to be doing. I guess it sounds pretty, y'know, *woo woo* to put it like that." She waved the fingers of her free hand in the air. "Or religious, or whatever. I don't mean it that way. It's what feels right."

He nodded, swinging his bare feet back and forth. She debated telling him to try to stay still, but thought they should stick with baby steps, at least for day one.

"Why remodeling?" she asked in return.

"It pays the bills. I'm studying civil engineering, and financial aid is only getting me so far."

As Chase began to paint the outline of his arms, she realized that some of Tyler's fidgeting wasn't only nerves; he was shivering. She got up, shaking the cramps out of her hand. "Let's take a break for a minute. You look cold."

He shrugged gratefully into his robe, and Chase tossed him a bag of chips.

"What's this for?"

"I promised you snacks, didn't I?" She opened a second bag for herself, lying on the floor to give her back a rest.

They ate in silence except for the crackling of the bags and the crunch of chips. When they were done, Chase got back on her stool, and Tyler shrugged out of the robe without being asked.

They didn't speak for a while. Chase found herself falling into the routine of painting, considering the sweep of Tyler's spine, the jut of his shoulder blades, the sharp line of his jaw. By the end of their two hours, he was starting to slouch from being stuck in the same pose for so long, and her hand had long since progressed from the first sting of cramping to feeling downright arthritic.

"Maybe we should wrap this up," she suggested. The whole base of the painting was done, blocked out into recognizable shapes topped with blocks of color that lacked any sense of detail. She could see it growing into the finished piece, but it was a long way from done.

"Can I see?" Tyler asked as he hurried back into the borrowed robe.

"You can see it when it's done, but only if you keep coming back," Chase promised with a knowing smirk. She packed her things up while he changed back into his clothes, then propped her canvas in a corner for safekeeping. He spent a lot less time getting dressed than undressed, and by the time he reappeared, Chase was still only half cleaned up.

"Do you need any help?" he asked.

She shook her head. "You've helped me a lot just by showing up. You're doing me a huge favor. My GPA and I really appreciate it."

He nodded nervously, glancing at the podium again before stuffing his hands into his pockets. "Well, um. Same time tomorrow?"

"See you here," Chase said, trying to sound cheerful. She abandoned her packing job for a minute and went over to him, touching his elbow lightly. "You're not going to ditch me, right?"

Tyler shook his head emphatically, flushing scarlet again. *If that boy isn't careful, he's going to pass out from the blood rushing to his head all the time.* Now that he was dressed again, it was tempting to tease him a little more, just to see him blush. It wasn't okay to tease a guy who was feeling shy and overexposed. But a fully-clad and disarmingly adorable guy?

No. She couldn't push it. Not when her grade was on the line.

As he scurried out of the room, Chase allowed herself a small sigh. Tyler was an obvious sweetheart, but she was willing to bet hard money that she'd never see him again. He'd clearly had to psych himself up just to stay the first two hours; by tomorrow, he'd have come up with some excuse for why he couldn't possibly sit for her again.

I wonder if Roberts will give me twenty percent credit for twenty percent of a painting? she thought morosely, changing out the trash bags before saddling up with her monstrous backpack.

TYLER

The walk up the stairs to the second floor of the art building for the second day of modeling was one of the hardest Tyler had ever done. His feet wanted to go one way, down and out of the building, but thoughts of Chase kept him slogging up the concrete. Not because of how cute she was—though, there was that. Not because of how funny she had been when she attempted to calm him down—though, that was endlessly sweet. But because of those last words she had said: *"You're not going to ditch me, right?"*

Those were the same words that ran through his mind every time some girl made an excuse to leave him at the punchbowl at a party, or used him to make some other guy jealous, or for a ride, or money, or whatever they wanted from him at that moment, only to leave the second they got it.

"You're not going to ditch me . . .?"

Like Becky at the prom the moment they went through the double doors, or Jane during their science project at the end of senior year, or Marie the moment he'd brought the beer over to her place to find he was the third wheel as she introduced him to the guy she had been dating.

"You're not going to ditch me?"

It was the mantra that drove him all the way back to the wooden door under the plaque on the wall that declared the room as Art Studio Three. It ran through his mind while the second hand of the hallway clock circled around, sweeping his nerves into a tight bundle, clicking off the minutes until Chase showed.

His pocket buzzed. His first thought—that she was calling to cancel on him—would have normally come as a relief. He was surprised to find he would be disappointed if it were the case. His feelings were mixed when he saw who it actually was.

"Where are you, dude?" Xavier asked when Tyler answered his phone. "I've been knocking on your door for like ten minutes straight."

"I'm out," Tyler reminded him, "on your stupid dare. Talk fast—I'll need to go as soon as she shows up."

"Ooh, so you got Cafeteria Girl's number? Way to grow a pair, Tyler!"

Tyler pinched the bridge of his nose and leaned back against the locked classroom door. "You mean Jenna, not Cafeteria Girl. She's a person, you know. And anyway, that's not who I'm waiting for. No, I . . . I did the other thing."

"What other thing?"

"The *other* thing. You know." Tyler lowered his voice, though not one student had come or gone in the hall since he had arrived five minutes earlier. "The *modeling* thing."

"The nude painting!" Xavier hooted with glee. "And what, did Jenna want to watch or something? I mean, you do you, buddy."

"Not Jenna. Chase. Chase is a girl. The artist. She's the one who posted the ad. I thought she was a guy, but—"

"*You're posing naked for a girl?!*" Xavier's laugh was so loud that Tyler had to hold the phone away from his ear. "Epic. Classic. Truly legendary. How much are you getting paid, you whore!" His gleeful laughter doubled.

Tyler's shoulder slumped. "I'm not getting paid."

"Not even taking you to dinner? You're an easy date."

"It's not like that," Tyler protested. "I've been naked almost the whole time she's known me."

"Exactly!"

"I've got to go. She could be here any minute."

"What does she look like?"

"What does it matter?" Tyler wanted to hang up, but wasn't this what Xavier had wanted? Tyler had proven that he wasn't boring. If this was all it took, he could be interesting for four more days.

"Just seeing if I should start answering the same ads when I see them. She single?"

"I don't know. Maybe? Look, that's not why I'm here."

"If she's single and she's good-looking . . ."

"I didn't say she was good-looking."

Xavier's voice turned sly. "She isn't?"

"Well, she *is*, but that's not the point either. Never mind. I'm hanging up now."

"Ask her out." Xavier's voice grew serious. "She saw you naked. She didn't run away. She *asked you to come back*. Two birds, one stone! Asking her out for dinner afterwards should be a cakewalk."

At least Xavier sounded reasonable now, and he wasn't being a total jerk. Besides, Chase *was* pretty. With her long chestnut-and-honey-colored hair, well . . . yeah. She was hot. But throughout the whole two hours yesterday, Tyler had barely been able to bring himself to look at her face. They had made eye contact exactly once, and in those two seconds, his heart had threatened to make a bid for freedom straight out of his chest.

Of course, he would *die* before he admitted that to Xavier.

Tyler looked up to find Chase heading toward him. "Gotta go, bye," he said urgently.

"At least get her nu—" Xavier managed to say before Tyler turned off his phone and jammed it into his pocket. He scrambled to his feet as Chase approached.

"You came!" she exclaimed in delight. "I wasn't sure you would."

He rubbed the back of his neck awkwardly, hoping she wouldn't notice the heat rising in his cheeks. "I told you I wouldn't bail. But I hope the janitor only comes on Mondays, as I'd really prefer not to have a repeat of *that* part." He tried to give her a smile, but his eyes refused to come off the toes of his shoes for some reason. Why had Xavier asked whether she was good-looking? Now he couldn't think of anything else. Well, aside from the sweet warmth of Chase's hand on his arm and her critical eye taking in his form without judgment.

It didn't mean anything, he told himself, but that actually didn't help. For Chase, their time together yesterday had just been an artist looking at her subject. For Tyler, it was like the first taste of water after a lifetime in the desert. Xavier would never let him live down the fact that one casual conversation with Chase was already Tyler's most intimate romantic experience.

Good thing Xavier wasn't there.

Chase dug through her pockets and produced the key to the classroom. He hadn't gotten much of a chance to look at her the day before, and she only existed as flashes in his adrenaline-filled memory, but he managed to finally rip his gaze from the floor to glance at her as she fiddled with the lock. Her pin-straight brown hair was pulled back in a messy ponytail today, although he was pretty sure it had been pinned up last night. Tyler had assumed that most art students were like the theater kids from his high school, with crazy outfits, brightly dyed hair, and an abundance of piercings. Chase was actually pretty tame, although everything about her appeared to be splattered with paint: her hands, her jeans, her phone, her bag, right down to her tennis shoes.

"Is all that stuff for just today?" he asked, indicating Chase's oversized backpack. It was so full the zippers groaned, and a giant notebook stuck out from the top of the largest section, looming over the top of Chase's head. "You'll mess up your back if you keep dragging that thing around."

"The glamorous life of an artist." Chase laughed, pushing into the room. "I'll know I'm a success when I can afford to have a chiropractor fix it."

While she set up her art supplies, Tyler laid out the sheet she'd brought for him before going back into the little room to change.

It was weird, getting naked in a classroom, made stranger yet by the fact that he could hear Chase thumping around in the main part of the room.

Maybe Xavier was right and he should ask her out. Casually, just as friends . . .

But we're not friends, Tyler reminded himself, *and wasn't she telling you that only creeps and weirdos responded to her ad?* What if asking her out put him in that category, and she was forced to choose between being uncomfortable for the rest of the week and sacrificing her grade?

Tyler shuffled out to the podium, hurried out of the robe, and settled himself gingerly on the sheet. Chase was busy doing something to her canvas, as if pretending to ignore him. It was nice of her to act like all this was no big deal, although they both knew she'd spend the next two hours staring at his naked back.

At least she wouldn't be staring at his naked *front*. The room was cold, and Tyler was nervous. That angle wouldn't be flattering under the circumstances.

Hitting on her now would definitely ruin everything. If he was going to do it, he would wait until the end of the week. If she rejected him now, he would still have to sit there moping until Friday. If she agreed to a date, then she'd be sizing him up for the rest of their time together, looking for flaws. Or worse, she would say yes to keep him there, only to disappear at the end of the week before he could have the chance to ask, *"You're not going to ditch me, right?"*

On Wednesday, Tyler's boss called to ask him to work a few hours in the evening.

"I'm busy," he said. "Maybe next week?"

"I'd hoped to wrap up the site by then," Dennis said. Tyler could hear the frown in his voice.

"Sorry, but I can't put this off. It's for a school project." There was no power on earth that could have dragged the truth out of Tyler at that moment. Xavier thought that the whole scenario was a riot, but Dennis was . . . well, *normal.* He'd think Tyler was an utter freak for doing this.

Either way, Dennis was obviously less than pleased. "Right. Just be sure you can make time for me next week. You're a great worker, Tyler, and I don't want to lose you, but if you can't make time to work, I can't keep you on the payroll."

"I'll make up for it over the break," Tyler promised.

He swallowed hard when he hung up, then gathered his things before heading out. It was silly, really, to pack for a nude modeling gig, but he'd have felt weird arriving empty-handed. Xavier probably would have told him not to bother wearing boxers under his shorts, either, but there were rules that had to be followed no matter what the situation. *Never go commando on a non-date* was one of them.

"Almost halfway there!" Chase said cheerily when they met at the classroom door. "You're a champion. I was thinking that you might decide to jump ship, but here you are!"

She had one dimple that only appeared when she smiled. A couple of times now, he had made himself look at her face. It was heart-shaped, and her eyes—when Tyler finally forced himself to look at them—proved to be brown and flecked with gold.

"Of course I came," Tyler said, shoving the thought of his missed work shift to one side. "I'm not going to ditch you now."

It rained on Thursday. Tyler was drenched by the time he arrived at the art building. He was practically frozen already and wasn't exactly looking forward to the idea of squatting naked in the classroom for the rest of the damp evening.

When he pushed on the door, he was surprised to find it was already unlocked. Chase was setting up a space heater next to the podium, and she had placed a cup carrier with two drinks on her stool.

"One's hot chocolate and one's mint tea," she said as she prodded the buttons on the heater. "Pick whichever one you want. I'd have brought us coffees, but it's kind of late for caffeine, right?"

Tyler took the cocoa. "Thanks. That's really nice of you."

"It's the least I could do." Chase looked him over, her hands on her hips. "Now, let's get you out of those wet clothes."

Four days ago, he'd have shriveled up and died with embarrassment over a line like that. This time, he just laughed.

On Monday, Tyler had wished that time would fold in on itself in parallax, just so he could escape to safety. By Friday, he was panicked that seven o'clock would come too soon. It was then or likely never. He had to ask her out before they went their separate ways—he had to say *something,* not the kind of cheesy line that Xavier would cough up but something memorable and witty.

Instead, he sat in silence for the whole first hour, his mind cycling through lines he would never actually say. *Feel like getting a coffee after this?* No, too bland. *Now that you've seen me without my clothes on, how about you buy me dinner?* Too dirty. *I've got twenty bucks if you've got twenty minutes—let me spend it on you and some coffee.* He cringed at the last one. Why would he even think something like that? This was why he was single. There was no good way to ask a woman out, so he didn't. Instead, he sat and mulled, feeling like the biggest idiot in the world.

"Almost done," Chase said on their last break. "You can actually put your clothes back on now, if you'd like. I'm just finishing up your face."

It would have been insanely weird of him to insist on staying naked, but Tyler was afraid of letting the evening get away from him. His mind sifted through another batch of terrible pick-up lines while he pulled his boxers on.

They went from bad to worse. Some of them were restraining-order-worthy. No matter how he looked at it, asking Chase out was a terrible idea.

"Tyler?" she called. "Are you done back there? I still need to get some of the face work done."

He went obediently, sitting sideways on the podium, letting his eyes drift toward her while she worked. Now that he didn't feel quite so self-conscious, he could let his eyes settle on her face. That would be better, wouldn't it? For the painting?

Tyler could convince himself to look at her if it was better for the painting. Her GPA depended on it, after all. Staring right into her eyes was too big of a risk, so his gaze settled a little bit lower. On her lips. Tyler hadn't cared much about lips before—things had never gotten that far—but Chase's lips were interesting. They looked soft. She was so focused that the pink tip of her tongue was sticking out between her lips, trapped between her teeth.

Mouths . . . mouths were interesting when you thought about them. Xavier used phrases like "swapping spit" or "sucking face," both of which were objectively disgusting. He might as well have called it "sharing germs." The idea of having someone else's tongue in his mouth was only slightly less disgusting than the idea of thrusting his tongue into someone *else's* mouth.

But Chase had a nice mouth. Objectively.

He was entering dangerous territory. Tyler forced his eyes away from Chase's lips, only to catch her eye. For a terrified moment, he wondered if she was looking at him because she had somehow managed to read his thoughts—but of course she had to look at him to paint him. Chase smiled at him, and Tyler smiled back but embarrassed and bashful. Would she like it, if she knew what he was thinking?

That question was impossible to answer. What did he really know about her, anyway? Sure, she had mentioned a few things about herself as they sat there, but she preferred to work in silence, probably afraid to spook him off by saying the wrong thing. For his part, it was hard to keep the pose and chat. The one thing he did know was that she was thoughtful and polite and a good aunt. *Is that a good basis for a relationship?* Tyler didn't know. He had no point of reference.

Tyler forced himself to take a deep breath, watching Chase work, wondering what she saw when she glanced over at him between brushstrokes.

At last she leaned back, letting her brush hand relax. She didn't seem to notice when the bristles rested against her thigh, adding another smear of paint to her already messy capris. "There, I think that's it. Do you want to see?"

Tyler hadn't thought of much else since he first asked on Monday and had been told he had to wait. But, for all he knew, Chase was a terrible painter. He didn't want to have to come up with fake compliments for a wreck of brushstrokes in a semi-coherent mess of a portrait. *Or what if she's great, and I end up having to basically compliment my own naked body? Or what if she's great, but when she looks at me, she sees something misshapen and unflattering, like that one painter, what's his name—Lucian Freud?*

"Having second thoughts?" Chase chuckled, clearly unaware he had entered a downward spiral. "You don't have to look if you don't want to. Though, I do vaguely remember how eager you were not five days ago . . ." She wiped her hands on a shop rag and pulled her ponytail tight as she looked at her work again. "I do have to say, though, it's probably my favorite thing I've painted this semester, and this isn't even the kind of art I'm hoping to do when I graduate."

The look on her face was enough. He heaved himself off the podium and moved around behind her, looking over her shoulder.

"Oh, wow," he murmured.

The portrait was absolutely him, but not just the outside of him: *all* of him. The mystical Tyler on the canvas looked peaceful, not at all the bundle of nerves that the *real* him had been. The paint stains on his fingers climbed across his body, lingering in the shadows as deep sapphire blues and seafoam greens, gleaming marigold and lilac where the light touched his skin. It was real and surreal and beautiful and fearless, and it stopped his heart, unfurling some clenched part of him he had unknowingly held tightly inside. The painting's eyes were focused on the viewer, and a shy smile lay curled at the corner of his mouth. A question was on the lips, held back but ready to be asked.

Too bad the real Tyler wasn't brave enough to ask it.

"What do you think?" Chase asked. There was no request for praise in the words, just honest desire for feedback.

Tyler swallowed. "This is what you see when you look at me?"

"I know I went over the top with the colors a bit, but there is something honest in it anyway. You don't think I captured you? I really thought I had." Doubt crept into her expression, and her usually steady shoulders slumped the smallest bit—not enough that anyone would have noticed unless they'd been watching closely.

"It's not that. This guy just looks, I don't know, brave?" He took a breath. "I want to be this guy."

"That *is* you." Chase folded her arms in satisfaction, admiring her work. "You stepped outside of your comfort zone to be here. I really can't tell you how happy I am with the final piece. Roberts is going to be thrilled. She's been bugging me about entering a portrait into the national show, and this is going to be perfect."

Tyler's stomach plummeted. "I'm sorry. What? A national show?"

Chase carried on as though she hadn't just delivered a verbal gut-punch. "Oh, yeah, it's a big thing once a year out in New York. Professor Roberts thinks I have a shot at placing. She's been hounding me to submit a piece. I had another one in mind, but this . . . This might be the best thing I've done to date." Chase nodded happily.

"No, no, no." Tyler backed away, holding his hands up between them, as if he could push the words away by sheer force of will. "Nobody said anything about a national show."

Chase blinked at him. "What would it hurt? No one you know will ever see it."

"I agreed to help you with a grade!" Tyler's voice cracked in panic. "I mean, my face is right there! And my rear is hanging out! No. No way."

"People were going to see it, you know. It is for a grade after all," Chase said, tilting her head to the side. She didn't seem to understand the problem at all.

How can she have seen me so clearly while she was painting me, but not see me at all right now? "Letting a professor grade it is not the same as displaying it in a national gallery!"

"It's my painting," Chase argued.

"And it's my body!" Tyler pointed a shaking finger at the canvas. "If you'd told me that you planned to put it out in front of an audience, I would never have agreed."

Chase looked back at the painting longingly. "But . . ."

"Please," Tyler stammered. "Please don't do this to me. I can't, I mean . . . please don't." The painting had become a mockery in a moment. All that bravery, captured in brushstrokes, as fake as the image itself. He was not that person. He shared a face with the man in the painting, but he would never be as confident as that guy.

"Whoa, hey, calm down," said Chase gently, refocusing on him, her hands coming up to his arms but not touching him. "I'm not going to send it in without your permission. My grade matters more than some contest, anyway. And you're right, it *is* your body."

Tyler looked back at the painting. It was really spectacular; even an amateur like Tyler could see that. Maybe, if she'd let him look fully away, he'd have considered it, but the face was too obviously his own. Anybody could recognize him. *Xavier* could recognize him. His *parents* . . .

His breath started coming in quicker and quicker drafts. The room had suddenly tilted, like one of those rides at the fair. Chase took a step and placed her hovering hands on his arm again. "Easy now. Take a deep breath. Relax. It's okay."

She walked him back to the podium. His breathing slowed with each gentle caress of her fingertips down his forearm to his wrist, then back up again. Usually, being touched by a girl he liked would have been the reason he flipped out, but Chase . . . Chase was different. She was trying to calm him down, not rile him up, and it seemed to be working.

"That's better," she said gently. "I won't do anything crazy without asking. I *do* have to submit the portrait to the professor, though, okay? And some of the people in my class will probably see it, but I'll tell Roberts that you don't want it displayed anywhere."

"I want it when you're done," Tyler blurted out. "I want to make sure that it doesn't come back to haunt me."

Her hand pulled away, and her face became unreadable.

"That wasn't part of the deal," Chase said. "I'm not going to hang it up in the commons or anything, but I need to at least add it to my portfolio. Don't make me waste a week and get nothing but a passing grade out of it."

That was probably a reasonable suggestion, but Tyler wasn't feeling particularly reasonable at the moment. "Once your grade is in, I want it back."

Chase took a step back and scowled at him. "Fine. Whatever. I'll email you once Roberts is done with it."

Tyler stood up, breathing hard again but not in panic—in disappointment of himself and in the knowledge that he'd ruined his chances with her. Clutching the front of his shirt, he squeezed the cloth and tried to regain his equilibrium. He felt as if he'd run a marathon—actually, he *had* run a marathon a couple of years ago, and this was worse.

With a frustrated sigh, Chase began to pack up her things. Tyler stood there, frozen in indecision, but there was nothing else to say. He ducked out of the room without another word, clambering down the steps to the first floor of the building.

Stupid. Stupid. Stupid, he thought with each impact of his descent, but it was too late now. He couldn't ask Chase out on a date after that kind of outburst, but there was no way in hell he was letting that painting go on display.

The worst part is, I think she actually saw me.

If he'd ever stood a chance with her, Tyler was pretty sure that he'd blown it.

This is all Xavier's fault, he thought as he slammed his palms against the crash bar of the art building's entryway. *If he'd never given me that ad, I'd never have come here, and I'd never have met Chase, and I'd never have wasted my time hoping that things could be different.*

That I could be different.

CHASE

Chase was already wondering if she'd made a mistake in how she'd brought up the New York show with Tyler. True, it was frustrating that he wanted to take the painting after the grade was in, and for what? He clearly wasn't going to display it in his living room. He might even destroy it. The thought of the wooden frame splintering and the canvas tearing, or worse yet, being burned, was too disappointing for words. It wasn't just one of Chase's best works of the semester—it was one of her favorites to date.

On the other hand, she probably shouldn't have brought up the idea of the art show like that while he was looking at the painting of his nude body for the first time. He'd been nervous all week. Of *course* he'd flipped. She'd have done the same thing if she'd been in his shoes.

She'd made an appointment with Professor Roberts on Monday to turn in her painting. It occurred to Chase that she should ask Tyler to come along. Maybe if he could see some of her other work, he would see how special this one was . . .

No harm in trying, right?

Chase pulled out her phone, navigated to her thread with Tyler, and then stopped to contemplate her words. She'd have to be cautious now if she was going to have any chance of changing his mind.

. . .

Hey, Tyler.

Sorry about tonight. I shouldn't have sprung things on you like I did, and I wish we'd ended on a happier note. If you're free Monday morning, I'll be back in Studio Three before turning the painting in to my professor. I'd love to see you there.

Meeting starts at ten a.m. Come a little early and I'll show you some of my other work!

Chase

That would have to do, as far as an apology went. It was probably better not to mention the art show directly—no point in reminding him the reason for their disagreement.

If he still demanded the painting after all this, she'd hand it over. His panic seemed silly to her, since nobody in New York would recognize his face. Still, Roberts *had* said something about the school newsletter, and although Chase didn't think it mattered, Tyler clearly did.

And since the painting showed Tyler's body, Tyler called the shots.

Even if the portrait *was* the best thing she'd ever painted.

$\sim$

That night, she dreamed in bright pastels and bold primaries. Tyler's hands were full of color, little rainbows spilling all across the room, and Chase was trying to catch them, but they kept escaping. She tried to stuff them into her pockets, hoping to save them for later, but they were nothing but light, and they slipped through her fingers.

As she chased them, Tyler kept watching her with that shy, self-conscious smile. When she finally looked up at him, his face turned serious as he asked, *"You're not going to ditch me, are you?"*

Chase got up early on Monday and collected her traditional, extra-large, double-espresso-shot red eye on the way to the art building. She unlocked the door to Studio Three for the last time. The class was over, and she wouldn't need to use it again until she picked up her work at the end of the semester.

Tyler hadn't responded to her email, and for all she knew, he was going to avoid her until it was time to take the painting and vanish from her life forever. The thought made her a little sad, and not only because of the painting itself. Tyler had seemed like a genuinely nice guy.

A handsome guy with a solid sense of humor and a body hardened by manual labor. Chase had spent the whole week staring at his bared skin, after all. Of course she'd noticed that he was fit. How could she not?

Chase pulled out the little stack of paintings she'd accumulated over the semester. Now that she'd had some time away from them, she could see what Professor Roberts liked about them. One of the charcoal sketches was smudged in exactly the right places to match the model's demure smile, and her gouache of the young woman from mid-semester was borderline effervescent.

None of them compared to the painting of Tyler.

She was sitting on the floor, surrounded by her work, when the doors slowly opened. Chase looked up, expecting to find Professor Roberts in the doorway, and grinned in delight when she saw Tyler standing there instead. His hands were shoved deep into the pockets of his worn jeans, and his cheeks were pink, but he returned her smile.

"You came!" Chase cried, leaping to her feet and tiptoeing between the canvases to greet him. She had thrown her arms around Tyler before she realized that this might be too much for him.

"Yeah," he said sheepishly as she released him. He didn't look upset by the hug, although the rosy blush in his cheeks had darkened to fuchsia. "I, uh, wasn't sure I was going to make it, you know, but class let out a little early . . ."

"Well, that's awesome." Chase stepped away, gesturing to the scattered evidence of her semester working in nudes. "Want to see what else I've done this year?"

Tyler bent down to examine the portraits. He didn't say anything right away, just looked at the closest one, then the next, and the next. When Chase tried to show her work to people outside of their department, they tended to say something like, *Oh, that's nice.* Other students tended to search for the right words, hoping to think of something erudite and insightful that would show off their knowledge of the creative process.

Tyler just looked.

Chase found herself watching him, trying to guess what he was thinking. His face was so expressive, so unguarded—she wished she could've had a chance to sketch him this week, focusing on his face and his posture and his sudden shifts in mood.

"They're not what I expected," he said at last.

"In what way?"

He bit his lip, letting his eyes skim over the whole collection again. "It might sound dumb."

"You worry about that a lot," Chase pointed out. "But we're talking about my art. I want to know what you see when you look at it. How can I ever get better if I don't know what people like and dislike?"

Tyler pointed to her full-frontal, watercolor male nude. "Well, take this one. I sort of thought you might be doing me a favor, you know, not making my portrait . . ." He blushed scarlet and cleared his throat.

How much redder can his cheeks get? Chase wondered in amusement. "Full frontal?" she offered aloud.

"Sexy," he blurted. "Or, I don't know, *sexual?* But none of these are, even the ones where you can see everything. They're matter-of-fact. And this one." He gestured to the gouache. "Like, her boobs just exist. They aren't special here. Not . . . I don't know. Am I making sense?"

"Boobs just exist," Chase repeated, laughing.

"I told you it was stupid."

"It's not stupid," she assured him. "And I think I get why you were worried now. The point of this type of art isn't to titillate or arouse."

Tyler squirmed uncomfortably, and it took a monumental amount of effort for her not to repeat the word *titillate* for the sole purpose of making him wriggle again. Part of Chase's brain told her to make him even more uncomfortable by using as many suggestive words as possible, but the louder part wanted to help him understand what she'd seen all week when she'd been staring at him.

"Most of the time, when we see naked bodies in things like advertisements or porn or anything that's trying to *sell* us something, it's to make us want to touch what we see," Chase said, unable to resist giving in to the temptation.

"Yeah, I get that," Tyler said in a strained voice.

"But my portraits aren't like that. They're about establishing intimacy with the viewer, showing them something personal and private." Chase picked up the watercolor of the male model. "When this guy walked into the room, he looked confident and cocky . . ." She shook her head at Tyler's reaction. "Stop smirking! You know what I meant. Anyway, he looked like your average dudebro. But after he stripped down, this other side came out, this kind of casual indifference. He was comfortable with himself. It was like he was sitting naked on the couch at home, instead of in front of a class."

Tyler chuckled. "You say that as if sitting around naked on your couch is normal."

"Isn't it?" Chase opened her eyes wide, blinking innocently.

"You let your butt touch the furniture?" Tyler shook his head. "At least you said couch and not kitchen table. Even so: horrifying."

"I would never put my butt on the kitchen chair. Too many toast crumbs," Chase joked. "Anywhere else is fair game to air out the undercarriage."

At the mention of Chase's butt, Tyler's eye twitched, but he soldiered on. "I've got roommates, so I won't be airing anything out. You won't catch me without at least boxers on."

"Oh my God, I bet you're a never-nude. I'm honored to have captured one of the only fully naked events of your entire life on canvas." Chase bumped her shoulder against his before putting the watercolor back. "But that's kind of my point. Most people have some kind of criteria about who gets to see their bodies, just as they have some criteria about who gets to know what they're thinking. These pieces are supposed to capture both of those things at the same time."

Slowly, almost unwillingly, Tyler's eyes climbed to his own portrait.

"You put my name on it," he said, noticing the little tag she'd written up to accompany the painting. His frown returned in an instant. "My real name."

Chase sighed. So much for her tactic of putting him at ease. "I can change it. Usually, we just use sequential numbers here in the classroom, so if you prefer, I can do that."

"I'd appreciate it." Tyler looked away from her, clearly trying to regain his composure.

"Easy-peasy." Chase fished a marker out of her bag and blacked out his name, flipped the card over, and wrote the number ninety-eight in broad strokes across the blank side before tucking the card into the wooden frame behind the canvas. "Better?"

"Thanks." Tyler sighed, looking at the painting again. "It's really good, you know. I mean, all of your work is beautiful. Maybe I'm being vain."

"You're not vain!" she assured him. "It *is* good. Like I said, it's one of my favorites to date."

Tyler hesitated, and a little spark of hope jumped in Chase's chest. Maybe he would change his mind, not about the show but about letting her keep the painting. It would be such a strong addition to her portfolio . . .

Chase began to gather up her artwork. It was almost ten, and she should be taking her painting over to her professor's office any minute now. "I need to get going, but my meeting won't take long. Walk with me?"

Tyler looked pleased. "Sure. I'm free until one."

There was an unspoken invitation, and Chase heard it clearly. He wanted to spend more time with her. He was, in his way, asking her to lunch, or more specifically, asking her to ask *him*. Tyler had been clear that he wasn't comfortable around people, but he was starting to come out of his shell with her.

"Hey," Tyler said at last, "I wanted to ask you something."

"Go for it," Chase said eagerly, hoisting her painting of him off the easel. Tyler followed her as she turned off the lights and locked the door.

Still, he hesitated, shuffling along beside her as they made their way down the hall toward the office.

"Look," Chase said gently, "it's almost ten, and I have to turn this in. Do you want to come in with me? I promise Roberts won't make it weird. She's going to be grading me on my technique, not on how much the piece looks like you."

Tyler stopped dead in the hallway. "Your prof is a woman?"

"Yeah." Chase narrowed her eyes. "Not all faculty are men, you know."

"No, I know. Can I wait in the hall?" Tyler asked, ruffling his hair mindlessly. "I'm sorry, I don't mean to be a drag . . ."

"You're fine." Chase patted his arm and wondered briefly how brightly he would blush if she kissed his cheek. Could he achieve burgundy under the right circumstances?

She left him there and trotted off into the office.

"Ah, Miss Zalinski." Roberts looked up from her computer as she stepped inside. "I must say, I've been looking forward to seeing this. Let's see what you've accomplished with your extra time."

In her excitement to hand the piece over, Chase knocked the number card loose from the frame. Roberts bent to pick it up, tucking it back into place before finally turning the painting over.

"Oh my," she murmured. "Chase. This is stunning."

"Thanks." Chase beamed, looking over the canvas once again. The more she looked at it, the prouder she felt. With its shy smile and clever brown eyes, the painting of Tyler felt like a third presence in the room.

"Remind me if I've got this right: you don't care for this class?" Her professor's eyes were bright with amusement. "Well, ennui certainly brings out something special in your work."

"Thank you," Chase said earnestly. "And thank you again for the extension." She handed over the key to the studio, and Roberts twisted it back onto her keyring.

"How is your sister doing?" asked Roberts, her eyes still skimming over the portrait. "Her boys didn't drive you crazy, did they?"

"She's doing a lot better, and I wouldn't say the boys drove me crazy, but I will say they hired an Uber and gave them directions."

"Well, I must say, I have no regrets about granting you the extra time. You've put that extension to good use." Roberts set the portrait of Tyler to one side. "You'll get this back at the end of the semester. I would expect a very positive grade on this project. You should be proud of yourself, Chase."

Chase's chest swelled with pride. She'd known the portrait was good, but being an art student often meant having even her best work criticized. Her professor's reaction only confirmed what Chase had already believed: this painting was special.

"Thank you again for everything." Chase got to her feet. "You're too kind."

She left with a spring in her step despite the enormous weight of her backpack, feeling utterly positive about how the whole day was shaping up. She would ask Tyler to lunch (her treat) as a thank-you for modeling. If nothing came of it, that would be all right. But maybe something would. There was no way of knowing. After all, she hadn't expected her painting to be great. What if there was more unforeseen greatness coming her way? If she waited for him to ask, they might be a hundred before he gathered the courage. Better to take matters into her own hands.

But when she stepped out into the hall, Tyler was gone.

∾

By the end of the week, Chase was getting annoyed. Not only had Tyler ditched her in the hallway with only a quick email saying, *Sorry, something came up*, he'd ghosted her ever since. At first, she wondered if she'd misread him, or if the low-key chemistry between them had just been her imagination. Either way, there was a difference between slow-burn romance and letting the fire go out.

This is why I don't date, she thought morosely.

On Friday, Roberts emailed her to ask if she was still willing to submit a painting to the show in New York. Chase mulled it over, finally settling on painting eighty-six, the gouache of the woman—it was probably her second-best piece, and even if Tyler had fallen off the face of the earth, that didn't mean she would go behind his back.

Still, it rankled, having to send in an entry that was good rather than great.

∾

Three weeks after she'd turned the portrait of Tyler in, Chase received her grade. As she'd expected, Roberts gave her an A.

That was all she'd needed, really. When Chase thought of the portrait now, she experienced a wistful ache of longing, but Tyler had made himself clear. He'd kept his promise, and she'd keep hers. After that, they could go their separate ways, and he could ghost whomever he liked.

She sent him a quick email on the last Friday of the semester, only five words:

Get your painting—ten a.m.

Chase

.   .   .

If she said anything else, she would undoubtedly tell him something she'd regret: her disappointment that he'd left unexpectedly, or her squashed hopes that there might be something between them. Nope, those five words would have to do. He could figure out the rest for himself.

She took her coffee to the classroom, stewing in her own frustrations all the way. Maybe he wouldn't show up at all. If he never responded, would it be all right to keep the portrait?

That train of thought derailed at the art room door, where she found Tyler waiting nervously, thumbs hooked through the straps of his backpack. His hair was mussed, per usual; it made her want to smooth it down with her fingers.

"Hey," he said. "How've you been?"

Chase had to fight the urge to roll her eyes. "Fine." *Which you'd know, if you'd bothered to stick around.* "You?"

"Okay." He looked down at his shoes, still nervous. Too shy to wait in the hall, too shy to reply to her email, too shy to ask her out—he might be handsome, but that wasn't going to cut it.

The other students were gathering their things too. A few waved to Chase as she entered, but she hadn't made a lot of friends in this class. Most of their work had been solo, and there was something about a class based in the study of nudity that rendered it hard to make eye contact with your peers while you worked.

Chase walked along the row of paintings, looking for hers.

"I thought they wouldn't be on display," Tyler hissed.

"It's not a display—not technically, anyway," she replied. "To keep the grades as fair as possible, Roberts will sometimes have other teachers judge them. Anyway, look around, most people haven't come through to get theirs yet. Hardly anyone will have seen it."

Tyler glanced over his shoulder at the cluster of students, frowning reproachfully. "Can we please just grab it and go?"

When she reached the Z's, however, her painting wasn't there.

"Did somebody steal it?" Tyler gasped.

"Nobody stole your nude," Chase said soothingly. "She might have taken it down early. Let's go ask the professor."

Roberts was talking to one of the seniors, a tall girl with black hair and purple highlights. Chase waited until the girl drifted away before approaching. For once, Tyler was right beside her.

"Hello, Chase," Roberts said, tilting her head to one side in confusion. "What are you doing here?"

"I'm picking up my painting," Chase replied. "Or I was trying to. It's not on my easel."

"Of course not," Roberts said. "It's in New York, remember?"

Tyler made a horrified noise deep in the back of his throat.

Chase swayed on her feet. It was as if she'd been punched in the chest; she could only imagine how bad Tyler felt. "There's been some misunderstanding. I said that you should send in painting number eighty-six."

"I did." Roberts nodded patiently. "And may I just say, it really is one of the most magnificent final projects I've ever had the pleasure to grade. You're the model, aren't you, young man? I recognize you from the portrait. What a magnificent likeness."

"That was number ninety-eight," Chase interrupted, as if she could argue reality back into the shape she wanted.

"Perhaps the tag got flipped over. But really, this one was the best piece in your portfolio. The show starts Monday, but it only runs for a week. If you need it back, you won't have to wait long—and given the size of the scholarships they're offering to the top four contenders, I can't imagine why you'd want to send anything less than your very best. Forget the school newsletter, Chase. If your piece places, you'll be on the cover of the *Magazine of College Arts*. Just think: your painting could appear in every university art room across the country!"

Chase didn't dare turn to face Tyler. She could already feel the panic radiating off of him in waves.

I bet he's achieved burgundy, she thought bleakly.

"Do you have the number for the folks in charge of the show?" Chase asked. Somehow, her voice sounded calm, despite the fact that she was trembling on Tyler's behalf.

And not only that. Exactly how big was this scholarship?

Roberts shook her head. "No, but it should be on their website."

Chase asked her for the URL and then typed it into her browser, which took an agonizingly long time to load.

"Yes, that's it." Roberts nodded, looking over Chase's shoulder. "All of the information should be there. I must say, I think you have an excellent shot at one of those top prizes."

Chase didn't know how to respond, so she didn't bother. Without saying a word, she looped her arm through Tyler's and dragged him away.

Tyler seemed to have stopped breathing. His eyes were wide, and a vein pulsed in his temple. The poor guy was clearly on the verge of losing it. She'd seen him nervous, certainly, but she'd never seen him flat-out panic like this.

"It's okay," she said in the same tone of voice she would have used to address someone who had just broken their leg. *I know it looks bad, but we can fix it.* "I'll call the gallery and tell them there's been a mix-up. I'll ask them to pull it from the show."

Tyler nodded mutely, and Chase dialed the number, already running over what she'd say.

"Hello," said a suspiciously robotic-sounding gentleman on the other end of the line, "you've reached the number for the Manhattan Student Gallery. Unfortunately, we are unable to answer calls at this time. Our gallery will reopen Monday at six p.m. for our national showcase . . ." Chase zoned out, waiting for the beep that would allow her to leave a voicemail, but it never came.

She slowly pulled the phone away from her ear. "Okay. New plan."

"You did this on purpose," Tyler said suddenly. "Right?" His hands were balled into fists, and his chest heaved. Someone needed to get him a paper bag to breathe into, or the poor guy was going to have a fit.

Chase squinted at him. "Are you serious? Why on earth would I do that?" She was impulsive, sure—her mother reminded her of that fact often enough—but she wasn't a *monster.* She had seen how much this mattered to Tyler.

"There's a big scholarship." Tyler crossed his arms. "That's what your professor just said."

"I asked her to send a different painting," Chase retorted. "She obviously got the numbers confused. Something that couldn't have happened, may I remind you, if you'd let me keep your name on the painting in the first place!"

"So now it's my fault?" Tyler demanded, and his eyes narrowed. "I should never have agreed to help you. I shouldn't have listened to Xavier . . . Oh, God, he's going to have a field day with this, isn't he?"

Arguing wasn't going to help, so Chase forced herself to think rationally. "It's not over yet. I'll try sending them an email."

"It's Friday morning right now. If they aren't answering the phone, I doubt they'll answer their email the entire weekend." Tyler groaned. "They won't get your email until after everyone sees the painting."

"They might," Chase insisted. "It's worth a shot. It's better than not doing anything, right?"

Tyler bent over, grabbing his sides, his breath coming in rapid gasps. "And your painting is so good, you're probably going to place in the top four. If you win, I'm going to absolutely die."

"Settle down." Chase was already typing out the email, half focused on his words and half trying to formulate her own. "It's not going to win."

"What happens if it does?" he demanded.

As Chase hit *send*, she bit her lip, remembering what Professor Roberts had told her when she'd first mentioned the show. "Well, if I win, I think it'll go on the cover of the school's alumni newsletter. And probably their web page . . . And in the *Magazine of College Arts . . .*"

Tyler actually sank down into a squat, hiding his face in his hands. He was only seconds away from wailing like a Greek widow in a performance of Euripides.

Chase knelt down beside him, ignoring the questioning looks of her classmates. "It's okay. Who's going to know? It doesn't have your name on it anymore. I mean, sure, I paint realistically and all, but it's not like people are going to go around trying to solve the mystery of the model."

"They won't have to," Tyler choked out. "They'll put it out there, and every girl and guy in the whole school will see that painting."

"I don't think anyone looks at that stuff but the art department." Chase could feel the conversation going off the rails, but what else could she do about it now? "Besides, it's not like you were on full display. The painting doesn't include your . . ." She gestured to her groin. "*Assets*."

"But it's obvious that I'm naked." Tyler covered his face with his hands. "They'll know that I was naked for the picture. And half my butt was in that picture!"

"Tyler," Chase said reasonably, "people have butts. Butts exist, like the boobs in that other portrait, remember? I've met plumbers with more visible crack than what's included in that portrait."

"You think this is funny?" Tyler demanded.

"No," Chase assured him. "I'm doing everything I can think of, but I'm not sure what other options we have."

She checked her phone. The gallery had already emailed her back, but when she opened it, the email turned out to be an automated "out of office" form reply.

"If people see it, my life is over," Tyler said. Suddenly, his head whipped up. "Unless they *can't* see it. Chase, we have to go get it back."

She shook her head. "Come on, Tyler, New York is like a twenty-hour drive from here. I don't have a car, and I certainly don't have the cash for a last-minute plane ticket."

When she'd been painting him, Chase had admired the open and expressive nature of Tyler's face. Now, she wished he could hide his feelings a little better. She'd seen him shy, she'd seen him cautious, she'd seen him happy. The look on his face now was something else altogether. He'd made up his mind.

Tyler was going to get that painting back or die trying.

TYLER

Tyler had spent most of his life wondering how people saw him. He could do very little to control what people thought when they looked at him, of course, other than to keep his appearance tidy and his demeanor professional. As for the Tyler on the inside, most people didn't take the time to stick around and ask questions to find out—they just glanced at him, made an assumption, and then disappeared.

But with Chase, he felt someone had *seen* him. Most of all, she had a relaxed, comfortable-in-her-own-skin attitude that had made it easy to be around her. When he talked, she actually *listened*. When he didn't talk, she let the silence linger, rather than pushing him into the sort of shallow social performance that always made his skin crawl. Chase seemed to *get* him without Tyler even having to explain what was going on in his head.

Which made his current meltdown all the more embarrassing. He might as well have been rolling on the floor like a toddler throwing a temper tantrum while the only girl he'd ever had the guts to flirt with looked on.

There was no helping it. As far as Tyler was concerned, his only current options were to get that painting back, or else sink deep into the earth and become the kind of legendary sewer-dwelling mole person that kept conspiracy theorists like Xavier up at night. Chase was right, of course—nobody would be *shocked* to learn that Tyler had butt cheeks, but that wasn't the point. Tyler could barely talk to most people, and suddenly, complete strangers were going to be able to look at his naked shoulders and chest? He always wore a T-shirt to the pool, for God's sake.

No, he couldn't let that painting get out. It was more damning than a naked selfie, partly because it was so damn *beautiful*. People would want to look at it, and in a roundabout way, that meant they would be admiring him.

"I have a car," he said when breath finally came back to him. Chase had managed to walk him to the corner of the room and sit him in one of the loose chairs that speckled the room. "I'll drive us to New York."

"Us?" Chase raised her eyebrows.

"I'm going to look like a crazy person," he argued. "If I turn up at the gallery, demanding to take custody of a naked portrait, they'll think I'm some sort of pervert."

Chase rubbed his shoulder. "First of all, it's not like it's courtroom evidence. I'm sure they'll at least take it down if they don't give it to you outright. Second, it is a painting of *you*. Surely you could prove that you're the guy in the portrait."

"By showing them my face?" Tyler asked. "Or by showing them my *butt*?" The fact that the portrait was so obviously of him was the main problem, after all.

Chase covered her mouth in a failed attempt to hide her smile. "I mean, I suppose that is always an option."

There was no way he would ever be brave enough to charge into a gallery and make a scene. How did you casually request the return of blackmail-worthy material from total strangers? Although that wouldn't be as embarrassing as if the portrait went viral, or if word of his shame got out to the general student body.

Tyler was pulled out of his spiral as Chase squeezed his shoulder. He sighed. "You can't go. I understand. It's okay. I guess I can have them call you to verify or something." He hated himself for surrendering so quickly. What if they didn't believe him? What if they said the artist herself had to be there? What if he didn't make it in time? Two thousand miles in a weekend by himself felt nigh impossible, but it was nothing compared to what awaited him at the finish line.

Chase held out her hand to help Tyler out of the chair she had sat him in. "Don't look so put-out. I'll tag along. It's sort of my fault that this happened, anyway. I can't very well ditch you now."

Tyler blinked. "Wait. Are you serious?"

"Sure, why not?" Chase shrugged. "The semester's over. I've got nowhere urgent to be. Although, I should tell you now, I'm pretty much broke."

"Me, too." Tyler shuffled back. "I guess I can borrow some cash from my friend Xavier, though."

Tyler looked around. Most of the other students had left, and the professor must have gone to her office, possibly to avoid the spectacle he'd made of himself. It was just the two of them now, standing in the room where he'd spent a week naked with her.

Not like that, he thought immediately, as if the memory might turn into something incriminating if he didn't keep it in check.

"We'll see what we can scrounge together." Chase checked her watch. "And I've got a credit card in case of emergencies. So, when do we leave?"

It was all happening so fast, just like it had when he turned up for her ad. Tyler didn't like adventures. He liked the steady, solid pace of a controlled environment, the same thing every day, no surprises. Now, there he was, begging a strange girl to take an emergency road trip halfway across the country to recover a nude portrait . . . *Jesus, it sounds like a Nicolas Cage movie.*

Still, this had been his idea. "It's a little after ten right now. It's gotta be like what, twenty hours to New York from here? Plus stops for food and rest. The sooner we leave, the better." Tyler pulled out his phone and checked the time to make sure that hours hadn't passed since panic had overrun him. Nope, it was still morning.

"I'll need an hour or so to take the rest of my paintings back to my apartment and pack for the weekend," Chase replied.

"I'll need to track down Xavier and grab some clothes too."

"Which dorm are you in?"

"Weaver."

"I'll meet you there," she said. "What time?"

Tyler stared at her. *How can I possibly know how long it will take me to get ready for something I've never done before?* "Noon? Is that enough time?"

"Plenty. And Tyler, I really am sorry," she said, tucking a strand of loose hair behind her ear. "But this is gonna be fun, don't you think?"

In fact, it sounded about as much fun as swimming in shark-infested waters, but there wasn't much he could do about it now.

Chase gathered up the rest of her paintings. Between the canvases and her giant backpack, she looked like a human mushroom: skinny stem legs on the bottom, threatening to overbalance with all the weight on top. She was already halfway out the door when she leaned back in, as if something else had just occurred to her.

"Oh, and Tyler?"

"Yeah?"

"I call dibs on the right side of the bed."

His parents were somewhere at sea in the Caribbean, and Tyler had taken a week off of work to model for Chase. Dennis's next check wouldn't come in until the following Friday. There was only one person who could help him now.

"Whaddup, dude?" Xavier drawled when Tyler dialed his number. "This too important to text or something?"

"I need to borrow some cash," Tyler panted. "Can you meet me at my dorm?"

"Hold up. What's going on? You okay?"

"Chase and I are going on a road trip, and I need some cash for supplies. I'll pay you back, I swear. I'm just behind on paychecks . . ."

"Slow down," Xavier said. "I'm gonna need more deets."

"I'll explain at the dorm," Tyler said, hanging up before Xavier could ask any more questions. He shot off a quick message to Dennis, saying that he had to go out of town for a personal emergency, which was basically the truth, after all. It was a good thing he'd been working overtime since he'd taken the week off to help Chase, and they were all caught up on projects for the moment.

Ideally, when Tyler traveled, he packed a few days in advance. That way, he had plenty of time to remember little details he might have missed on the first pass. This time, he was reduced to making a hasty list as he jogged to the dorm: socks, clean underwear, a few pairs of pants, spare shirts, toothbrush, deodorant, a sleeping bag, a poncho, a flashlight . . .

By the time he reached his dorm, he'd compiled a comprehensive list, which he ran over and over in his mind, adding to it as he went. It was easy enough to go around the room, tossing things into his duffel bag, but the nagging feeling he might be missing something haunted Tyler. What if somewhere in Ohio, he realized he'd forgotten his phone charger? Or what if he needed something he hadn't thought to pack? There were too many variables to account for, and Tyler simply couldn't keep track of them all.

When the bag was full and half of his dresser stood empty, Tyler retreated downstairs to his little gray Honda. It was already ten till noon. He was stuffing the overfull bag into the trunk, after having pushed the unused paint rollers and pans from work aside, when Xavier jogged up.

"Hey, sorry I took so long!" his friend said as he popped off the curb and looked at the thick canvas sack lying in the shallow well of the car's trunk.

"Where have you been?" Tyler demanded. "You live, like, two minutes away and it didn't sound like you were in class."

"Whoa. Who is doing who a favor here, buddy?" Xavier chuckled. He held out a plastic bag with the local pharmacy's logo printed on the side. "I had to make a detour. I knew you'd feel embarrassed stopping at the drugstore yourself, so I took the liberty of stopping for you."

Tyler frowned at the bag. "What is this?"

"Supplies." Xavier's accompanying wink was so exaggerated that it looked more like a spasm.

Tyler opened the bag and almost dropped it in shock. "Dude. What is *wrong* with you?"

"Don't act like I gave you a sack full of snakes. If you're going to take an, *ahem*, 'road trip' with this art girl, you need to be prepared."

Tyler stared down at a box that, according to the label, contained the largest supply and variation of condoms he had ever seen. He reeled back in horror, all but dropping the bag. "I need to borrow *cash*, Xavier. For things like gas and food."

"Say no more." His friend opened his wallet and handed Tyler half a dozen crisp twenties. "Wine her and dine her, my dude."

"Is that all you have?" Tyler asked nervously.

Xavier pressed his lips together and rolled his eyes. "What do I look like, the Bank of America?"

"I don't mean to sound ungrateful. Thank you." Tyler shoved the bag back toward him. "And you can keep these."

With a world-weary sigh, Xavier opened the passenger door and stuffed the box inside the glove compartment. It was so large that he had to crush the corners down to get it closed.

"You'll thank me later," he promised, tucking the empty bag into his pocket.

Tyler hid his face in his hands and tried to breathe normally. After years of quietly worrying that something might go wrong, his poor brain was on the verge of overwhelm. *It might very well be easier to think of ways this could go* right. *That would make for a much shorter list.*

"Don't get too stuck in your head," Xavier said. "I know it can be stressful, especially since this is your first time, but don't worry. Art Girl has already seen the whole package, you know what I mean? And she's still interested."

"*Chase* doesn't see me that way," Tyler argued through his fingers.

"She said that the whole point of the painting is to see the person, not their sensuality."

"That's great for you, right?" Xavier mused, leaning back against the passenger door. "You seem like you'd be into that."

"Xavier."

"Hey, I'm not making fun. I mean, what are the odds that the first girl you get serious about actually *likes* you for you? You're lucky. It's fate. Actually, you should be thanking me for pointing out that flyer in the first place."

"Xavier," Tyler repeated.

His friend went on as though he hadn't spoken. "You've got to be careful, though. If your first time was bad, and it was with a random hookup, no problem—ghost her. But if you actually like this girl, you're gonna want to put in the effort." He made a thrusting movement with his hips and waggled his eyebrows. "Text me if you need tips."

Tyler stuck his fingers in his ears. "Please stop talking."

Xavier slapped his back. "Don't stress, Tyler. If you're feeling over-whelmed, just tell her to direct you. Chicks love that."

At that moment, Tyler's name echoed across the parking lot.

"Tyler! Hey!" Chase grinned at him as she wove between the lanes of parked cars. For a moment, he thought she had *only* brought the backpack of art supplies before realizing she also had a small bag slung over her shoulder.

"Is that going to be enough for the whole trip?" he asked skeptically.

"I can always wash stuff on the road." She turned to Xavier and stuck out her hand. "I'm Chase. Who are you?"

"*Enchantée*," Xavier said, bowing at the waist as he shook Chase's hand. "I'm Xavier. I would say that I'm Tyler's best friend, but I made that as a default by being his only friend."

Chase laughed. "So you're the troublemaker?"

It was slowly dawning on Tyler that a prolonged conversation between Xavier and Chase could only end in a barrage of embar-rassing stories he would never be able to live down.

"Can I help you with your bags?" Tyler asked, hoping to cut the conversation off before anything terrible happened.

"Aw, such a gentleman," Chase said, "but I've got it."

As she bent over to dump her bags in the back seat, Xavier nodded sagely. "Like I was saying, Tyler, some women just *know what they want*. Better to *follow her lead*." His smug facial expression wouldn't have been out of place in a Monty Python skit.

Please stop, Tyler mouthed.

Xavier shook his head and opened his mouth to say something else when Tyler spoke up to drown him out. "Okay, let's get this show on the road."

"Ready when you are," Chase said. She had let her long hair down and was now trying to get it under control with a hair tie. There was something so feminine about the way she moved—the tilt of her wrists and the way she leaned one hip back on the car door—that terrified and enthralled Tyler all at once. They were going to be in the same car for almost a week. His haste to reach New York had wiped all ideas of the return trip from his mind.

He couldn't think about that now. If he did, he would never get up the nerve to pull the car out of the lot. One thing at a time.

Tyler turned to his friend. "Thanks for seeing us off, Xavier. And I'll pay you back as soon as my next check comes in."

Xavier looked disappointed that he couldn't continue to banter at Tyler's expense, but he gave a small smile and waved as his friend slid into the driver's seat. Chase collapsed into the seat next to Tyler, grinning excitedly. She had her phone out, already pulling up the directions.

"This is going to be a blast!" she exclaimed.

Tyler reversed out of the space, wondering how she had it in her to be so excited. Shouldn't she be the nervous one, getting ready to head off along the highway with a total stranger? How many *Dateline* episodes started this way? Unless *she* was the sociopath . . .

Seeing him so vulnerable while she painted his soul onto canvas must have given her the upper hand.

"Okay, we're getting onto I-70." She looked up at him. "Do you know the way, or do you want me to direct you?"

"I can get us there," he assured her.

In the rearview mirror, he caught a glimpse of Xavier making a series of increasingly suggestive gestures in the reflection.

Tyler pressed his foot against the gas pedal, leaving his willfully perverted friend behind.

It was time to save his own butt.

Literally.

CHASE

All her life, Chase had been told she was impulsive. In other people's mouths, this word had often sounded like an insult, but Chase always took it as a compliment. If you didn't strike out on your own, nothing interesting ever happened.

Her mother would have called her impulsive today—but that would have been nothing new. Mrs. Zalinski would probably have approved of Tyler more than she did of her own daughter.

"Your friend is pretty interesting," Chase said as they pulled onto the highway. She leaned her seat back and tucked her spare hoodie under her head like a pillow. "I can totally picture him bullying you into answering my ad."

"Xavier's not a bully." Tyler kept his eyes on the road, merging carefully. "He's just, you know, got a lot of opinions and ideas, and he's not afraid to express them. I'm sure you'd like him." He seemed to second-guess what he was saying. "Actually, I'm *not* sure. He can be . . . *single-minded.*"

"I'm gonna go out on a limb and guess that he isn't super comfortable with girls, either."

Tyler risked a brief glance over at her in surprise. "No way—he's had a ton more experience than I have."

"Only because you're shy." Chase closed her eyes, listening to the soothing rumble of the road beneath her. "Trust me, guys like him are just masking all their own insecurities. He's definitely someone who spends a lot of time cultivating an image."

She waited for a clever retort, but Tyler spent a long moment considering her words. "I never thought of him that way. I always assumed he was fearless."

"Nobody's fearless." Chase chuckled. "People who seem like they are? Totally faking."

"What about you?"

"Me? I'm not fearless."

"Oh, come on. Name one thing that so much as slows you down."

Chase shook her head. The hair tie was coming loose again, but she didn't bother trying to fix it. "I barely know you. You don't get to know my kryptonite yet."

"That hardly seems fair," Tyler retorted. "*Everything* is my kryptonite, and you already know that."

Chase smirked. "But that's BS, obviously. I mean, look at you. You say that you can't talk to girls, but you're talking to one right now, and you don't seem to be having any trouble with *that*."

Tyler fell silent, keeping his eyes on the road. Chase briefly wondered if she'd crossed a line, but he didn't seem angry.

This was a guy who listened to what people told him. She'd have to be careful. If she said the wrong thing even one time, he wouldn't roll past it. He'd stew in it until it drove him crazy.

When it became apparent that he wasn't going to respond, Chase broke the silence again. "I want to ask you something, but you don't have to answer. That day in the hall . . . why did you ghost me?"

"I didn't ghost you," Tyler said at once.

She shrugged. "You didn't wait, and then you didn't respond to my email, and I didn't hear from you again until I told you that I had something you wanted. Is that not, in fact, the literal definition of ghosting?"

"It sounds bad when you put it that way," he told her.

"It felt bad at the time."

"I'm sorry," Tyler said, and he sounded like he meant it. "My boss called me in. I had to pick up some extra shifts the last few weeks to make up for . . ."

Chase waited patiently, and after a moment, Tyler wrinkled his nose.

"To make up for all the shifts I missed during our sessions," he said at last.

"Hold on." Chase sat upright so fast that her seatbelt locked. "You missed work so that you could model for me?"

Tyler seemed embarrassed to admit it. "Yeah. Kind of."

"But we worked at night!"

"We've been working our current site on a swing shift." Tyler checked the rearview mirror before passing a semi. "Our most recent contract has us repainting offices, and we do it at night so that the buildings can stay open during business hours. Besides, a lot of the guys are gig workers, like me. Most of us have school or another job in the meantime."

Now that she looked at him, she could see the graying circles under his eyes and the weary set of his jaw. "Why didn't you tell me that another time of day would have worked better for you? You need to stand up for yourself sometimes, Tyler."

"Isn't that what I'm doing right now?" he replied. "Isn't that why we're driving all the way to New York?"

He sounded more resigned than annoyed, but by Chase's accounting, he had a right to be both. Tyler had done nothing but bend over backward to help her, and in return he'd only asked for one thing: that nobody else see the portrait. She should have been more careful, more respectful of his wishes.

They rode in silence for a while. Chase had never been good with silences, but Tyler didn't seem to have that problem. She made herself sit in it, accepting a little discomfort as penance for her behavior.

The city was long behind them before Chase finally spoke up again. "Water."

"Are you thirsty?" Tyler asked. "I have some bottles in the back seat."

Chase shook her head, looking down at the hem of her shirt. "No, I meant . . ." She sighed, bracing herself for the confession. "So, one summer when I was a kid, I rode this crazy-huge waterslide. I thought it would be fun, but the minute I hit the pool at the bottom, I totally flipped out. I'd never been that far underwater before, and I hated it. Now I avoid water completely. Oceans, lakes, pools, even deep bathtubs—it doesn't matter—I can't handle it. Showers are fine, but the moment I'm submerged up to my neck? I panic. And it's dumb, I know, because the more you panic, the more likely you are to drown, but I can't rationalize my way out of it. There. Now you know my kryptonite."

Tyler nodded seriously. "Thanks for telling me."

"That's it?" Chase tilted her head, looking at him from another angle. "You're not going to tell me that I need to get over it, or that a swimming coach would help me, or that I just need to dive in and get over it?" Chase snorted. That was the kind of crap her mother would say—that the fear didn't matter. That Chase needed to be more in control of her emotions. That she'd never really been in danger in the first place.

"God, no! Are you kidding? Have you met me?" Tyler shook his head in astonishment. "I never leave my comfort zone."

"I don't know. Seems like you've been stepping out of your comfort zone lately. Let's agree not to go scuba diving anytime soon."

"With sharks?" Tyler gave an exaggerated shudder. "No way. Those things will eat you without a single ounce of regret."

"Speaking of eating . . ." Chase wriggled around in her seat to look into the back. "I brought snacks. Do you want anything?"

Tyler lifted one hand away from the wheel to rub his eyes. "Is there a chance you have a Monster or something in that bag? Anything with caffeine in it would be great."

"Do you want me to drive?" Chase offered. She did, in fact, have a couple cans of cold-brew coffee from her emergency supply, but even *she* drew the line at driving while exhausted. "You look like you could use a break, and it's not like I'm doing anything vital at the moment. If you see a gas station at one of the exits, or a rest stop, we can always switch."

"I don't know . . ." Tyler stifled a yawn. "I mean, I'm tired, but you're not on the insurance, and it's my fault we're here anyway . . ."

Chase pulled out one of the cans, popped the tab, and set it in the cupholder for Tyler. He immediately took a swig.

"I agreed to come with you," Chase reminded him, tearing open a bag of cheese puffs. "I did *not* agree to die in a fiery wreck because you fell asleep at the wheel. Besides, it's my job as the passenger to keep you awake. If you insist on driving, I'm going to have to keep you alert."

Tyler smirked and took another slurp of coffee. "Do your worst."

Chase licked some of the electric-orange cheese powder off her fingers. "Okay, let's do a round of Would You Rather. Would you rather listen to nothing but country music until you die, or never hook up with anyone for the rest of your life?"

"Easy." Tyler's mouth quirked up into a shy smile. "I like country music."

Chase groaned and let her head thump back against the headrest. "God, I should have guessed that. Your turn."

"All right. Would you rather . . ." Tyler yawned hugely and shook his head.

She watched him while he tried to think of a good question. His face was never still. One second, he'd half-smile, and the next, he was scowling and narrowing his eyes. Everything he thought was written across his face as clear as if he'd said it aloud: he'd had a funny idea, then rejected it, then started the search for another. How was it possible for a person to be so unguarded, especially one as shy and self-conscious as Tyler?

"You're staring at me," he said.

"Your face is really interesting," she told him. "I like looking at it. Now either come up with a good question, or admit that you're too tired to be responsible for our general health and well-being."

"We're not even to Limon," Tyler protested.

"There's a lot of road between here and New York. Don't worry, you'll get plenty of time behind the wheel."

"You're stubborn," Tyler complained.

Chase put her feet up on the dashboard, preparing to shake the last of the cheese powder into her mouth. "Takes one to know one," she said.

Tyler fell asleep within a few minutes of surrendering the driver's seat. He was a snorer, too, but he looked so exhausted that Chase didn't have the heart to disturb him.

Chase turned on the radio, scanning through the stations as the miles rolled by. She skipped past the country stations—Tyler might like it, but too many lyrics about drunken macho patriotism and girls in cut-off blue jeans made her break out in hives. She skipped the pop stations, too, fully aware of her own impulse to belt her favorite lyrics at maximum volume even in confined spaces. In the end, she split the difference, settling for throwback eighties rock.

Tyler had only taken a few sips from the open can of cold-brew, and there was no point in letting it go to waste. Chase finished it off before sitting back, relaxing her shoulders, and tapping her hands on the wheel in time to the beat of "Don't Stop Believin'."

Unlike most people in her family, Chase actually enjoyed driving. Sarah would complain like a wet hen if she was forced to spend more than half an hour behind the wheel for *anything*; although to be fair, if Chase had to deal with her nephews screeching in the back seat, she would probably feel the same way. Someday, when she could scrape together a decent savings, she wanted to be able to travel. Driving was hypnotic. Relaxing. Even if Tyler's car had decent cruise control, Chase wouldn't have bothered with it. She liked being rooted in the moment. Before she knew it, she'd passed the Goodland exit. They were making great time.

As she mumbled the lyrics to "Billie Jean," Chase spotted a billboard advertising the World's Largest Ball of Twine. Tyler was still asleep, so she pulled up the map on her phone, turned on voice recognition, and whispered, "Cawker City, Kansas."

It was only a slight detour. Cawker City lay along Route 24, which ran parallel to the interstate. If they followed the side roads, they could rejoin I-70 near Topeka.

Chase had visited the twine ball once before with her father. She'd been almost thirteen at the time and had complained about how lame the whole enterprise was. As they'd stood looking over the nearly nine-ton twine ball, her father had whispered to her to close her eyes. When she obeyed—after rolling them so far back in her head she'd seen stars—Chase had heard the soft *shink* of scissors, and then felt a scratchy length of cord being twisted around her wrist. Her father had told her to be quiet in case anyone caught them, and the two of them had hurried back to the car, giggling like mad.

She'd found out later that he'd bought the twine at the gift shop when he'd gone in to use the bathroom, but the memory of the thrill she'd felt as they'd sprinted across the parking lot had stayed with her. Maybe she could give Tyler a memorable experience of his own, something to push him further out of his comfort zone without actually forcing him into a life of petty crime. They had plenty of time to get to New York. One little detour wouldn't hurt.

As she turned onto the Exit 45 off-ramp, Chase smiled to herself. After all, if you were going to be impulsive, you might as well do it right.

TYLER

Sleepless nights spent painting offices had taken their toll. The moment Tyler's eyes were closed, he was all but dead to the world, waking once or twice only long enough to turn his head to the other side, or wipe a spot of drool from his lips. His exhaustion, combined with the rumble of the engine beneath him, kept him comatose for hours.

Tyler slept so deeply that when the car finally pulled to a stop, it took him a moment to understand where he was.

"Chase?" he mumbled in the direction of the familiar figure in the driver's seat. *This is a weird dream*, he thought blearily. *Why would we be in a car, anyway?*

The nightmare of the situation came flooding back to him: a painting in New York, a trip across the country, the fear of embarrassment if he ended up on art magazines from coast to coast. He sat bolt upright, nearly knocking his head on the roof of the Honda. "Where are we?"

"Cawker City, Kansas," said Chase proudly. "Home of that magnificent wonder!" She gestured up a small hill toward an enormous, squat lump sitting under an open-sided protective roof. The sign next to it, barely readable to his sleep-bleary eyes, declared it as "Cawker City's

Ball of Twine. World's Largest." His confusion only intensified. What were they doing parked in front of who-knew-how-many tons of twine rolled into a forty-three-foot ball?

Tyler stared at it for a moment. He felt more stretched and knotted than the massive ball of string itself. "What? Why?"

"Because man is driven by creative urges he cannot deny," Chase said grandly, unbuckling her seatbelt. "This twine ball was created in the same spirit as the *Mona Lisa*, the Eiffel Tower, and the *Thirty-six Views of Mount Fuji*. We make art because we must, either in paint or in steel or in the humblest form of fiber arts."

Tyler rubbed his eyes. "Okay . . . but why are we *here*?"

"We're here on pilgrimage, obviously. Stop bellyaching and get out of the car," she said, already halfway out the driver's side. Nearly bouncing off the asphalt road, she popped open the rear door to his Honda and then snatched her art bag out of the back seat.

With a sigh, he crawled out of the passenger seat. If they were only in Kansas, he couldn't have slept long, but he was already feeling better. Actually rested. Which was more than he could say after the power naps he'd been taking the last few weeks as he juggled work and classes.

"These highway attractions are so weird. Anything to get you to turn off the interstate and get your gas in their town, I guess," he said as they followed the walkway up to the display.

"It's a little off the highway," Chase admitted. She'd tucked one of the smaller sketchbooks under her arm and thrown her art bag on one of the black-and-white benches surrounding the squat ball of brown rope. She had given up on the hair tie altogether. The smaller sketchbook unfolded into the crook of her arm, the flat side of which was exactly long enough for it to start at her palm and end with the spine perfectly in the crook of her elbow. It perched up at an angle from there, and she kept it open with the neat trick of tilting the tall half into her bicep. A piece of charcoal appeared in her other hand like magic. "My family stopped here once when my dad was still alive, so when I saw the billboard, I had to come. We're not far off course, I promise."

"Not far?" he repeated. "How far is 'not far'?"

She looked away sheepishly. "Forty-five minutes."

"Chase!" he exclaimed, stopping in his tracks. He pulled out his phone and checked the time. Had they passed through a time zone? "We're, like, six hours into a twenty-odd-hour drive! We can't afford to make detours like this!"

"We have plenty of time!" she argued.

"Yeah, but we're short on cash, and gas costs money." Tyler scrubbed his hands across his face. "Oh, man, we're going to be stranded in some weird little town with no way to pay for gas, I just *know* it . . ."

Chase looked suddenly sheepish. "I didn't think of that. I'd have asked what you thought, but you were asleep. You snore pretty loud when you get tired enough, by the way. Besides, look at it! I . . ." She gestured helplessly toward the twine. "I had to."

Tyler shook his head in bewilderment. "But it's *twine.*"

"Exactly." Chase grinned. "Nobody expects great things from twine, do they? But think about it: one day, a guy decided to make something, and after he died, a bunch of Kansans got together around his twine-based legacy and said, *You know how we're going to leave our mark on the world? We're going to keep hand-rolling almost nine tons of twine into a work of civic art.* And then they did. Imagine all the planning, all of the *hours* that have gone into this. All of the people whose hands touched it, all the way down to the middle."

"Are you making this up?" Tyler asked, narrowing his eyes at her.

"No," she said as they stepped under the roof of the gazebo. "I read the sign coming in. Some guy started making it in the fifties, and when he died, he gifted it to the town. They add to it every August." She plopped down on one of the benches and started scratching the charcoal in rapid strikes onto the open page of her sketchbook.

Tyler bit his lip, feeling the seconds slipping through his hands. "Chase . . ."

She held up a finger, the chalk already blackening her fingertips. It gave him the quick, nervous thought of criminals and rule-breaking.

Her hand went back to the sketchbook, roughing out quick shapes he couldn't make out from the angle where he stood. "Just look at it," she repeated with a nod toward the massive round roadblock she'd thrown in their way. "Take in its majesty. Give me like five minutes and a bathroom break, and then we can get back on the road, okay? We won't even have to backtrack to I-70. I've got a plan. Trust in the plan, Tyler."

He sighed and stuffed his hands into his pockets, looking over the giant twine ball. It was taller than either of them, rising almost to the underside of the decent-sized red-roofed gazebo. Either Chase was messing with him, or she really *did* think it was magnificent.

As far as Tyler was concerned, it was just . . . brown and in their way.

He pinched the bridge of his nose. Would it be rude to yell at Chase for making an unplanned stop? He was glad she had agreed to come with him to New York, but to have wasted time without asking him? Wasn't that rude too?

If Xavier had pulled a stunt like this, Tyler wouldn't have been surprised. On the other hand, his best friend might be irritating, but at least Tyler had the guts to call him out on it. He didn't know Chase well enough to do something like that.

While she sat scratching away in her book, Tyler examined the twine. There was only so long that he could look at it. Aside from its sheer mass, there was nothing spectacular about it. Twine was too ordinary to hold his attention.

When he looked back over his shoulder at her, Chase was smiling down at the sketchpad. *She* had no problem being captivated by something ordinary.

Which was probably a good thing, as far as Tyler was concerned. Maybe he could hold her attention, too, even now that he was no longer posing for her.

It'd be pretty bad if he turned out to be less riveting than a pile of handmade string.

Chase stood up abruptly, stretching her back and shoulders. She scooped her art bag off the bench and fought the oversized drawing pad—the one so large it stuck out of the top—to make room for the smaller sketchbook. She noticed something in the bottom of the bag and smirked as she fiddled with it unseen.

"Now for my bathroom break," Chase declared.

The little visitor's center was closed, but a port-a-potty luckily stood outside—likely the pair were not the only evening visitors who happened by every so often. While Chase made use of the limited facilities, Tyler took out his phone and checked their route. They actually weren't that far from the highway. That was a relief on two fronts: he didn't have to confront Chase further, and they really weren't that far behind on time.

The port-a-potty door opened, and then Tyler saw Chase approaching from the corner of his eye.

"We're just going to stay on Route 24, right?" Tyler asked, not looking up from his phone.

"Nah, there's a shortcut," said Chase. She was bent over the twine ball, examining it closely.

Tyler didn't look up until he heard the sharp *shnick* of scissors being closed. His mouth fell open in horror. With a look of total glee, Chase wielded the scissors again and leaned back from the twine ball, holding up a long and dangling thread in one hand.

"What are you doing!" Tyler demanded.

"Taking a souvenir." Chase winked, brandishing her shears. "I wouldn't want to forget our little rendezvous at the Twine Shrine."

"That's gotta be illegal."

"Yup," said Chase, tucking her scissors into her bag. "We've desecrated a national monument." She grabbed his hand and pulled it closer, wrapping the length of illicit dark fiber around his wrist.

"What are you doing?"

"Linking you to the crime," she said, finishing the knot. "Do you think they have cameras out here?" She leaned in conspiratorially. "I guess we have no way of knowing. Better make a run for it. If we get arrested, we'll never make it to New York in time. And now you're the one carrying the evidence, so if you try to throw me under the bus, they'll never believe you."

"Arrested?" he echoed in horror, his premonition about seeing black fingerprints and crime coming true.

"They can't hold us if they can't catch us." She tugged on Tyler's hand, and the two of them bolted down the walkway toward the Honda.

She shouldn't be running with scissors, Tyler crazily thought. How could he trust Chase after a stunt like this? She was obviously manic. Or a maniac. Or both. She could have been lying about the painting too—maybe she felt that as long as she didn't get caught, she could do whatever she liked. It was clear she didn't care about civic decency, at any rate, so why would personal privacy be any different?

Tyler flung himself into the driver's seat. He didn't wait for Chase to buckle her own seatbelt before he peeled off through the sleepy streets of Cawker City.

Somewhere along the way, Chase had started laughing. Now she was bent over the dashboard, thumping her palms on her thighs and cackling like a madwoman.

"What's so funny?" Tyler demanded, trying to calm his pattering heart. He had to drive like a normal person now. According to the documentaries he'd watched, plenty of criminals got caught well after their original crimes for basic driving infractions—just look at Ted Bundy and the Oklahoma City Bomber. If they could only make it out of Cawker before the police caught up with them, they should be okay. *Unless they got a photo of your plates.* God, he'd feel like an idiot if he ended up keeping his nude portrait out of an art show only to get his mug shot splashed all over the internet in the process. What was the statute of limitations on twine vandalism, anyway?

"Your face." Chase snorted, still shaking with laughter. "Priceless."

"Look." Tyler did his best not to snap at her, but the words did have a little bite. "You're supposed to be helping me fix your mistake, not getting us in *more* trouble. Why would you think that *this* was worth it?" Without looking away from the road, he held up his arm. "All that talk about art and creation, and the first thing you do is destroy it!"

Chase fell silent.

He risked a glance over at her. She was staring at his wrist, her mouth twisted to hold back some emotion. Had he gone too far? Well, she certainly had. Tyler shot a look of disgust at the blue yarn wrapped around his wrist.

Blue?

Tyler checked the road, then held up his wrist for closer inspection. Sure enough, a length of blue yarn was knotted around his arm.

"What is this?" he demanded.

Chase let out another howl of laughter. "You totally fell for it! You really thought I'd cut it, didn't you?"

"You didn't?" he asked.

"Of course not. How much of a vandal do you think I am? I had some blue yarn in my bag." Chase wiped tears from her eyes, still giggling. "It would have been better if the store was open, and I could have gotten some *real* twine. Too bad I didn't have any on me. I bet you'd never have figured it out then. My dad did the same thing to me, only he bought a twine piece beforehand. I practically sprinted to the car. You *actually* did." She wiped tears of laughter from the corners of her eyes again.

"You were just messing with me?" he asked, fingering the loose knot of yarn.

"I couldn't help myself."

"And we're *not* on the run from the cops?"

"Not unless you have a secret history I don't know about." She chuckled.

Tyler eased off the gas and let out an exasperated puff of air. "You and Xavier *would* get along."

Chase's phone chimed, and she looked out the window suddenly. "Slow down! We're turning left up here."

He frowned at the map on his phone. "Are you sure we can't just stay on US-24?"

"Come on, Tyler. You're going to miss the turn. I told you there was a plan, didn't I? What else did I say?"

"You told me to trust the plan." With a sigh, Tyler obeyed.

They didn't talk for a while, and Chase reached into her art bag at her feet and pulled her sketchbook out again. The soft scratching of her pencil on the paper made his shoulders relax. He reached out and pulled the yarn bracelet on his wrist like he was plucking a guitar string.

"If you're that mad about it, I can cut it off," she said. "The yarn, I mean. I thought it would be funny, but if it's not . . ." She folded up her sketchpad for a second and looked in her bag, dragging out the scissors.

"That's okay. I'll keep it as a reminder that you aren't to be trusted." Tyler shot her a sudden look, worried she might have misunderstood that he was joking. But Chase was smiling as she dropped the scissors into the bag and reopened the sketchpad. She leaned against her own door and tilted the paper into the dusky light.

I want to be like her.

The sudden realization made his head ache; he didn't want to be quite so over-the-top, but he'd love to be a little braver, a little more easygoing, a little more confident.

"You're going to take a right up here, and then a left pretty soon after that." Chase closed her notepad. "And I'm sorry if I really scared you. I thought it would be fun. A cheap thrill."

Tyler sniffed. "It was kind of fun, I guess."

"Really?" She leaned her seat back again, nestling into the cushions. "I'm glad. That's the whole point of living, isn't it?"

"Would you rather eat a hagfish, or a dozen raw grubs?" Chase asked.

Tyler scowled. "What's a hagfish?"

"It's a deep-sea creature that's basically a never-ending snot supply. They also kind of look like that squid guy from *SpongeBob*."

"And why would I eat *either* of those things?"

"Choosing between two equivalently bad experiences is the whole point of the game." She scoffed. "If I asked, *Would you rather eat a hagfish or a cheeseburger?* I wouldn't learn anything about you."

"What if I hated cheeseburgers?" Tyler asked. It was fully dark;

they'd left Cawker City behind more than an hour ago. "Or what if I'd sworn off beef?"

She considered this before shaking her head. "I think by definition humans have sworn off hagfish, but I'll take your non-answer as an answer. You'd starve. If it were me, I'd eat the grubs."

Tyler was searching for a witty retort when he saw the sign: *Road Closed Ahead.*

"You've got to be kidding me," he grumbled, bringing the small Honda to a lurching stop on the narrow two-lane road.

Chase's eyes widened as she pulled out her phone to double-check. "No way. The app doesn't say anything about a road closure."

Tyler gestured to the sign. "Well, I guess it's wrong."

She groaned and tapped at her phone for a minute before biting her lip. "I'm not getting a signal."

"Cause we're dozens of miles from civilization," Tyler said. There were no other cars on the road, at least. Other cars honking at him always made him nervous.

"We'll have to make a U-turn," said Chase in a small voice. "And we need to go back to Route 24."

He turned the car around in a three-point turn, doing his best to keep the wheels on the asphalt. The last thing he wanted was to slide down into the culvert. Being trapped on a small rural road with no phone was the start of at least three horror movies he could name off the top of his head.

"Are you mad?" Chase asked. "You look mad. I'm really sorry, Tyler."

"I'm fine," he muttered. "Let's just not take any more detours, okay?"

Chase nodded glumly and reached for the radio. "You said that you like country, right? I accept this as my penance." She fiddled the dial until she found a top-twenty country station.

They drove back the way they'd come, no longer talking. The silence didn't sit easily with Tyler, but Chase seemed to be giving him space, and he wasn't sure what to say.

A half hour later, they stopped for gas at a little family-owned store, hardly more than a shack. Chase sat in the car while Tyler paid for their fuel in cash. He tried not to think about how much farther along they'd be if they'd stuck to the route, counting his meager stack of bills once more. They hadn't just wasted time; they'd wasted money they didn't have.

By the time they finally pulled out onto I-70, the radio had cycled through the entire list of top country hits. Chase's forty-five-minute detour had cost them more than two hours and almost a quarter of their cash.

CHASE

C hase was exhausted, but she couldn't sleep.

Tyler hummed along with one of the country songs on the radio. Chase had never heard it before tonight, but after only a few hours, she felt like she knew every song on the top-twenty charts by heart.

Finally, when the repetition became too much, she reached over and flipped the radio off. "How are you doing?"

"I'm starving," Tyler admitted, "but I'm holding out."

"I feel like the biggest idiot in the world. Like I really let you down. Like I don't deserve to be Navigator-in-Chief. We're almost eleven hours into this drive, and we haven't even reached Topeka."

"Well, we *are* low on gas again," Tyler said. "And I could really use a minute or two to stretch out the old legs. Maybe when we get close to Topeka, we can take a little break."

Chase nodded. "That sounds great. I'm glad we're talking again, too."

"We could have been talking this whole time. I really wasn't as mad as you think I was. I'm kind of . . ." He shrugged helplessly. "Quiet. As a person."

"Do you need me to keep you awake?"

"As long as I don't have to play *Would You Rather* for a few hours, I'm happy to talk."

Chase crooked one arm behind her head. "Have you ever been to New York before?"

"When I was a kid, my parents took me. I remember everything feeling big. It smelled awful, and it was so *dirty*. I couldn't imagine living like that."

Chase shot him a shrewd look.

"Okay, yes, I realize how that sounds." Tyler laughed self-consciously, adjusting his grip on the wheel. "Probably if you took someone who lived in New York City and dumped them off in the backwoods, they'd feel the same way I did."

Chase examined him thoughtfully. "Did you grow up in the woods? Do you know how to tie a bunch of cool knots and, like, purify water and whatever? I've always wanted to learn to do that kind of thing. Ooh, and identify wild herbs and navigate by starlight and know which side of trees moss grows on, and . . . Well, whatever else people do in the woods. Are you secretly a lumberjack? Can you teach me your tree-cutting ways?"

A slight grin tugged at the corner of Tyler's lips. "No. I was being facetious. I'm a city boy, just not a *big city* boy. To be honest, I'd probably be afraid of the woods too. It's full of blood-sucking parasites and bears. Plus, what if you identified herbs wrong? You know that guy who died in Alaska from eating wild plants? The guy from the movie—Chris something. I couldn't eat lettuce for a week after that."

"You once saw a movie about someone who died from eating a wild plant and you decided to give up salads?"

"Only temporarily. And I would never eat a wild plant."

Chase grinned. "Are you afraid of cilantro?"

"I don't *like* cilantro. You know what I do when I go to the grocery store? I *don't buy cilantro*. And I know my salad greens don't have deadly nightshade or whatever mixed in." Tyler quirked an eyebrow at her. "But, hey, you want to go tasting the wild plants, be my guest."

"You know that tomatoes and eggplants are nightshades, too,

right? And potatoes, I think." Chase tapped her phone a few times before nodding. "Yup, and peppers. And *tobacco*."

"Are they deadly?" Tyler asked, looking worried.

Chase lowered her phone. "Did you just ask me if potatoes are deadly? Don't you think someone would have noticed by now?"

Tyler winced. "Uh. Maybe?"

"You're too much." Chase kicked her feet up onto the dash with a grin. "How come you're so reluctant to try things?"

"I'm not reluctant," he retorted. "Just reasonable."

"Sure, with some things. Like, when we were talking about sharks? I get that. Although, there are a lot more car accidents every year than shark attacks, and you don't seem too nervous about driving."

"Yeah, but I drive all the time. It hasn't killed me yet."

"Nothing's killed you yet," Chase pointed out. "But you're still *overly reasonable* about things."

"I guess it is pretty silly of me," he mumbled. "This is why I don't really talk about it."

"I'm not making fun." Chase wiggled in her seat so she could look at him, reinforcing that she truly was not teasing by giving him her full attention. "And I'm not criticizing, either. I'm *curious*."

When Tyler didn't reply, her stomach sank a little. This time, she'd pushed him too far. After all, it wasn't like he owed her an explanation for his overabundance of caution.

Stifling a twinge of guilt, Chase settled back in her seat. "You know, when I was a kid, I used to get into all kinds of trouble. I wanted to try everything. When I was, I dunno, six? Old enough to know better, anyway, I realized that I didn't know what a dodgeball tasted like, so I licked one."

Tyler laughed in surprise. "Gross."

"I like to know things, even if they don't make sense. And I don't always think in a straight line. So when I press you and ask these questions, I'm not making fun. I actually want to understand."

He tapped his fingers on top of the steering wheel before responding. "It's safe. That's about all I can tell you. If it ain't broke, don't fix it. And there's a lot of risk-reward analysis involved. I like not being eaten by sharks more than I like swimming, so I don't go in the ocean. I like not getting attacked by an axe-wielding maniac more than I like sleeping in the woods at night, so I don't go camping. I like not getting tetanus more than I like licking mysterious playground equipment, so I . . . don't do that."

"Pretty sure dodgeballs don't give you tetanus." Chase chuckled. "Of course, I did have the rubber taste on my tongue for hours afterwards."

Thankfully, she had the good sense not to turn that into a sex joke.

It was nearly midnight by the time they pulled into the riverside gas station just outside of Topeka.

"Hey," Chase said suddenly as she glanced at the clock, "it's official."

"What is?"

"You've now officially spent more time in my presence clothed than naked." She held up her hand for a high-five.

Tyler rolled his eyes, blushing only slightly this time. "I am not high-fiving that."

"Don't leave me hanging," she said. At last, reluctantly, Tyler held up his own hand and slapped his palm lightly against hers.

"You call that a slap?" Chase laughed. "You have to be a little rougher than that." Unable to stop herself this time, she leaned closer. "A little *harder*."

For someone as tired as he obviously was, Tyler hopped out of the car rather quickly.

Chase slipped out her door and groaned as she lifted her arms above her head and bent down to touch her toes.

"I think my butt was starting to fuse to that seat," Chase complained.

"At least you were wearing pants, Miss I-sit-naked-on-my-home-furniture."

"I'm never going to live that down, am I?"

"Not while we're driving across the country to rescue *my* naked bottom, no."

"Fair point." She twisted her hips to one side until the joints popped, and she sighed with relief. "All right. It's my turn to cover the gas. Do you mind grabbing us some more snacks before I'm reduced to eating my own arm?"

Tyler chuckled. "I'll see what I can scrounge up."

He left her to pump the gas, and Chase watched him fondly as he made his way into the twenty-four-hour gas station. He was really growing on her. After a lifetime of bad dates with guys who were inevitably hot messes, Chase was a little surprised to realize that in the current duet, she was the hotter and messier one.

She took her purse out of her huge art bag and stepped around to the driver's side, dug out her card, swiped it in the reader, and then tossed the handbag on the roof of the car. Its long strap trailed down over the window. Tyler still seemed pretty awake, and Chase was beginning to think she really *should* take a nap. If he was ever going to trust her behind the wheel again, she should be well-rested enough to help make up for lost time.

Once she had the gas pump going, Chase reached for the windshield cleaner squeegee and got to work. There were bugs smeared all over the glass, and it would be nice to prove she was capable of being thoughtful and actually thinking ahead. For once.

She was just finishing up the driver's side when a man cycled past. *Kind of late for a bike ride,* she thought, but who was she to judge? Everyone had their own story, and she'd certainly had to head out for a late-night snack run more often that she'd like to admit. For all she knew, he worked there.

Chase kept squeegeeing, stepping back to admire the results. It would be a lot easier to drive through the night if they could actually see where they were going.

The bike rolled past again, right next to the car this time. She looked up, and the rider made eye contact with her as his arm shot out, snatching her purse off the car roof.

"Hey!" she screamed. "Get back here!" The biker ignored her, pedaling faster, her purse clutched to his chest. He wobbled side to side as he stepped hard on the pedals, trying to gain speed. The bicycle bounced onto the road from the parking lot, heading across the street toward the bridge that ran over the Kansas River.

Chase didn't stop to think; her feet were already moving. She pelted after the bike faster than she'd ever run in her life.

As she passed the building, Tyler stepped out onto the tarmac with an armful of snacks. His brown eyes widened in shock, but Chase didn't have time to worry about him.

Even running at full tilt, she was already well behind the bike. Her mom hadn't raised a quitter, though. With a primal scream that came from the very core of her being, Chase threw the squeegee like a tomahawk. It whipped, rubber end over plastic handle, in a slicing spiral.

She'd meant to hit the rider, but through the magic of happy accidents, the squeegee flew into the spokes of his front wheel. The thief was flung forward over the handlebars.

"Drop my bag!" Chase snarled as the man scrambled to his feet, trying to pull the squeegee free at the same time. It wouldn't come. He dropped the bike and started running.

He was fast too. Apparently, his little tumble over the handlebars hadn't been as rough as it looked. He was barely limping.

I should aim for the head next time, she thought, springing after him.

Chase caught up with him as he passed the edge of the bridge, grabbing for the strap of her purse. "Give it back!"

The thief tried to kick her legs out from under her, and the two of them went sprawling onto the pedestrian walkway along the side of the bridge.

The man got to his feet, sprinting a few more yards out over the water before she managed to catch up again, swiping at his arm.

"I'm not going to call the cops!" she shrieked. "Just give me the bag!" Her fingers wrapped around the handle of the purse, and she gave it a sharp tug.

She caught a glimpse of Tyler running up to them just as the thief elbowed her hard in the gut. With the purse still clutched triumphantly in her hand, Chase overbalanced. Her hip bumped the rail as she went over. A moment later, the muddy water of the Kansas River closed over her head.

For a second, Chase was stunned.

She hadn't had time to take a deep breath before she hit the water. The current pulled at her, and she hung underwater for a moment while her scattered senses regrouped. When her lungs started to burn, she flailed to the surface, choking on the muddy water that had already filled her nose and mouth.

The current had carried her a little way downstream. The bridge seemed miles away, and it shrank quickly as she was pulled along. Tyler rushed out onto the walkway, his arms empty. She tried to call out to him, but she choked on the water that was intent on filling her lungs. Her feet kicked, barely keeping her above the surface, but she made no headway to the shore.

I'm going to die out here. I can't touch the bottom, and I never learned how to swim—why didn't I bother?

Chase paddled harder, trying to swim against the current back toward the bridge. She went under again for a moment and came up choking, her eyes burning with the sting of muddy river water.

I'm going to die in Kansas.

And Tyler's just going to watch.

To her lasting shock, Tyler didn't hesitate. He dove over the side of the bridge at a full sprint. The water stole him from sight with a splash before he popped to the surface again, gracefully swimming over to her with long, powerful strokes. Within seconds, his hands hooked under her armpits, and he began to tow her back to land. Instead of fighting the current, he swam with it, letting it push them downstream, at an angle, ever closer to the edge of the river.

Chase kept struggling, trying to help, doing anything she could think of to get them out of the water.

"Relax," Tyler said. "It's harder to hold you when you keep squirming."

Her fight-or-flight instincts had kicked in, but Tyler sounded so calm. So self-assured. His grip tightened on her, and Chase decided to trust him.

When they reached the bank, Chase dragged herself up onto the rocky shore, still gasping for breath.

"Are you okay?" Tyler asked, pushing her wet hair out of her eyes.

"My purse," she gasped, holding up the spaghetti-thin leather shoulder strap with two broken brass clips on either end. "All my stuff was in there. My credit card, my phone, my ID, they're all gone." The purse's body had been on the strap as she hit the water but had somehow broken free in her panicked flailing, leaving her with a useless strip of leather.

It was easier to talk about the purse than admit she was still panicked by the idea of going under for good.

Tyler grimaced sympathetically and looked out over the water. In the darkness, it was impossible to see anything. Chase knew it was hopeless, but that didn't stop her from scanning the current, just in case.

"It's gone," he said. "But are you okay?"

Her mouth tasted like dirt, and she was shivering so hard her teeth clacked together. But she felt physically whole. "I'm okay," she finally said. "I'm okay."

Tyler slumped onto the rocky embankment and wiped the water from his eyes and the mud from his face, blowing out a shuddering sigh of relief.

"Thank you," Chase said, her voice quivering—whether from the shock or the cold, she wasn't sure. "For following and for diving in and . . . and thank you." She hugged her knees tighter to her chest, trying to keep out the chill. Her ears were ringing, and although she was safe now, the memory of the water pressing in on her chest and tugging at her legs made her shudder.

"Are you sure?" Tyler asked.

"I . . . I . . ." Chase sucked in a breath, partly just to prove to herself that she could. There was no water. No rush of cold liquid clogging her lungs and throat. "Y-y-yes . . ."

"Hey." Tyler leaned closer and squeezed her arm. "Count backward from ten."

"Huh?" Chase blinked at him. "Why?"

"It always helps me relax," Tyler said. "Slowly. Count your breaths. Ten . . . Nine . . . Eight . . ."

Chase did as he told her, feeling her shoulders relax incrementally with each passing breath. By the time they reached *one*, she really did feel better.

"Can you get up?" Tyler asked gently as he unfolded himself from the rocks and wiped his hands down his soaked front. "We need to dry off."

Chase nodded absently and let him pull her to her feet.

They walked back to the gas station, where their snacks and drinks lay scattered on the concrete. Tyler must have dropped them when he followed.

"Are you okay?" A worried-looking gas station attendant peeped her head out of the doorway. "What happened?" Her eyes widened when she took in their bedraggled appearances.

"Somebody grabbed her purse and knocked her in the water," Tyler said. Chase was glad he'd been the one to answer—her teeth were rattling so hard that she wasn't sure she could speak.

He left Chase by the door, returning with her duffel before ushering her through to the women's bathroom. Despite being as cold as she was, he was calm and collected.

"Take as long as you need," he told her.

She nodded slowly.

The bathrooms were surprisingly clean. Chase ducked into a stall and stripped off the drenched clothing while biting back tears. Her hands were shaking, and the reality of what had almost happened was starting to sink in.

Would I really have died for a purse and credit card? she thought angrily, trying to steer her emotions away from fear and remorse. *Why did I think confronting him would be worth it? I should have just let him go.*

She dug out a T-shirt and shorts and finished changing before she headed over and squatted down under the heated hand-dryer. She hoped to dry her hair enough that she could stop shivering. She didn't want Tyler to see her panicking. Chase didn't like *anyone* seeing her scared, but for some reason it felt especially important that Tyler not know how freaked out she was, although she couldn't have said why.

When she finally emerged from the bathroom, Tyler was standing at the counter, having already changed in the other restroom.

"Do you want me to call the cops?" the attendant asked, looking anxiously between the two of them as if she were hoping they would say no but wanted to follow the proper protocols.

Tyler looked over his shoulder toward Chase. "Your call."

"And put us another few hours behind?" Chase laughed bitterly. It was her fault they'd lost time in Cawker, and her fault that they'd both gotten dunked.

"*This* is a bigger deal," Tyler said. "Than the other thing, I mean. If you want to stay here and deal with this, the other thing can wait." He seemed to mean it too.

Which probably meant he actually *was* as freaked out as Chase, but he was hiding it better.

Chase considered his expression before turning to the attendant. "Do you have surveillance cameras here?"

The attendant grimaced. "Not out there right now. Sorry. The exterior cameras broke a while back, and the new one hasn't come in yet."

"Then there's no point," Chase said, turning back to Tyler. "We might as well keep going. It's not like I'm going to be able to identify that guy, and my purse is at the bottom of the river. We wouldn't gain anything by hanging around."

They thanked the attendant and headed back to the car. While Chase got into the passenger side, Tyler put the nozzle back and closed the gas cap. It felt like a hundred years since they'd pulled off the interstate, and she was thankful for whoever had invented the automatic stops on gas pumps. Otherwise, they'd be drowning in gasoline.

Drowning. Chase shuddered. Of all the dangers she could have been forced to face tonight, why did it have to be water?

Tyler dug around in the trunk before producing a down sleeping bag.

"You're shaking," he said kindly.

Chase accepted the offering and unzipped the side, spreading it over her lap. "You're so prepared."

"Not that prepared." Tyler held up his phone. "I didn't think to take this out of my pocket earlier. I'm pretty sure it's dead."

"And I was just about to ask you to let me borrow it so I could call and cancel my credit card." Chase groaned. "So no phones and no credit card. What do we have?"

"About a hundred wet bucks and some cheap snacks."

"What do we do now?"

Tyler opened his wallet, spreading out the damp bills on the dashboard. "You tell me. Do we go back?"

"Back?" Chase asked in surprise. "You mean back to Colorado?"

"I'm thinking of it more as a tactical retreat," Tyler corrected. "Besides, you're the one who faced your worst fear tonight."

"And you're the one who rescued me from it." Chase nestled down in the sleeping bag, already feeling pleasantly warm. "We're a good chunk of the way there, right? More than a third? No point in going back now. We came here on a mission."

"You're sure?"

Chase nodded. "I'm game if you are. Heaven knows I can survive a few days on cheap crackers and gas station coffee. Wouldn't be the first time."

He ran his fingers over the damp blue length of yarn, seeming to think things over. "Are we doing the thing where we egg each other on despite the fact that it might not be in our best interests?"

"I know I am." Chase grinned.

"Then let's go." With a determined nod, Tyler started the engine, leaving the damp bills to dry on the dash. He turned the heat up without asking. "But first, I better get us the analog version of Google

Maps." He grabbed one of the squishy bills off of the dashboard and reached for the handle of his car door.

While she waited, Chase snuggled deeper into the sleeping bag and closed her eyes. She repeated the little exercise that Tyler had given her. *Ten. Nine. Eight . . .*

Her eyes snapped open as Tyler stepped back into the car, a paper map clenched triumphantly in one hand. "There we go. All set. Ready to resume your duties as Navigator-in-Chief?"

Chase nodded, accepting the map with all the solemnity of a knighthood. "Thank you, milord." She clutched the map between both hands, eyes still fixed on him. "And thank you again. For earlier. Not just the diving but for making sure I was okay. The counting thing helped."

"Doesn't it?" Tyler smiled.

"Do you rely on that a lot?" she asked curiously.

"Only when things get to be too much." He turned the key over in the engine. "In other words: yes."

She laughed softly. "Hey, Tyler?" she said, as she pulled the toasty sleeping bag up to her chin, feeling the first blushes of sleep cloud her mind. He paused and looked over at her. His hair had begun to dry, curling around his face like a pale brown halo. *I want to sketch it,* Chase dreamily thought. "Were you scared when you jumped in the water?"

"Sure."

"Then why'd you do it?"

"Risk-reward analysis," he said in a voice so soft that Chase thought she might be imagining it. "Like the *Would You Rather* game we keep playing. I like knowing you're all right more than I like keeping my feet on dry land. So I jumped."

TYLER

I t was still dark when Tyler pulled into a rest stop near the Illinois border. According to the clock, it was nearly six a.m.

Chase blinked at him, rubbing her eyes sleepily as she squirmed in her seat. "What's going on?"

"I need a break," Tyler said. He put his seat back as far as it would go.

The early spring air was still cold, or he'd have considered sleeping on one of the benches outside, just for a chance to get out of the car. Not away from her, but away from the body-deadening rumble of tired shocks and uneven pavement. As it was, he tossed and turned, trying to get comfortable in the too-small space, the steering wheel rubbing him one moment, the brake catching his toes the next. It was too cold in the car to be comfortable. Tyler rubbed his shoulders and biceps to force a little heat into himself.

A few minutes, he told his body. *Come on. Five minutes of sleep. That's all I ask.*

After ten minutes of this, Chase pulled the sleeping bag off herself. "I got it warm for you," she said.

He shook his head. "You should keep it. I'll be okay."

Chase ignored him, shoving the whole downy zippered blanket

over the console at him before rolling to one side and nestling against her duffel bag as though it were a pillow. Within moments, her breathing became slow and even again.

Tyler lay awake, watching the cars on either side of them come and go. Whenever he closed his eyes, he imagined Chase disappearing beneath the dark water of the Kansas River again and again.

How come you're so reluctant? she'd asked, but he had heard the true question: *Why are you so scared of everything?* Probably because he could always imagine the worst outcome of a situation, no matter how far-fetched it was. The danger of her drowning hadn't been some remote worry. It had been terrifyingly real.

An event like that certainly puts things into perspective. Watching the beams of headlights play over the roof of the car, Tyler instinctively imagined the worst that could happen if Chase's painting ever saw the light of day.

He'd be humiliated, sure. But then what? He'd been humiliated before, and he'd eventually gotten over it. The painting would be on a bigger scale, though. People on campus would recognize him. Someone would tell his parents. And Dennis. And if the painting won, it would go into that national magazine and probably online, and everyone knew that once something was on the internet, you could never get rid of it. The painting would haunt him forever, turning up in job searches and background checks, and if he ever got in trouble with the police, they'd be able to find it, and they'd say, *This is Tyler, and he's the pervert who modeled for a total stranger in college, so with this undisputed history of public nudity, we rest our case, your honor . .*
.

It was irrational. He knew that. But his fear was still real, even if it made no sense. He still had to get that painting back.

He had told Chase that jumping off the bridge had been a matter of risk-reward analysis, but the truth was he hadn't thought at all. Seeing her flip over the guardrail and hearing the terrifying splash of her body hitting the water had awoken something primal and unfamiliar in the core of him. One second he was on the bridge, and the next he was looking down to water rushing up to meet him. There was no thought in his mind as he splashed through the rushing water, only the desperate need to get Chase to shore.

Gradually, he became aware that the car was shaking. He checked to make sure that the engine was off before looking over at Chase.

She was shivering.

"Take the sleeping bag back," he said softly, pushing it toward her.

Chase shook her head stubbornly, still facing the passenger window. "Then you'll just be cold."

"I told you, I can handle it."

She rolled over toward him, and a pair of headlights illuminated her face for a moment. Her hair had dried into a tangled mess made flat and disheveled by the unforgiving canvas bag she had turned into her pillow. Trails of dried dirt from the river peeked out in patches near her hairline. The small amount of sleep she had managed to glean had not erased the dark smudges under her eyes. Chase gave him the perfect smile, and she became the most beautiful thing he had ever seen. "This is dumb. Why don't we share the sleeping bag?"

Tyler blinked at her.

"Let's sleep in the back seat," she said.

"Together?"

"I promise I'll keep my hands to myself," she said in playful innocence.

The thought of lying down beside her, sharing a sleeping bag in such a small space, made Tyler's already straining heart threaten to break through his rib cage. Just like it had when he'd read her email inviting him to view her portfolio: *I'd love to see you there*. The way it had when she had first seen him nude without a blush of embarrassment of her own. The way it had when she had unselfishly volunteered to take this wild journey with him.

Chase could do things like that, could throw heavy words around like they weighed nothing, could ask him to sleep beside her like it was no big deal. Tyler himself had trouble thinking of anything that *could* be a bigger deal. How did this kind of thing come so easily to her? It was pathetic, really, how much he wanted her to like him, even when he was convinced he'd never have the guts to do anything about it. His mouth went suddenly dry, and he found himself looking at her legs and her hips, before changing his focus to the little piece of blue yarn tied around his wrist.

His mind went to the giant box of condoms in the glove box. *No,* he thought wildly, *I can't . . . We're not . . .*

If Xavier knew that he'd had the chance to get this close to a girl he really liked and had turned her down, Tyler would never hear the end of it.

It doesn't matter what Xavier would want, he told himself. *What do I want?* Another glance at Chase's sleepy face was enough to convince him that she literally meant *sleep.*

He couldn't "sleep" with her, but just plain sleeping? He could probably manage that.

"Okay," he said, diving off the figurative bridge.

Chase smiled at him again before opening her car door and getting into the back seat. She lay down, looking up at him, her head just below his headrest.

There wasn't a lot of room left back there beside her. They'd be really, really close.

"Remember when I got so cold in the art room?" he asked.

She nodded. "Right after that lady walked in on us."

Tyler groaned. "Don't remind me. I'd rather forget that ever happened. Anyway, I was going to say, you turned the heat up to keep me from shivering. That was really nice of you."

"You're stalling," Chase said. "It's okay if you'd rather stay up there. I'll just be lying here . . . slowly freezing to death . . ."

"I'd always heard art students were dramatic. I wonder who starts rumors like that?"

Her laughter followed him as he opened the car door, stepping out into the cold night. Even then he hesitated.

"You're making a big deal out of nothing," he mumbled to himself in the darkness. "It's a nap. People nap together all the time."

Maybe some people did, but not people like Tyler. Not with people like Chase.

He opened the back door, and she wiggled over to make room for him.

"I won't bite," she promised. "Not this time, anyway." Tyler recoiled, but Chase reached for him. "No! I'm kidding. Come on."

Warily, Tyler slid in.

The seat was cramped, and she shifted again to make more room for Tyler. It was awkward at first, and it required quite a lot of shifting around and sliding their limbs against each other. Tyler was quietly going into anxiety-induced organ failure when they finally settled in side-by-side.

"I don't fit," Tyler complained.

Chase hoisted herself up on one arm. When Tyler didn't move, she reached out and dragged him closer so his shoulder rested against the back of the seat.

"But where will you . . . ?" Tyler began. He stopped abruptly as Chase settled in against him, resting her head on his shoulder. They were touching all along their bodies now—through their clothes, of course, but he could still feel her warmth. Still feel her breathing. Hell, when he held his breath long enough, he could feel her heartbeat.

"Tyler?" Chase asked.

He let out a noise like helium escaping a balloon.

"Oxygen is your friend," she reminded him.

"Right," he gasped. "Uh-huh. You're totally correct."

She sat up again, leaning over him to reach for the sleeping bag. She tugged it a few times, hauling it back toward them, using him as leverage as she did so. When it came free, she tucked it carefully around them.

"There," she said. "Is that better?"

This is how people are supposed to feel at prom. This scared-but-excited thing? This is what I was supposed to feel every time I sat next to a girl that I thought I liked. Tyler shifted slightly. "Yeah."

"If you're falling off the edge, you can roll on your side," she pointed out sleepily.

He did as she suggested, but that only made things worse. Now his chest was pressed against hers, her face inches from his own . . . It was like they were about to kiss. But they definitely weren't.

Right?

"Tyler?" Chase said.

"Yeah?" His voice wobbled, threatening to break.

"*Breathe.*"

"Yes. I should . . . yes."

"You're okay," she told him, rubbing his arm. "Count down from ten. I promised: I won't bite. Okay? You're safe with me. I'm not going to do anything you don't want."

He closed his eyes, pinching his mouth as though he were in pain. "You don't have to do that."

"Do what?"

"Be nice to me. Comfort me. I know what I'm like."

Her hand stilled on his arm. "What are you like?"

"A coward," he said at once, like the word had been bouncing around inside his head for days, maybe even years. "Boring. Forgettable."

Her fingers trailed down to the loop of blue yarn at his wrist. "That's not how I'd describe you."

"But it's true!" he insisted. "The only reason you put up with me at first was for the grade in your class, and the only reason you came along with me on this road trip was because I guilted you into it."

"Name one thing you haven't been brave enough to do."

He got very quiet. Her eyes were bright in the dim glow from the lamps that lined the parking lot.

She'd seen him naked, hadn't she? He could be honest with her about this.

"I didn't ask you out," he mumbled.

Chase tried to meet his eyes, and when he looked away, she lifted herself up on one elbow until he was forced to meet her gaze. "What are you talking about?" she asked.

"The day that you dropped the painting off," he said, "you'd sort of invited me to lunch, and then you left me in the hall when you turned in the painting in your one-on-one, and I thought . . . I thought, *Tyler, you big dummy, if you don't ask her out, you're going to be kicking yourself for the rest of your life.* And then I had to go to work, and I started to panic, and I couldn't quite get the guts to reach out again."

"Oh," she said. "I didn't know."

"Didn't you?" he asked. "Because when you invited me to come look at your work, you said you'd *love to have me there.* And I know you probably typed it without thinking, but I kept reading it over and over again and wondering if you'd meant more than that . . . which is stupid, I know." He swallowed hard, thinking he should probably just shut up. "I spiraled out of control, overanalyzing a simple sentence. And then I thought, *You're being a freak, Tyler. Just talk to her—it's not like she declared her love for you, you idiot. Just explain why you had to leave.*"

Chase let herself back down onto the seat. "I had no idea all of this was going on in your head."

"How could you have known?" he asked. "It's not like I told you."

"That explains why you didn't ask me." She looked back up at him. "What about now?"

"Now?" he echoed.

"Sure. I get that all of this stuff was going on for you up until Friday, and what happened with the painting probably put a damper on things, but . . . what about now?"

He swallowed so loud that the sound echoed through the enclosed space. "*Now.*"

"Why don't you ask me out now?" she said, lifting her eyebrows. Even in shadow, she was beautiful. She wasn't going to force him to do anything, but if he wanted . . .

Tyler's chest had begun to rise and fall unsteadily as he stared at her. No doubt she could feel it, but he couldn't stop himself.

"What would your answer be if I asked?" he asked. Her fingers went back to tracing lazy circles around his wrist, following the line of the yarn.

"Asked what?" she teased.

"I already told you, I'm not brave enough to do it," he said.

Her fingers traced their way up his forearm, over the hem of his T-shirt near his collarbone. He didn't pull away.

"Tyler?"

"Chase?"

"I have a confession to make." She leaned closer, until their faces were only a few inches apart.

"A confession?" Tyler squeaked.

"I want to kiss you, but I don't want to scare you. And if you're uncomfortable asking me out, then I understand that you probably don't want to kiss me, either. But I thought you should know."

"Oh." His pulse began to race under her fingertips. "You do?"

She nodded. "I have for a while. Since we're coming clean about this sort of thing, I figured I should tell you. If you *did* ask me out, there's a high probability that I'd agree to at least one date."

Tyler had started shaking somewhere along the way. It was nothing like how he'd shivered after being doused in the water—he felt warm all over. Hopeful. If Chase liked him, too, then he'd been worrying for nothing.

"Sorry," Chase said, misjudging his silence. She pulled her hand away and shrank back; there wasn't much room between them, but she was clearly doing her best to give him space. "I don't want to pressure you into anything—"

"I think you should do it," he blurted.

She was quiet for a moment.

"I think you should do it," Tyler repeated, more firmly this time. "I'd like you to. I *want* you to."

Chase chuckled and relaxed again. "Is that so?"

Tyler nodded, making himself lean in. Not all the way but halfway.

Chase's hand returned to his neck, then slid up into his hair. Tyler closed his eyes.

"If you don't like this, we can stop. It's fine."

Most people probably did this as teenagers. It had sounded terrifying at the time, but now Tyler could see the advantages of kissing someone as clueless as he was. Chase had probably kissed all sorts of people. She knew what to do with her hands and her lips and her—oh,

God, her *tongue*. What if she tasted like river water? What if *he* did? What if she decided she hated kissing him and wanted to get as far away from him as possible?

"What if I do it wrong?" he whispered.

"Then we'll keep practicing." She leaned closer, not quite closing the distance between them. "Cost-benefit analysis. Just do what you did then. Just go for it."

"You could do it," he told her.

"Yeah, but then I'll be wondering if I'm doing something you hate. If you're going to change your mind, then I'd rather you do that *before* I shove you out of your comfort zone."

That was sweet of her and also desperately unfair. Tyler usually only did frightening things when someone pushed him.

This time, it looked like he was going to have to push himself.

He took a deep breath, as if he were about to dive underwater, and closed the distance between them.

Tyler had resigned himself to the fact that his first kiss, when it happened, probably wouldn't be anything special.

He'd been wrong.

Chase's lips were as soft as they'd looked, and she tasted like coffee and powdered cheese. Her hand stroked the back of his head, calming him in the same way her touch always did. He kissed carefully, waiting for guidance, wary of demanding too much.

Tyler was used to the voice in his head that scolded him and warned him and made him terrified of failing. Now, that voice was silent.

He felt the moment when Chase smiled against his lips.

"Am I awful?" he murmured, pulling away. He kept his eyes closed, terrified of seeing her face.

"No," she assured him. "No, Tyler—kissing you is not awful in the least. In fact, I would go so far as to say that I enjoy it."

That was when the flashlight beam hit the back of Tyler's head.

"Folks, I'm going to have to ask you to get out of there," said a woman's muffled, weary voice from outside of the car. "Do you know how many times I've had to break up couples in the act? Let's not let this go any farther."

Tyler lifted one arm to block the light. Chase laughed evilly and reached up for the door handle.

The strange woman took a step back, and Tyler scrambled out of the back seat. His feet got tangled in the sleeping bag, and he couldn't seem to disengage himself from Chase—their legs kept getting wrapped around each other. It took her throaty laughter to clue him in to the fact that she was doing it on purpose.

Tyler finally emerged, still shielding his eyes from the light, unable to formulate a coherent reply. The woman stood a dozen paces away, a crisp uniform cutting a dark silhouette against the safety lights behind her. It was impossible to determine her age or what the uniform declared as her occupation; the brightness of her flashlight obscured the details.

"I know it's dark out," she went on, "and I know that being alone in a car with someone can get heated. We all need to recharge. But this is a public space, and I'm not going stand by and watch yet another couple get it on in my parking lot."

"Wh-what?" Tyler stammered. "No, ma'am, I would never . . . We would never . . . Chase, tell her."

He turned to his traveling companion, expecting her to jump to his defense, and instead saw something shift in her eyes when he said, *we would never.*

"It's such a shame you came by when you did, officer," Chase said loudly from the back seat. "It was going to be our first time sleeping together too."

"Chase!" Tyler gaped at her.

The officer turned off her flashlight and shook her head. "I was young once. I know how it is, but this isn't the place."

"There's nothing to know!" Tyler insisted. "This wasn't going to be the place!"

"Did you have another place in mind?" Chase asked innocently.

"That's not what I meant!"

Chase looked past him at the officer. "It was so cold. I wanted him to warm me up . . . if you know what I mean."

Tyler covered his face with his hands. "Chase. Please."

Without the flashlight blinding him, he could make out the officer's uniform. She was some kind of park warden. "Look at you, son. You're so red, you're practically glowing. My advice to you is that if you can't handle getting caught, don't get frisky in public in the first place."

"It's my fault, officer," Chase said, poking her head out of the back seat. "I'm the one who kissed him."

"I'm going to have to ask you two to leave," the warden told them. "If you still want to get down and dirty, you can do it on someone else's beat."

"We don't," Tyler mumbled helplessly, but the warden had already turned away, shaking her head as she went.

Tyler turned back toward Chase, who was grinning from ear to ear as she pulled herself out of the back seat.

"My turn to drive," she said. "I got a decent nap in already."

Tyler narrowed his eyes, but when Chase held out her palm, he handed over the keys.

He got in the back, tucking the trouble-making sleeping bag around himself as Chase pulled out of the parking lot.

"Why would you bait her like that?" he asked with a sigh, shifting around among their snacks and trash, trying to get comfortable.

"*I would never . . .*" she said in a fairly good imitation of him.

"That's not what I meant. I can't believe you would imply such . . . tawdry things."

"*Tawdry?* You're lucky I didn't ask her for a favor."

"What favor could you *possibly* ask her?" Tyler demanded.

Chase winked at him in the rearview mirror. "If I could borrow her handcuffs."

Tyler rolled away from her. "You're a monster."

"I was only messing with her. Besides, I didn't say one word that wasn't true. If she wants to make assumptions, who am I to correct her? It's not like we were doing anything wrong."

"She thinks we were."

"Who cares what she thinks? We'll never see her again, and it'll give her a funny story to tell her friends. If she's going to stop me from kissing a guy I really like, then she deserved the runaround."

Tyler ran his thumb over the yarn around his wrist but didn't reply. *A guy I really like.* Tyler was that guy. When had that happened?

Xavier was going to go bananas when he heard about this. Tyler wouldn't tell him the details, but he'd get a kick out of the warden's unfortunate timing.

"Get some sleep back there," Chase said, more gently this time. "We'll be on I-70 at least until Pennsylvania. I swear on my honor not to leave the highway for anything other than gas."

Tyler pulled the sleeping bag tighter around himself and closed his eyes. The memory of Chase's lips on his followed him into his dreams.

CHASE

Chase had stopped for gas outside Indianapolis, paying in cash with one of the wrinkled twenties Tyler had tucked into their cupholder. He slept through the whole ordeal. When her attention started to wander after they got back on the road, she tuned in to a series of local radio stations, listening with amused interest to whatever stories the personalities thought were important. Most of them were only the kinds of things that small Midwestern towns would find enthralling, and Chase ate it up.

She was feeling good today. Happy. Maybe the mix-up with the paintings hadn't been the worst thing, not if it got her closer to Tyler. He'd been so adorably awkward last night.

And, sure, he wasn't the best kisser in the universe yet, but he'd been earnest. They could work with that.

It was nearly nine in the morning by the time Tyler woke up in the back seat. He stretched his arms as much as he could, bringing the yarn on his wrist up to his face and looking at it like it was a watch. "No big ball of twine this time?"

"I keep my promises," Chase assured him. "We just crossed the Ohio border and we're still going straight on I-70. We're okay on gas, but I could do with a bathroom break. And some breakfast." She paused as a glorious thought struck her. "And *coffee. All the coffee.*"

"We'll get you the good stuff," Tyler promised, leaning up between the seats. "The finest coffee the dollar menu has to offer."

"It can taste like compost as long as it has caffeine," Chase told him sincerely.

There were no stops for the next few miles, and she was starting to regret not using the bathroom at the last gas station. But she'd felt weird enough about leaving Tyler in the car to run inside and pay for gas; she would have felt twice as nervous leaving him asleep while she used the bathroom too. It wasn't like he was going to get snatched away, like that dipstick in Topeka had snatched her purse, but still. What if he woke up alone and thought she'd abandoned him?

"There's a McDonald's coming up," Tyler said, pointing toward an amenities sign as they passed.

"Thank God," Chase muttered. "Your car just lucked out in ways you'll never understand."

Between her screaming bladder and her caffeine headache, Chase was already shaking by the time they pulled off the exit. It was another mile and a half to the McDonald's, and Chase's lead foot jiggled on the gas pedal, aching to drive at highway speeds even on the two-lane roads.

"It's crowded," Tyler said as they drove into the restaurant's parking lot. "Who knew that at ten a.m. on a Saturday, all the cool kids would be at McDonald's?"

"Us and about two hundred Ohioans, apparently."

The lot was full, making them circle the building like lost sharks. The thought of water was a bad idea, and Chase had to pee so badly that her eyelids were actually twitching. After a veritable eternity, a mom and two kids wandered out of the restaurant, to-go cups clutched in their hands. The sight of the liquid sloshing around in the translucent plastic almost did her in.

Chase pulled up right behind their Nissan and waited as patiently as she could for the kids to crawl into the car and subject themselves to an endless ritual of strapping-in. Remembering the production of car trips with her own nephews, she managed to keep herself from laying on the horn.

At last, the Nissan backed out, the woman waving apologetically in her mirror. Chase gave her a thumbs-up and tight grin that felt borderline maniacal.

Just as she nosed into the spot, a giant silver SUV whipped in from the other direction, nearly hitting the passenger-side door of their car.

"Oh, come *on!*" Chase snarled, tapping the gas to gain another two inches. The SUV didn't budge.

"Let him take it," Tyler said. "We can wait."

Instead of answering, Chase thumped her palm against the horn and gestured for the man to get out of her way. He was wearing sunglasses and either talking into his car's Bluetooth or cussing her out.

"It's our spot!" Chase exclaimed, although the man clearly couldn't hear her.

"It's a public spot," Tyler said calmly. "It's not worth it. Just back out. I think that Prius is about to pull out anyway."

Instead of putting the car in reverse, Chase slammed her thumb on the button to open the passenger window. "Get out of the way!" she screeched across the seat.

The other driver ignored her.

Chase was tired and hungry and still shaken from her tumble into the river not twelve hours earlier. Thinking about the man on the bike only made her angrier—he'd gotten away scot-free, and now *this* arrogant dude with his loud, gas-guzzling, overcompensating-for-something SUV had the *audacity* to try to block her out of a space she had waited for *so patiently* . . .

Little red dots were dancing behind her eyes as she leaped out of her seat, slamming the door behind her. Tyler watched open-mouthed as she stomped around the car and pounded on the other driver's window. The big, bearded man began to roll the window down, not even bothering to look at her.

"Sorry, Pete, I'll call you right back." He turned off his car's Bluetooth and twisted around to smirk at Chase, sliding his sunglasses down to get a better look at her. "Listen, lady, I can do this all day. Are you gonna get out of my way or what?"

Mr. SUV was a beefy guy, with pecs that bulged through his V-neck tee and arms as big as Chase's waist. His thinning red hair was swept up into an attempt at a mohawk, and blocky tattoos ran up and down his arms.

Chase didn't care how built the guy was or how tough he wanted to seem. At that precise moment, all she wanted to do was slap the stupid, smug grin off his face.

"I waited for that space," Chase told him. "Move."

"If you back out of *my* spot, I can pull in and let you by." Mr. SUV's blue eyes twinkled. "You're holding up traffic, lady."

Sure enough, the SUV's awkward angle was cutting off the drive-thru line, and half a dozen cars were already waiting. One of the cars honked, setting off a chain reaction of horns that echoed through the lot.

"Then I'm sure they'll appreciate it when you finally move," she shot back.

Mr. SUV shook his head. "Calm down, sweetheart. No need to get hysterical. Pretty sure your fun-sized car can't take me, though, so you might want to rethink that attitude."

"And I'm pretty sure that everyone can tell that your powder-blue monster truck is just false advertising for your unimpressive manhood." Chase stepped right up to his window, jabbing her finger at him. "We were here first, and if I don't get to the bathroom soon, I swear to God that I'll crawl in there and pee on your seats."

Mr. SUV cackled, looking over Chase's shoulder through the open passenger-side window of their car toward Tyler. "Your girlfriend's crazy, man. You need to learn to keep her in line, or someone else is going to have to take her in hand."

"Chase—look out." Tyler had crawled into the front seat. Slowly, careful not to scrape his passenger door along the bumper of the SUV mere inches away, he backed out of the space.

"At least your boyfriend has some common sense." Mr. SUV

shoved his sunglasses back on. "Maybe you could learn a thing or two from him."

Chase stood frozen with rage until the other driver shooed her away. "Gotta pull in, and I'd hate to hit you," he said, rolling up his window. "Tell your man thanks for the spot."

She turned her back, stomping over to the car.

"You want to use the bathroom?" Tyler asked as she got in. "I can circle the block, or wait for another spot to open while you head inside." He was using the same gentle, rational tone he'd employed after he pulled her from the river, clearly trying to put her at ease.

It wasn't working.

"If I have to go into the same restaurant as that guy, there's going to be a murder," Chase snapped. She glared at the giant dude with the manchild mohawk as he swaggered across the lot into the restaurant, willing her eyes to develop laser vision so she could light his hair gel on fire.

"Then why don't we go across the street to the Pilot gas station?"

Chase's upper lip twitched. "Sounds great."

As they pulled out, Chase briefly fantasized about keying the unattended SUV, maybe in a vulgar shape, right on the hood . . .

"Chase?" Tyler asked. "Are you okay?"

"Oh, sure," she snapped. "I'm great. You know what I love? I love when some guy acts like an entitled jackass, talks to me in a *super* condescending voice, and then my friend throws up the white flag and lets the other guy get away with it. Yeah, Tyler, that makes me feel *really good.*"

"You have every right to be mad, and I didn't agree with his behavior . . ." Tyler started.

"Oh, gee, lovely. Do I have your *permission* to get mad?" Chase crossed her arms. "You know, if you didn't want to get involved, that's one thing, but the fact that you took his side is a total betrayal."

"I didn't take his side!" Tyler protested. "There was a line, people were getting upset, and he clearly wasn't listening. I wanted to do the rational thing and diffuse the situation."

"So I'm being irrational now?" Chase unbuckled her seatbelt as they pulled into the lot of the Pilot, taking one of the many open parking spaces. "Well, I'm glad we sorted that out. Hey, maybe you should make out with *him*, since you're so quick to come to *his* defense." She knew that bringing their kiss into this conversation was a bad idea, but the words just popped out. Jocksy McMuscles had said that someone needed to get her in line. What if Tyler agreed?

What if Tyler, like her mother, thought that Chase was just *too much* sometimes?

"Hey." He reached for her arm but wisely hesitated. "I don't agree with the stuff he said, but I didn't see the point of causing more drama or getting in a fight."

"Sometimes you have to fight," Chase declared. "You let people walk all over you all the time. You're a nice guy, Tyler, but sometimes being 'nice' isn't enough. You have to stand up for yourself. You have to put your foot down eventually."

"What did you want me to do?" He actually looked annoyed. Of course his stubborn side *would* come out now, when he was facing off with her rather than the driver of the SUV. "That guy was, like, twice my size! He might have talked down to you, but we both know that if I'd have gone after him, he'd have been a lot less amused. Did you want me to get the crap beaten out of me to defend your honor over something that dumb? It was a parking space, Chase. Let him have it."

She shook her head and opened her door. "I need to use the bathroom. The guy has his space now, so everybody's happy, right?"

Chase didn't wait for him as she stormed into the Pilot, making a beeline for the bathroom. When she finally made it into a stall, she actually sighed aloud with relief.

As she washed her hands, Chase wondered if she'd crossed a line. She'd definitely taken some of her anger at the bike guy out on Mr. SUV. And that was fine—he more than deserved it.

Tyler didn't. Sure, it was annoying that he'd backed down so easily, but he was there for her when it mattered. She remembered his swan-dive off the bridge near Topeka, the way he'd taken charge while she stood shivering in the parking lot, the way he'd finally relaxed when she said that she liked kissing him.

He didn't need to be confrontational. Chase was assertive enough for the both of them. If she wanted him to respect her, he at least deserved the same courtesy.

"He's gonna hate you if you keep this up," she told her reflection. "So maybe tone it down, all right? Not all the way but a little."

The girl in the mirror looked exhausted and irritable, with her messy hair flattened on one side. No wonder Mr. SUV hadn't taken her seriously. She looked as bedraggled as she felt.

Chase leaned against the counter, stretching her back out for a moment while she still had a little privacy.

This trip wasn't shaping up the way she'd hoped last night. They should get back on the road.

The sooner they got to New York, the sooner they could go home.

TYLER

Tyler rifled angrily through the racks of chips. The breakfast sandwiches at one of the restaurant kiosks smelled magnificent, an ambrosia of cheese and grilled sausage and yeasty bread.

But that tempting smell led to a no-doubt delicious sandwich that probably cost at least five bucks. Money they couldn't spare.

He shouldn't be letting Chase's words get to him like this, but they sounded so much like Xavier's that Tyler couldn't help but wonder how true they were. If his best friend and his crush felt the same way about him, maybe it was a sign that Tyler really *did* need to change.

If Tyler didn't get it together, Chase would get bored with him too.

Chase approached, a giant cup of coffee in one hand and a single donut in the other.

"Less than three dollars," she said, indicating her meal. "Not exactly the healthiest thing, but it'll hold me over. And we should grab a map of Ohio while we're here, right?"

Tyler nodded without speaking and turned back to the chip rack.

"I'm sorry I went off on you like that," she said in a much quieter voice. "But that d-bag in that overcompensating SUV really got my goat, you know?"

"That didn't stop it from sounding like you meant it."

Chase raised her shoulders up toward her ears in an uncomfortable shrug. "Maybe I did? Kind of? I mean, some backup would have been nice, but I guess challenging a powerlifter in a fast-food parking lot isn't the best way to assert yourself . . ."

Tyler nodded, grabbing a pack of off-brand cheese crackers. "Yeah, I guess."

"Hey." When he tried to move past her, Chase blocked him. "I'm not saying this right. I'm trying to apologize. I know that I've riled you up a few times, but you've never gone off on me like that. Ignore what I said—you really don't need to change."

"But it would be cool if I did."

"I didn't say that."

"Didn't you?" He gestured across the parking lot toward the McDonald's on the other side of the road. "In fact, I'm pretty sure that you said so *explicitly*."

"Tyler . . ."

"Can we pay for this stuff and go?"

Chase shuffled to the side, and he pushed past her, still simmering with annoyance.

She's going to ditch you, just like Xavier threatened to, if you don't do something, the frightened little voice in his head told him. *The moment you're back at school, she's going to drop you. Nobody's ever going to like you. Nobody wants to be around you because you're not worth the effort, and let's be real, you're not a good enough kisser to make up for your other deficiencies.*

"Hey." Chase was back at his side with a map held alongside her coffee. "We should pay. Are you getting anything else?"

"I'm good. We've got water in the car." He couldn't bring himself to meet her eyes. After all, he knew what he'd see there: the same disappointment he'd seen in Xavier's eyes when he'd called Tyler a coward.

Chase followed him to the counter, where a pimply teenage boy rang up their purchases. Altogether it cost almost eight dollars, and Tyler scowled down into his wallet. If she had sucked it up and waited for another spot to open or let him drive around the parking lot while she went inside, they could have had hot food off the dollar menu for half the price.

Or maybe he really should have challenged that SUV driver. Maybe it was his fault for not putting his foot down.

Chase sipped her coffee as they headed back out to the car. "Do you want me behind the wheel again for this leg?"

"I can handle it."

She was probably glad they hadn't slept in the back seat together, now that she knew he wasn't man enough to fight a stranger on her behalf.

Tyler slammed the door of the car and took a couple of long, deep breaths. He was already aching from what was starting to feel like an eternity in the car and far too little sleep. If he could have gone off alone to stretch his legs, even for half an hour, he might have been able to sort through his thoughts.

Because you like to run away from your problems. That's all you want now . . . another chance to run away. Chase is right about you.

He started the engine and made sure no one was coming, then backed out of the parking spot. Chase sat beside him, nursing her coffee and sneaking little glances his way.

He flipped on the turn signal, planning to turn right to get back to the highway. Would Chase have used one? Or was following the rules of the road not *assertive* enough for her?

That isn't fair, the reasonable part of Tyler's brain told him. Aside from her tendency to fall for kitschy tourist traps, she'd been a perfectly good driver so far. She was only mad because she was tired and cranky from spending so much time on the road and probably still freaked out from that fall from the bridge. *The whole situation has you on edge . . . Isn't it possible that she's just worn out and not really mad at you?*

The trouble was, Tyler didn't really want to listen to the *reasonable* voice. Ever since Chase had gone off on him, he'd been spoiling for a fight.

The drive back to the interstate seemed to be taking an awfully long time, much longer than it had taken them to get to the McDonald's.

"Um, Tyler?" Chase said after a few minutes. "I think we may have come the wrong way."

"We didn't pass the sign for I-70 yet," he said stiffly. "I would know. I was looking."

Chase pulled out their map of Ohio, squinting first at cross-street signs as they went through an intersection, then down at the map. It seemed to keep unfolding forever, like some kind of cheap magician's trick, until at last it took up the whole dashboard.

"Okay, here we are." Chase prodded the map. "Which way did we turn when we came out of the parking lot?"

"Right."

"Hmm. Looks like we should have gone left."

"I went out the way we came in," he snapped.

"That's the problem, though. We crossed the street after the . . . uh, after we left the McDonald's lot. We're gonna need to find someplace to turn around."

"We're fine," he insisted.

"But we just passed McCaffrey," she said, jerking her thumb over one shoulder. "Which means we're somehow headed south, instead of reconnecting with I-70 . . ."

"Show me," he insisted.

"Pull over."

"Show me."

"Tyler," she said reasonably, "I'll show you if you pull over, but we're on these itty-bitty back roads and you need to watch while you're driving."

The words themselves weren't a problem, but Tyler was on the verge of boiling over, chafing against everything she said—especially her tone, which had become patient and motherly and painfully condescending.

"I don't think you're reading it right," he insisted, looking over to where her finger rested on the paper. "So if you could just *show me*—"

"Tyler," she said and then louder, "*Tyler*. Tyler, look out!"

"Stop yelling!" he said irritably, looking up in time to see the edge of the road rolling toward the passenger tires.

The wheels caught the gravel berm, and when Tyler tried to jerk the steering wheel back, he overcompensated. The car skidded a moment before spinning down the embankment into a concrete culvert. There was a loud snap, followed by a screech of metal. The wheel jerked in Tyler's hand. By the time they finally came to a grinding stop, Tyler's ears were ringing, and his nose was filled with the stench of burning rubber. The steering wheel lay at an awkward angle in his lap, limp and useless.

For a moment, he sat there in stunned silence, unable to process everything that had just happened. He had the surreal feeling that there must be a way to skip back in time several seconds and undo the accident, like reloading a video game to the save point after an unsuccessful boss fight.

When his brain finally clicked into gear, he turned to Chase. "Are you okay?" *Please let her be okay. Please don't let me have hurt her because I was being a spiteful idiot.*

"I'm fine," she said. "What about you?" She was sitting bolt upright in the seat, her wide eyes focused on some vague point directly ahead. Her voice was eerily calm.

"I crashed the car," he said stupidly, as though she hadn't been there, as if she couldn't see the detached wheel or hear the anguished grinding of the engine beneath them.

"Turn it off," she said. When he didn't move, she pointed to the key. "Leaving it on won't help, and if the engine was damaged, it might . . . well, I think it might blow up, but maybe that's some BS I've picked up from watching too many action flicks."

He did as she told him.

"Good," she said, "good."

Chase looked down at her lap, and only then did Tyler realize that the glove compartment had fallen open somewhere along the way. Now her lap was full of insurance paperwork, plastic utensils . . . and a novelty-sized box of assorted condoms.

Gingerly, she lifted the box in both hands, turning her head toward Tyler. He shriveled in his seat, squeezing his eyes shut.

"Xavier gave them to me," he murmured. "It was supposed to be a joke."

"Well," she said calmly, "at least you came prepared."

They sat there for a moment in silence, and then Chase began to laugh. Within moments, she was bent over in the seat and gasping for breath as she stuffed the condoms back into the glove box.

"What's so funny?" he asked. He was still shaky from the crash, and the mortification that came with her discovery of Xavier's tasteless gag gift didn't help.

"Would you rather . . ." she tried to ask, but her words were swallowed in another burst of crazed laughter. It took a few more tries before she managed to string the full sentence together. "Would you rather die in a car crash, or have a painting of your butt displayed in a national gallery?"

Tyler stared at her, and she stared back, struggling to hold it together. After a long moment, she lost it again, her hysteria echoing throughout the car.

"What part of this is funny?" he asked, and she gestured broadly to encompass the road, the car, the map, the two of them.

When she finally managed to gather herself and wipe the tears from her eyes, she opened the door and stepped out of the car, scrambling up the embankment to the main road.

Tyler sat there, frozen and mortified, as Chase tried to flag down a passing car. After the third person refused to stop, Tyler finally talked himself into opening the door. Given the car's angle, he could only open his side partway and had to shimmy through the too-small crack or risk smashing the door on the concrete lining of the culvert. From the outside, the car looked okay, which would have been more comforting if he hadn't felt the wheel free-spin when he squeezed out of the door.

"Are we trying to hitch a ride?" he asked.

"We need a phone. We have to call a tow truck." Chase's voice was still full of suppressed laughter, as if Tyler hadn't almost killed them by attempting to be more assertive. He couldn't understand. If *she'd* driven off the road, he'd have been furious. How come she'd been ready to throttle him over a petty parking lot squabble, but a car crash that was entirely his fault seemed to have brought her back over to his side?

If she wasn't going to leave before, she will now. She'll realize that I'm a disaster and that she should stay far, far away from me.

A fourth car zipped past, ignoring Chase's urgent waving. Tyler was barely able to summon the energy to lift his arm.

"This isn't working," she said. "Maybe one of us should show some leg and see if that helps."

"You or me?" Tyler asked flatly.

She chuckled. "Both of us, maybe. Double our chances."

It took another ten minutes of waving to get someone to pull over. Their savior was a rusted pickup truck with a faded bumper sticker that read *Nothing Runs Like a Deere.* They had to jog a little way up the road to the place it had pulled over, where the shoulder widened again.

"We had an accident," Chase told the driver, an older man with a concerned expression. From the back, a young boy peered curiously at them. "Our phones are dead—would you mind letting us call a tow truck?"

Tyler waited while the driver Googled a local mechanic, then handed over the phone so Chase could do the talking. In a perfectly pleasant voice, she explained that they needed someone to come tow them out of the ditch, giving them directions with the pickup driver's help. Somehow, the way she described their situation made it sound like it was something that had just *happened* to them, a veritable act of God.

I did this. I did this. I did this, Tyler's mind repeated in a self-mocking mantra. He could feel himself shrinking, bowed under the weight of his guilt. It was entirely his fault. He'd had something to prove, and he'd let that get in the way of his common sense.

He couldn't stop imagining all the things that could have gone wrong, or all of the horrible things that might have happened to

Chase if they'd fallen farther, or hit a tree, or if the car really had exploded like she'd said. The fact that she was standing right in front of him without a scratch on her didn't make a difference. Something *could* have happened, and he'd have been entirely to blame, all because he couldn't take a little criticism.

Tyler's heart pounded so hard it made him dizzy, and he clutched at his shirtfront, as if putting pressure against his chest could counteract the squeezing sensation that was building in his ribcage.

Chase returned the phone and jogged back toward him as the driver pulled away. "No problemo," she said lightly. "The tow truck guy said he'll be here in ten minutes. We're lucky he's so close. Hey, Tyler? Are you all right?"

He nodded, but he couldn't make himself look at her face. *I did this.*

"Are you having a panic attack?" She put one arm around him, rubbing her palm in slow circles on his lower back. "You're gonna be fine. Take a deep breath. That's it . . . Count down from ten."

He did as she asked, but this time his tried-and-true method didn't seem to help.

Chase nodded, patting his back. "Now, tell me three things you hear."

"You," he said. "And, um, cars. Wind, maybe."

"And two things you see?"

"You. And my totaled car that I drove off the road because I was acting like a *total freaking idiot* . . ."

She stifled a laugh, but her hand kept moving. "That's really not the point of the exercise, but at least you're not hyperfixating anymore, so, you know . . . that's a win?"

"I could have killed us," he said helplessly.

"But you didn't. We're both fine." She stared down at the car and shrugged. "I mean, we're stranded in small-town Ohio with no phones, no car, and basically no money, but aside from that, we're golden."

CHASE

Chase desperately wanted to make fun of Tyler for orchestrating a setback that put her twine detour to shame, but he was obviously in shock, and teasing wouldn't help this time. Instead, she made herself sit quietly with her sketchbook while the tow truck driver dragged Tyler's car back onto the road and drove them to a nearby small town, whose weathered sign proudly declared it, *Everett: Population 1,200.* The gas station the tow truck pulled into had one pump attendant, one mechanic, and one owner . . . all of which were the same man.

The attendant/mechanic/owner was a squat, balding fellow with a potbelly and a snaggletooth. He came out to meet them as the tow truck pulled up to the cement block building. It had a single-bay garage, and the lone pump still sported analog dials for the price readout. A hand-painted sandwich board sign at the end of the short drive declared the business as *Earl's Fuel and Fixin's.*

"You're in luck," the garage owner said as he stepped out of the open bay door and stretched his lower back. "The shop just opened, and I don't have anything lined up this morning. Name's Earl, like on the sign." He held out a hand that was already streaked with grease, either fresh from early morning work or the remnants of older stains that had never washed away. Chase—who knew a thing or two about spilling her medium all over herself and had the stains on her shoes to prove it—shook it without hesitation.

"I'm Chase," she said. "And the guy having a mental breakdown is my partner in crime, Tyler."

Tyler lifted his hand in mute greeting.

Chase carried on. "Nice to meet you, Earl. I hope you have some good news for us."

The mechanic leaned around her, wrinkling his nose as he assessed the damage. "Let's hope she's not totaled. You don't want to get stuck trying to buy a car on short notice."

Chase was painfully aware that her driver's license and credit card were lying on the bottom of the river outside Topeka. "No," she said, "I certainly do not."

Tyler paid the tow truck driver and came over to stand next to her as Earl wriggled under the Honda. For a guy with such a prominent beer gut, he certainly was spry.

"How much did he charge?" Chase asked in a low voice.

Tyler had gone terribly pale. "I have exactly twenty-two bucks left, plus whatever quarters are floating around in the cupholders."

Chase grimaced. "Okay."

Tyler stared at her as if she'd grown a second head. "How is that okay?"

"It's not," she admitted. "It's a nightmare. But it's what we've got, so . . . okay."

"Good news!" Earl reappeared from under the vehicle and flashed them his snaggle-toothed grin. "Unless there's something else wrong that I can't see from here, y'all are only looking at a busted tire rod. If I can find one of those at the junkyard, I can get you back on the road by tomorrow morning."

Tyler made a little sound like a punctured balloon.

"That's great," Chase said, matching Earl's upbeat tone. "Out of curiosity, how much does a tire rod cost?"

Earl pulled a grease-stained handkerchief from his pocket and wiped his hands uselessly on it, staring toward the heavens as he did some mental math. "Well, if I can find one today down at Jason's Junk-yard, you'll be looking at labor plus maybe fifty bucks . . . so probably about two hundred all together. Now, if I have to order one, you'll be waiting into next week, and it's going to cost you a heckuva lot more than that. But let's keep our fingers crossed. You folks have been lucky so far."

"Lucky," Tyler repeated in a tiny voice.

Chase turned to him. His face had gone slack; he looked like a wax statue that had been left out in the sun on a hot day. "Don't panic," she said gently. "We've got until tomorrow morning to come up with the money, and we still have until Monday evening to get to New York."

He stared at her vacantly, all the symptoms of shock playing on his slack expression.

"Thanks, Earl," she said, turning back to the mechanic. "We really appreciate your help. Do you have a bathroom I can use?"

"In back." He thumbed over his shoulder at the white block build-ing. "Grab yourselves a couple cans of pop on your way back. You kids seem like you could use a pick-me-up."

Chase left Tyler standing in the gravel lot and pushed through the door. The main part of the shop looked as if a bomb had gone off right before a herd of elephants trampled through, but the bathroom was clean and smelled strongly of Pine-Sol.

Most of the large coffee she had bought at their ill-fated stop at the gas station earlier was on the floorboard of Tyler's car, since the cup had flown out from between her knees as the Honda hit the culvert. She really didn't need to use the restroom, but she'd gone back there to have a moment to think. She could tell that Tyler was on the verge of a breakdown and that he was counting on her to be the sane, calm one.

Bad mistake, buddy, she thought with a grim smile. *You don't know what you're in for.* The implications of the crash and Earl's solution were still sinking in. They needed money for the car, something to eat, a place to stay the night, and a way to travel around and get those things all without phones. At least they had Tyler's ID, but without any other resources, it was just a piece of plastic.

As the concerns cluttered her mind, she tried to imagine what Sarah would do in her shoes. If Sarah could juggle two boys, Chase could come up with a solution to a little thing like a car accident.

Her sister would say to take things one stage at a time. More than anything else, they needed money. Chase would focus on solving that problem before moving on to the next one.

She splashed some water on her face, fixed her hair, and strode back out toward the front door, two cans of Dr. Dazzle in her hand. Maybe Earl could point them in the direction of a restaurant that would be willing to pay them cash for a day's worth of work.

As she opened the door, a colorful flyer caught her eye. She paused, squinting at the advertisement that some poor, design-challenged entrepreneur had typed entirely in Comic Sans and decorated with generic clipart of corn and tomatoes.

"A farmers' market, huh?" Chase peeled the flyer free from the gummy tape that held it in place before stepping outside.

Tyler was sitting on one of the faded yellow parking bumpers. She handed him a can of the soda and the flyer at the same time.

"What's this?" he asked, flipping the flyer back and forth as if expecting to see something written on the back.

"There's a farmers' market on Saturdays here in Everett. I think we should go."

"Are we going to get an Amish guy to whittle a new steering wheel for us?" Tyler's smile was strained, but at least he was joking around again.

"I had something better in mind." Chase went over to their car, which had been disconnected from the tow truck and rolled into the open garage bay during her refresher in the bathroom. She pulled the massive backpack out from the back seat and debated grabbing the duffel bag as well, but there was no telling how long the walk would be. Besides, she was on her next-to-last change of clean clothes, and she was saving those for when they got to the city. Hopefully, she could sneak in a shower between now and then so she wouldn't look like such a hot mess when they went to get the painting back.

"How close is the farmers' market?" she called to Earl, who was pouring cups of coffee for himself and the tow truck driver in the back of the garage.

"Not far." He waved vaguely to the right as if the block wall next to him wasn't there. "About a mile down that-a-way, big signs, you can't miss it. Not a lot else to do here on a Saturday, and it's a nice enough day, so everybody and their brother will be out and about."

Tyler got up from his seat on the bumper curb, still frowning at the flyer.

"You know," he said slowly, "the whole reason I met you was a flyer like this."

"My font was more tasteful, but yeah." Chase winked at him. "And that was the best decision you ever made."

"What exactly is the plan?" Tyler asked.

Chase shrugged. "Not sure. But it seems like our best option, doesn't it? It's not too far, and maybe when we get there, we'll find something that gives us an idea." *You're being impulsive again,* her mother's voice warned her. *You don't have much time. You should make a plan before you go running off. Think, Chase . . . that's all I ask.*

Well, technically, Chase *did* have a plan. She was going to scope out the terrain. They couldn't come up with a plan of attack until they knew the lay of the land, right?

Tyler gazed mournfully into the open garage door at the crooked tire remains of his small Honda. He took a long swig of the Dr. Dazzle and looked down at the paper flyer hanging droopily in his fingers. "Hopefully, someone there is selling miracles."

"More importantly," Chase added as she shouldered her art bag, "hopefully someone is selling miracles for less than twenty-two dollars."

TYLER

Thanks to the movies, when Tyler pictured a farmers' market, he envisioned long rows of tidy tents overflowing with organic heirloom squash and populated by bearded, flannel-clad hipsters and thirty-something women in yoga pants pushing their dogs in strollers.

Small-town Ohio was a lot less pretentious than that. To Tyler, the event taking place along Main Street looked more like a flea market that just happened to include produce. A couple of stalls offered green onions and asparagus and strawberries, but there were also card tables piled high with stuffed animals, children's clothes, VHS tapes, handmade potholders, novelty spoons, and one older gentleman smoking a grape-scented cigar in front of a table full of hand-welded metal sculptures.

The most impressive thing about it was its sheer size. It dominated the small town square, filling every sidewalk with wares and the closed-off streets with customers.

"Who even owns a VHS player anymore?" Chase asked under her breath.

"Nobody, it looks like," Tyler answered. "They don't exactly appear to be flying off the tables."

Families were wandering around, some of them with dogs in tow, enjoying a lazy morning of haggling with their neighbors. Chase nearly stumbled into a small group of young boys who were dodging through the thick crowd with wads of singles clutched in their little hands. Tyler instinctively steered Chase away with a hand to her lower back before he realized what he was doing. Once she was out of harm's way, he dropped his hand immediately. *Just because she kissed you the other night doesn't mean that she wants you touching her now.*

"So, what's the plan?" Tyler asked.

Chase sighed, settling down on one of the few empty benches that lined the sidewalk. "Put out a bowl and go busking? I was sort of hoping that we'd get here and an idea would just spring into our heads. Do you have any hidden talents I don't know about? The voice of an angel, or a fully developed one-man dance routine?" She flashed him a wicked grin. "I guess you could always do a striptease . . ."

"Not in front of the kids," Tyler said, feeling completely normal for the first time all morning. "But why are we talking about *my* hidden talents and not your very public ones?"

When Chase squinted at him, he gestured toward her backpack.

"Oh, I don't know," she said skeptically. "I study fine art, and you know us artists, we never really intend to *sell* anything."

Tyler snorted.

She ran her hands along the edge of the biggest sketchpad, the one that was so large it stuck out the top of her backpack. "What are you thinking? Just auction off my art one piece at a time?"

"How many blank pages are in there? That big one, I mean." An idea was slowly taking shape in his mind as he looked around at the families wandering past.

"Most of them. It's so awkward to hold, I really only use it for assignments. I tend to stick to the little ones when I'm just doodling."

"And how fast can you doodle? Speaking as a guy who sat still for your ten-hour painting . . ."

Chase laughed. "You didn't sit *that* still." She nudged him playfully with her elbow. "And I do life sketches all the time."

Tyler got up, looking around with renewed purpose. There was a little church at the end of the block. A young Black man wearing a short-sleeved button-down with a clerical collar was standing at the space outside with tables of what were likely donated items spread out in front of him.

Tyler almost asked Chase to go talk to the preacher, but he stopped himself. The memory of trying to read the map while he had been driving came unbidden to his mind. When Chase had told him to be more assertive in the gas station parking lot, she had likely meant he should get comfortable asking strangers for directions or standing up against bullies, not insisting that he be in control of every aspect of the journey. This was his chance to show that assertiveness in its proper form. He took a deep breath and strode over to the church, already running through what he'd say in his head. Chase followed.

"Excuse me," he said as he reached the preacher. *Or is he called a pastor in this denomination? Father?* Tyler never knew the appropriate title. "I'm hoping to talk to someone, and I'd appreciate it if you could point me in the right direction."

The pastor looked up at him hopefully. "Does the person you're looking for happen to be our Lord, Jesus Christ?"

Tyler froze, his mouth still open, unable to think of a single suitable response.

The pastor chuckled. "Yeah, didn't think so, but it's always worth a shot."

"My husband thinks he's funny," a pregnant blond woman said, coming out of the church with an armload of pamphlets and two kids in tow. "What can we do for you?"

"Who's in charge? Of the market, I mean," Tyler added hurriedly, seeing the glint in the pastor's eye. "Not, you know, in a divine way."

"That would be Luellen." The pastor pointed to a tall woman wearing a baseball cap and a T-shirt that proclaimed *Nothing Beets Eating Local.*

Chase nodded, narrowing her eyes. "She *looks* like a woman who uses Comic Sans."

Tyler, who had already talked to more strangers today than he did in the average week, strode over to Luellen. She was frowning down at a clipboard, and Tyler had the distinct impression she was trying to look busy and important. He waited politely until she finally deigned to glance up at him.

"Is it too late to get a space for the market?" he asked.

She looked back at the clipboard. "Well, we don't usually do same-day registration . . . but Carl's in Florida this week, so I guess you could take his usual space. Assuming you can pay the fee, that is."

Tyler closed his eyes. "And how much is that?"

"Twenty bucks."

That was pretty much everything they had left. He snuck a glance at Chase, who shrugged nonchalantly, more curious than anything else.

Reluctantly, Tyler opened his wallet, extracted the last wrinkled twenty, and placed it hopefully in Luellen's open palm.

She nodded. "Very good. You'll be next to Dean. Don't let him talk your ear off." She pointed back toward the church and the vacant spot next to the preacher and his family.

"Care to tell me your master plan?" Chase asked excitedly on their way back over.

He didn't answer yet. If she wanted him to be assertive, she could live with the suspense. He was also a little bit worried she'd say no—although, come to think of it, when had Chase ever turned down an opportunity to do something new and exciting?

Tyler approached the pastor again. "I'm really sorry to bother you, but do you have a couple of chairs we can borrow?"

The older man nodded sagely. "'Ask, and it will be given to you; seek, and you will find; knock, and it will be opened to you.'"

The older kid, a boy who looked like he was around eight, rolled his eyes. "Dad . . ."

"Nobody appreciates my sense of humor," the pastor said wistfully. "Matt, would you and your sister please grab a couple of picnic chairs for our new friends?"

The boy got to his feet, running up the steps to the church, and his little sister hurried after him. When they came tottering down the steps a moment later, the folding wooden chairs clutched awkwardly in front of them, Tyler hurried to retrieve them.

"Wow, thank you, Matt," he said. "That was really helpful. And what's your name?" he asked the little girl.

"Virtue," the girl said shyly, hiding behind her brother.

"Well, Virtue, let me tell you, you're a world-class chair carrier."

She beamed up at him before hurrying back to her mother, giggling.

As Tyler set up the butt-pinching wooden chairs, the pastor looked over at them curiously. "I haven't seen you folks around here before."

"We're just passing through," Chase told him. "We had some car troubles, and we're a little strapped for cash."

"Ah . . ." The pastor's eyes twinkled, but Chase beat him to the punch.

"*The Lord is our shepherd and we shall not want*, right?"

The pastor laughed heartily. "I must be getting predictable."

Chase grinned. "Hey, I may not have been to church since I was in high school, but I didn't forget *everything*."

Tyler flinched; she probably shouldn't be making fun of the guy's faith. The pastor didn't seem to mind, though. "Well, my new goal for the day is to get you in church again," he told her. "And I think my odds are pretty good, since we're the closest building with a public restroom."

"Devious." Chase shook her head. "But brilliant."

Tyler cleared his throat as Chase looked over at his modest setup.

"So do I just start drawing?" Chase asked, reaching for the big notepad. "Maybe some life sketches of the market? Like snapshots of the area, or should I sketch from my imagination?" She fidgeted, as if her fingers were already itching to draw.

"Not quite. Did you ever go on vacation somewhere really touristy?" Tyler was thinking of the summers when he and his dad had visited the state fair in Pueblo. "Sometimes there are people that sketch you, right, and they'll make your nose crazy big, or give you caterpillar eyebrows . . ."

"Caricatures." Chase smiled. "I actually *hate* that style, but I think I can come up with something. You think enough people here will be interested?"

"Give me a sheet of that big paper and a marker, and we'll find out."

Chase dug around in her bag until she found a Sharpie, and handed the pad over. She'd been right about it being clumsy to hold, and in the end, Tyler had to set it on the ground and bend over it to write his message in blocky letters. *Cartoon Portraits: Only $5.*

"Nice to see that the degree I'm working toward is going to pay off before I'm even out of college." Chase chuckled.

"Beggars can't be choosers." Tyler capped the pen and handed it back. "You wouldn't happen to have tape in there, would you?"

Chase looked down at the bag and wrinkled her nose. "Scotch, duct, or washi?" When Tyler's mouth fell open, she grinned. "Just kidding. I only have washi." She fished out a roll of bright blue tape patterned with silver moons, and Tyler taped the sign to the back of her chair.

"Now what?" Chase asked.

Tyler stood back to admire his work. "Now we wait, and we pray that I didn't just blow our last twenty on an idea that won't pan out."

Chase looked over at the little church. "Well, if we're praying, at least we've come to the right place."

CHASE

Chase had never sold her work on the street before, but the idea was slightly thrilling—getting to talk to people while she worked, testing her timing skills, capturing a variety of new faces and expressions on paper . . .

She was sure it would be a lot of fun, if even one person had been interested.

Her stomach had begun to rumble. It had to be about lunchtime, but with only two dollars to their name, neither she nor Tyler had breathed a word about getting something to eat. Instead, she doodled in her small sketchbook, trying to look compellingly artistic.

"You should move to the shade," Tyler said, and Chase looked up to see that the sun had moved. One of the trees outside the church was now shading a bit of the sidewalk, and she scooted her chair over into its shadow.

Potential customers walked by, and a few people had actually looked at the sign with interest, but Tyler seemed reluctant to *talk* to any of them. At one point, Chase looked up to find him gone; a moment later, he tapped on her shoulder and handed her a cold bottle of water that was still sweating from lying on ice.

"Where'd you get this?" she asked.

He shrugged, sipping from his own bottle. "There's a taco truck over there. I figured, hey, what's the difference between having *two* dollars and *no* dollars? And the difference is that we don't die of dehydration." He took another swig from his bottle, then went back to busking—or, more accurately, he went back to standing awkwardly at the front of their booth and making half-hearted attempts to talk to anyone who happened to walk by.

The pastor's little girl, Virtue, came over to examine Chase's sketchbook. "Can I see what you're drawing?"

Chase winked at her. "Better yet, how about I draw you?"

The little girl's eyes widened. "But I don't have five dollars!"

"It's okay," Chase told her. "The first one's on the house. Think of it as advertising."

The girl pulled herself up onto the other chair, swinging her feet back and forth, her hands folded in her lap as though she were having her picture taken.

Chase wasn't really great at standard caricature—she'd tried a couple samples for her cartooning class, but she felt like they exaggerated the wrong things. Even when she got it right, they were intentionally ugly. Their whole point was to be irreverent, but in Chase's opinion, people had no problem seeing the things they didn't like about themselves without any help at all, thank you. She wanted to show the beautiful parts of things.

Her pencil skimmed over the paper, mapping Virtue's curly hair, her chubby cheeks, and her huge, dark eyes, which became more exaggerated on the page. She was still cartoonish, but with all her best features expanded rather than diminished.

Not that it took too much effort. She was naturally adorable.

"What's your favorite food?" Chase asked, adding a little shading with the flat edge of her graphite.

"Ummmm . . ." Virtue considered the question with all the seriousness that a five-year-old could muster. "Strawberries?"

Chase sketched a couple of plump cartoon strawberries around the edges of the portrait and tore it loose from the book. When she saw it, Virtue squealed.

"I'm chibi! Can I show my mommy?"

"It's yours," Chase told her, smiling at the girl's unexpected knowledge of Japanese concepts. "You can do whatever you like with it."

The girl sprinted back to her parents, proudly displaying the illustration. "Mommy, look, I'm chibi!"

"I don't know what that is, sweetheart, but you look adorable," her mom said.

"Wow, that's really something," Pastor Dean added. He looked genuinely impressed. "Maybe you should do a sketch or two to set out for display. It's hard to sell people something they can't see." He widened his eyes and pointed a meaningful finger skyward. "*Trust me.*"

"That's a good idea." Chase started on a second drawing, this time one of the pastor's wife. "You're Dean, right? And you're . . . ?"

His wife carefully rolled up the portrait of Virtue for safekeeping. "Jo Beth. I know, it's about as Southern as it gets—I'm named after my grandmother."

"I'm Chase, named after the time my dad almost got caught in a bank heist." She laughed at their expressions. "He used to tell me that all the time, but I'm *pretty* sure he was joking."

Dean nodded. "Well, it sounds like you won't be up for a high-speed car chase anytime soon. You got somebody taking a look at your vehicle?"

"Earl." Chase pointed back down the road, figuring it was a small enough town that they'd know whom she meant. "But we're a little low on money, and we need to get to New York by Monday night. We were hoping to drum up some cash today, but . . ." Chase gestured at the empty chair, and at Tyler, who was still waving halfheartedly at people as they passed. "It's not looking great."

"Your boyfriend needs to figure out a way to get people's attention," Jo Beth said. "He's too shy. It's really sweet how he takes care of you. He was good with the kids . . . He just needs to be like that with other people too."

"Yeah." Chase finished up the portrait of Jo Beth and looked over to where Virtue and Matt sat on the church steps. "Hey, do you mind if I borrow them?"

"You can have them," Jo Beth told her, putting one hand over her stomach. "My hands are already full, and we still haven't finished the baby's room."

Dean faked concern. "Do I get a say in this? I don't know if we should be giving away our kids to total strangers. Surely we should at least charge a fee."

"Agree to disagree." Jo Beth cocked an eyebrow. "Actually, I'm thinking we should pay her to take them off our hands. But yes, by all means, if you think they can help you, put them to work!"

"Matt! Virtue!" Chase waved the two of them over, and Virtue came running. Her brother followed at a more casual pace, adjusting his glasses as he did and clearly making an effort to look more grown-up.

"Are you going to draw Matt too?" Virtue asked.

"Maybe later. For the moment, I need your help with something." Chase lowered her voice, looking around as if to make sure that nobody was listening in. "See, the thing is, my friend is kind of bad at talking to new people. He gets scared."

Virtue nodded seriously. "I get scared, too, sometimes."

"Not me," Matt said proudly. "Dad says I'm an *ex-tro-vert*." He sounded out the word carefully, then grinned, revealing his braces. "That means I *like* talking!"

Chase gave him a thumbs-up. "That settles it. Matt, you're in charge. I want people to know that I'm drawing pictures. Can you go show Tyler how it's done?"

Matt nodded, and Chase handed over her second portrait, the one of Jo Beth. He took it in both hands, holding it up by the top corners, and marched over to where Tyler stood.

Tyler appeared surprised by his new companion and turned to look at Chase in confusion. A moment later, Matt shouted, "Pictures! Get your pictures here!"

"Pictures!" Virtue exclaimed, holding up the cartoon of herself that she'd retrieved from her mother. "Cute pictures! Get 'em here!"

Chase smiled when Tyler's face lit up. Seeing the kids' enthusiasm seemed to spark something inside him, and in an instant, his whole demeanor changed.

"Want a portrait?" Tyler cupped his hands around his mouth. His voice echoed through the market, and people immediately turned to look. "Get your portrait drawn here. Professional artist on-site, accepting commissions now!"

"Only five dollars!" Matt added.

"Only five dollars," Virtue repeated.

"That's right, only five buckaroos," Tyler called out in response to the kids' unbridled enthusiasm. It quickly became a game of one-upmanship between the three of them as they sought the attention of anyone and everyone around them. Tyler seemed to forget all of his usual fears as he playfully enjoyed the banter.

"See?" Jo Beth said. "All he needed was a little encouragement." She reached into her purse and handed Chase a five. "That's for the one you did of my daughter, by the way, and don't you dare say no. You earned it."

Chase tucked the bill into a pocket of her backpack. "I appreciate it."

Egged on by the kids, Tyler was trying different voices and accents. "Ladies and gentlemen, step right up, and let the talented Miss Chase recreate your likeness in pencil!" he called out like a carnival barker. "Only five quid for a memory that will last you a life-time!" he added in a serious British dialect.

"Do an Australian voice," Virtue said with a giggle.

Tyler immediately complied. "G'day, mate, come get a pic done 'fore you go home and throw your shrimp on the barbie!"

Not to be outdone, Matt responded with his attempt at a Southern accent. "Ain't no better drawin's than what our Miss Chase will make fer ya."

"Oui, oui, Mademoiselle," Tyler fired back, doubling down on their impromptu game, "surely you want to get your portrait done by ze arteest?" All three began giggling.

"I think he missed his calling," Dean said. "Should have been an auctioneer."

"Should have been a carnie," Chase countered, leaning forward to rest her chin on her palm as she watched Tyler fondly. She knew how nervous Tyler was and how much time he spent worrying what people would think, but as he and the kids egged each other on, his worries seemed to disappear. All he needed was a little encouragement—freaking out at him had done more harm than good. If only she could remember that the next time they ran into trouble, they'd be much better off.

Trouble, she suspected, was inevitable, but hopefully she could keep her cool in the future.

And hopefully Tyler would forgive her for her meltdown earlier. If she was lucky, they'd get a chance to kiss and make up.

He doesn't mind being himself with people he trusts.

The thought made her do a double-take, but before she could think on it in much detail, it was interrupted by the arrival of an older couple. They approached Tyler, interrupting the stream of his patter.

"Can we get a portrait together?" the man asked. He and his wife had their arms linked, and Chase's fingers already itched to draw their smiling, weathered faces.

"Five dollars apiece," Matt informed them, becoming a little business manager in a split second. "That's ten for the picture."

The old man pulled out his wallet without a second thought.

"Do you mind standing?" Chase asked. "I'll be quick. I want you standing just like that, as close as you can get."

They shuffled together, the woman tipping her head slightly to one side to rest her cheek on her husband's arm. A true caricature artist would have exaggerated their wrinkles, the man's Roman nose, the woman's almond eyes. Chase focused on their smiles, the way they kept stealing little glances at each other, the way their bodies almost formed a heart shape as they stood so close. She made the couple on the page look a little more realistic than the sketch of Virtue, trying to capture the feeling she got when she looked at them.

When she was done, Chase handed the paper over, and the woman covered her mouth. "Why, Andy, it looks exactly like you!"

"She left out my liver spots," the old man complained, winking at Chase.

"Oh, nobody needs a reminder about your liver spots," his wife told him, admiring the picture. "She did real well on the eyes, though. And she made me look ten years younger. You're a very talented young woman, dear. Good luck today!"

The old man, Andy, pulled out his wallet and slipped out another ten-dollar bill and handed it to Chase as a tip. It had been so fun to sketch them that she was tempted to hand it back, but she was in no position to refuse it.

It had only taken her about five minutes to sketch the couple, and there was already a line forming. Tyler had given up on his sales patter and was sorting everyone into an orderly queue. Next up were two women and their new baby, followed by a middle-aged couple with their squirming puppy. Every sketch was a little different, not only because the faces in front of her changed, but because the energy changed too. When the iron sculptor came over from his booth to get his portrait done, Chase made it look like he, too, was welded together from discarded parts; he smiled when he saw it and handed Tyler an extra five.

Chase fell into the rhythm of drawing, focusing only on the faces in front of her. By the time the line dwindled, Tyler was hoarse from calling out to strangers, the sun was going down, and Chase's hand was cramping so badly she could barely hold the pencil.

"How'd we do?" she asked Tyler.

He held up a wad of small bills. "Two-fifty," he said in wonder. "It's kind of like magic, isn't it? Like we pulled money out of thin air."

"I'm *so* glad I've gone into crushing college debt for the chance to make a cool two-fiddy." Chase beamed up at him. "That was a good idea."

"Yup," Tyler said absently, still focused on the bills.

Chase shook her head and moved closer, laying her hand on his elbow. He went still, finally looking up at her. "I'm telling you that you did a great job, okay? I need you to hear that. It matters more than any of the stuff I said this morning, all right?"

Tyler nodded, meeting her eyes this time. When they'd first met, she'd have said his eyes were brown, but in the afternoon light, she caught unexpected flecks of green and gold. "I hear you."

"Good." She turned back to her backpack. She'd used up half the pages from the big sketchbook, and it slid back into her bag a bit more easily than it had come out.

"Did you get enough to cover your repairs?" Jo Beth asked as she helped her husband fold up their own tables.

"And gas too." Tyler fanned himself with the money. "And maybe, if we're lucky, we can afford a couple of things off the dollar menu along the way."

"You know where you're going to stay tonight?" Dean asked. He was working on breaking down the pamphlet display, handing things to the kids as he went. Matt and Virtue carried everything back into the church piece by piece.

Tyler's smile faded, and he looked down at the money again. "What's the cheapest hotel in town, do you think?"

"Closest hotel's back along I-70," Dean said and turned to his wife. A silent conversation passed between them. "Although . . ."

"They could stay in the church," Jo Beth said, and Dean nodded.

"Wow." Chase playfully narrowed her eyes at Dean, shaking her finger at him. "You really *will* do anything to get me in church again."

The pastor's smile widened, and he pumped his arm in the air as if he'd just scored a goal.

"You could have dinner with us too," Jo Beth offered as she grabbed one of her husband's wrists and lowered his arm. "I'm not promising anything fancy, but I bet I can beat McDonald's."

Chase turned to Tyler, who was still frowning at the money. "I don't want to take advantage of your kindness," he said.

"Maybe there's something we can do for you in exchange?" Chase suggested. "Something we can help with around the house?"

Dean shook his head. *"Do not neglect to do good and to share what you have, for such sacrifices are pleasing to God."*

"I don't want to argue with you, honey," Jo Beth said, tapping a finger to her lips in thought. "But someone needs to paint the baby's room, and I wouldn't say no to a little help."

Dean bit his lip, then turned to Chase. "She has a point."

"Well, it just so happens that in addition to being a world-class carnival barker, my associate here happens to be a professional painter." She patted Tyler's back, and he nodded modestly.

"I'm happy to help," Tyler said. "Chase, you can skip if you want. I know your hand cramps up if you use it too long."

"Thanks, but I don't mind helping." She wasn't big on the fuzzier feelings, but she felt a sudden ache in her chest at the realization that Tyler cared about how she was doing and seemed to be genuinely supportive. In fact, he'd been supportive and thoughtful ever since the car accident.

How many times had he done little things to take care of her, or to see how she was feeling? He didn't always do things her way, but he *was* always looking out for her. He'd jumped in a river for her, after all.

If she wasn't careful, she was going to end up really liking the guy.

Tyler's smile turned awkward, and Chase realized she'd been staring at him for a long time. She finally made herself look away.

"You two make such a cute couple," Jo Beth said, exchanging a knowing smile with her husband.

Chase didn't deny it this time, and she noticed Tyler didn't, either.

"Thanks," she said. "Now, let's get that room painted."

"Sounds like a fair exchange to me," Dean told them, turning the card table over and folding in the legs. "Help me get the chairs inside, and I'll stop by the hardware store on the way home for supplies."

Tyler lifted one chair over each arm. "I've got the rollers, padre, if you've got the paint."

TYLER

Tyler hadn't seen his niblings since Christmas, and being around Dean and Jo Beth's kids at the market all day had made him miss his family in a way he hadn't expected.

The pastor's house looked a little worse for wear on the outside, but the garden was tidy, and from the moment Tyler stepped inside, it felt like home. The walls had been painted a warm eggshell color that made the whole place feel ever-so-slightly soft, and they were lined with family pictures, finger paintings, macaroni art, and a variety of craft projects. A large wall clock was faced with a painting of Jesus in pastel robes staring off toward the timekeeping mechanism and was captioned with the words, *Jesus, would you look at the time?*

"That was a Christmas gift from my brother," Dean explained as he kicked off his shoes. "I think he was yanking my chain, but the joke's on him, because I love it."

"Is he looking at the clock?" Jo Beth called from the kitchen. "Tyler, tell him it's tacky."

Tyler shifted his grip on the painting supplies they'd snagged from his car. Dean had driven Tyler by Earl's garage on his way to the hardware store, and Tyler had collected his pans and rollers from the trunk. He leaned closer to Dean and lowered his voice, tipping his chin toward the clock. "To be honest? I think it's pretty funny."

Dean winked, then spoke up again. "How come nobody appreciates my sense of humor?"

"Because you're corny!" Jo Beth called back.

Dean chuckled and took the supplies from Tyler. "I'm going to take these up to the nursery for later. Make yourself at home, all right?"

Tyler removed his boots and set them by the door, then went into the kitchen. It was warm and sweet-smelling, a mixture of baked goods and spiced leftovers from meals past. Chase was chopping lettuce into an enormous bowl while Jo Beth stood beside the stove, overseeing a large pot.

"I hope you like spaghetti," she said. "My kids are picky eaters, and I've learned to pick my battles."

"I love spaghetti," Tyler assured her. "You want me to take over? I think I can manage watching water boil. Or, you know, averting my eyes *until* the pot boils."

Jo Beth stepped away from the stove. "Usually, I wouldn't put our guests to work, but my ankles have been killing me, and I'll take any excuse to get off my feet. Thanks, you two." She withdrew to the dining room on the far side of the wall and checked in on the kids, who appeared to be completely engrossed in a pair of coloring books.

Standing in the kitchen alone with Chase felt oddly domestic. What would it be like to live with her? To share a space with her?

Slow down, Tyler. You hardly know the girl. You have kissed her once, *which is the exact same number of times you've crashed your car with her in the passenger seat. Maybe tone it down?* Still, when Chase smiled over her shoulder at him, he was tempted to lean in for another kiss, just to see if she'd be willing to kiss him in broad daylight.

By the time they all settled down at the table, Tyler's stomach was growling. He'd been too angry to eat much this morning, and he was running on fumes at this point. It took a surprising amount of effort not to wolf down his supper like a starving animal.

"You did a great job today," Chase told Matt as the family worked their way through the food. "You really whipped this guy into shape." She nudged Tyler with her elbow as Matt puffed up with pride.

"How did you two meet?" Virtue asked.

Tyler choked on his pasta, and the preacher shot him a curious glance.

"I drew his picture," Chase said innocently.

"Oh, like you did for me!" Virtue nodded as though this made perfect sense.

Tyler cleared his throat and took a long drink of water.

"Kind of like that, yeah," Chase told the girl. "But yours turned out way cuter."

Maybe it was because of how easy Dean's family was to talk to, or a side effect of the unselfconsciousness of the little kids, but Tyler experienced a disorienting sense of déjà vu in their company. It was as if he'd brought Chase home to meet his family, which really didn't make any sense, as he had no point of comparison for what it would be like to bring a girl home. He certainly hadn't brought Becky Blackstone around to spend time with his parents, and as Xavier had so heartlessly reminded him, she had been his only romantic experience prior to Chase. Still, seeing the way Chase slid seamlessly into this household made it easy to picture her in his.

Too easy. What would she say if she knew what he was thinking? Would she laugh in his face, or . . . ?

It was actually impossible for him to imagine any other alternative. He could see Chase fitting in with his family, but he couldn't imagine her settling for him, not in the long-term. When they were on a road trip, sure. But when they were back at school, where she had options?

Nah. No way. She struck Tyler as the sort of person who bored easily, and if Xavier had proven anything, it was that Tyler couldn't keep up.

$\sim$

"This is such a cute room!" Chase exclaimed.

"We just renovated it," Jo Beth said, examining the blank walls.

"We'd been talking about adding a craft room, but . . . best-laid plans and all that." Her hand went to her stomach so casually that Tyler wondered if the movement had been subconscious.

He laid his painting supplies out while Dean opened the freshly bought cans of paint, then carefully stirred the mint-green mixture.

"The kids really like you, Tyler," Dean said. "Seems like maybe you're more comfortable with them than you are with other people." It was a statement, but Tyler could hear the question inside of it.

"I guess I'm an introvert," Tyler said.

"I used to be like that." Dean took his paint tray and started working around the doorframe. "You know, back in high school, I was so shy that I could barely talk. I failed a final project in English because I flubbed the presentation—everyone was looking at me, and I completely clammed up. It was weird, too . . . I knew every single one of those kids, but having all their eyes on me at the same time was more than I could handle."

"What changed?" Chase asked. She was on her knees, feet tucked under her, keeping the roller steady as she skirted the baseboards.

"He met me." Jo Beth chuckled.

"Jo B's a little on the extroverted side." Dean's laugh made it sound like this was a colossal understatement. "Tell you what, marrying an extrovert will rub off on you. These days, my job is literally talking to people. I get up in front of the congregation each Sunday, and I haven't panicked once."

"Not in front of an audience, at any rate," Jo Beth teased.

"So the secret to making Tyler come out of his shell is to find him a firecracker of a woman," Chase said, grinning over her shoulder. Tyler tried to focus on painting so that no one would be able to see his expression.

"Sure doesn't hurt," Jo Beth replied.

Dean nodded with all the world-weariness of a middle-aged dad. "And if that doesn't change your mind, kids will finish the job. You'll be too tired to worry about things like secondhand embarrassment or if people are staring at you while you clean ice cream off your daughter's best shirt."

Neither Tyler nor Chase had said a word about not being a couple. At first, it had felt like an inside joke, but now Tyler found himself wondering where the line between "together" and "not together" really fell.

You only feel that way because you've been stuck in a car with her for the last two days. It's messing with your mind. You kissed her once. You still haven't asked her out. Yesterday morning, they'd barely been acquaintances. Everything had gotten so intense since they'd climbed into the Honda . . . That was why he was making more of their relationship than was really there.

Needy.

Clingy.

Desperate.

The words rattled around in Tyler's skull, making him shrink in on himself any time he thought them.

It was only a small room, but by the time they'd gotten the second coat on, Tyler's eyelids were already drooping.

"I'm sorry, y'all, but I'm fading." Jo Beth appeared pretty beat too. "Dean, are you okay taking them back to the church?"

"Of course, honey. Why don't you go to bed? We'll take care of things." Dean kissed his wife's cheek, and she smiled gratefully.

"You should sign the corner of the wall," Dean said. "Artists sign their work, right?"

Tyler still had the Sharpie Chase had given him earlier, and they knelt down in the corner to sign their names. Tyler went first, and when Chase added her name, she put a little plus between them. Almost like their names belonged together, not out of mere coincidence, but by choice. She added a quick sketch around their names. For a moment, Tyler thought it was a heart, but then he realized it was a picture frame.

You're getting sappy, he scolded himself. Probably because he was so tired. *We're only together until we get that portrait back.*

They poured the extra paint back into the can and put the half-full paint can with the three other empties.

"You got a good place to dispose of this?" Tyler asked.

Dean looked guilty. "My usual plan is to hide stuff in the basement until hazardous waste pickup day rolls around again, or until I forget it's down there—whichever comes first."

Tyler held out a hand. "I can take them. We've got a disposal site at work."

Dean perked up. "I appreciate it. Well, shall we get you two set up for the night?"

While Tyler cleaned the paint trays in the bathroom sink, Chase and Dean collected some pillows and blankets from the linen cupboard. Dean drove them back to the church and helped them carry everything inside. There were emergency cots in the basement, and Dean stayed to get them all set up.

"I'll swing by before the service tomorrow and give you a ride out to Earl's. We'll get you back on your feet and going in no time. I hope whatever's got you headed to the Big Apple is worth all this trouble?"

"We're headed there for an art show," Chase said, looking at Tyler. "My professor entered one of my pieces, and . . . it's a whole thing."

Tyler pressed his lips together, hoping she didn't bait Dean the way she'd baited the ranger the night before. The memory of their kiss made his skin prickle; no doubt she thoroughly regretted it by now.

Dean was oblivious to Tyler's silent agony. "Too bad I can't go with you! I'd love to see more of your work."

Chase shot Tyler a wicked grin, and Tyler shuddered. This was exactly the reason he didn't want that stupid painting getting out into the world . . . The wrong people would see it, and they'd make a lot of assumptions about Tyler that just weren't true.

When neither of them responded, Dean shrugged. "Well, I hope you get some sleep. You know where to find everything. Oh, and promise me one thing?"

"Sure," Tyler said. "What's that?"

"Leave room for Jesus." Dean winked and jogged toward the stairs before either of them could protest.

"I hope you didn't show him that enormous box of condoms

Xavier gave you," Chase stage-whispered once they were alone. "Otherwise, he'll probably be up all night praying for us."

Tyler squeezed his eyes shut. "Of course I didn't. Although something tells me he'd take it better than most people in his line of work."

"True." Chase dropped her art bag onto her cot. "You know, if my grandmother's pastor had been that cool, I might have gone to church more. As it is, I don't think I've set foot in one since I was fourteen."

"Someone I knew got married a few months ago." Tyler lay down on his cot, rolling onto his side to look at her. "That was the first time I'd been to church in years."

Chase sat down on her own cot, legs crossed, and pulled one of her small notebooks into her lap. "Oh? And did seeing them tie the knot give you wedding fever?"

"Kind of the opposite. My cousin got married, and she's . . ." Tyler trailed off. "Okay, so you know how I get anxiety about normal people?"

Chase snorted as she began to sketch. "She was a bridezilla, huh? You know, I used to hate that term. It always struck me as super sexist, but then I went to my second cousin's wedding a couple of years ago, and . . . yikes."

"She's like that all the time," Tyler confessed. "And—uh, is it rude to talk badly about a bride on her wedding day?"

"Only on the day itself," Chase said cheerfully. "Anytime afterward is fair game."

"I don't think she and the groom were a good fit." Tyler lifted one shoulder. "But what do I know? It's not like I'm in a position to give anyone relationship advice."

Chase tilted her head to one side. It was nice to talk to her like this, to have an excuse to keep looking at her, made easier by the fact that she was focused on whatever she was drawing. He kept secretly hoping she'd get up from her cot to come sit beside him and kiss him again. Even a quick peck. If she would touch his arm for a moment, it might be enough to reassure him that she wasn't still mad about their fight earlier.

Personally, Tyler had all but forgotten about it until that very moment. His mind was occupied by other, more important things.

When did we stop telling people that we aren't a couple? What are we now, anyway? If you kiss someone once, does that count as "friends with benefits"? The question was on the tip of Tyler's tongue, but he couldn't quite force it out. If she knew what he was thinking about her, that might make the rest of their trip awkward. Surely, telling her, "The moment I met you, I thought, *Here's a woman worth breaking the Unwedding Vow for*" would make her run for the hills. It sounded like the kind of cheesy line Xavier would whip out two seconds after meeting a cute girl.

Even though Tyler found that he meant it.

"I thought your hand was cramped," he murmured.

Chase smiled. "Yeah, it was, but I can't help myself. Sometimes I just have to get it out, like an exorcism. But don't change the topic. Did attending that one wedding give you anxiety about weddings in general?"

"Not anxiety, but . . ." Tyler took a deep breath and ran the fingers of one hand over the cold aluminum cot frame. "What if I fall for someone who's a bad fit for me, and neither of us realizes it until it's too late?"

Chase smiled gently, still sketching away. "Divorce is always an option." Her hand stilled, and she met his eyes. "But that's not what you mean, right? You're worried about your judgment."

"Mm." Tyler frowned. "Yeah, I guess."

"People get married for all kinds of reasons," Chase said. "My sister is one of the lucky ones, but some people rush in blindly. Honestly, I think some folks are happy to marry the first person they come across."

Tyler's mouth snapped shut. It was a good thing he hadn't said that cheesy line about the Unwedding Vow, if *that* was how Chase felt.

"But you're a thinker, Tyler," she went on. "You're not someone who makes snap decisions, and I don't think you'd be attracted to the kind of woman who'd turn out to be a bridezilla. You have better taste than that."

No. Apparently, I'm attracted to the kind of woman who would think I'm a loser for falling too hard, too fast.

Chase was already engrossed in her sketchbook again, and Tyler's exhaustion sat on his shoulders like a weight. He let his eyes drift shut as he rubbed his thumb over the yarn that still hung from his wrist.

He fell asleep to the sound of her pencil darting back and forth across the paper.

CHASE

C hase woke to the sound of running water.

"Tyler?" she mumbled, rolling over to look for him before remembering that they were in a church, not the Honda. She'd dreamed they were sleeping next to each other. Before he'd fallen asleep, she'd toyed with the idea of crossing the room and kissing him, but he'd been so shaken after the accident that she didn't want to push him too hard.

I'm the kind of girl who rushes into things. Like I told him, he's a thinker. If I'm not careful, I'll end up pushing him away.

Instead, she waited until he was asleep. On her way past him to use the bathroom one final time, she'd allowed herself the small luxury of running her fingers through his messy blond hair.

Now, she sat up and rubbed her eyes, feeling genuinely refreshed for the first time in days. A bubble of hopeful happiness rose in her chest, and for a moment she couldn't think why. Then the cramp in her hand reminded her of their success the day before. She'd enjoyed drawing all those strangers, but the look of triumph on Tyler's face as he fanned himself with the bills had been far more satisfying.

He was always handsome, but seeing him smile without reservation had been breathtaking. Usually, he kept his lips closed, but when he'd really smiled, Chase could see his teeth.

Not that she was keeping tabs on his lips. Or his mouth in general. Nope, she only noticed because she had an artist's eye for details.

Tyler's cot was empty, the borrowed blankets tossed aside. After a moment, it occurred to Chase that he must be using the church's shower. Pastor Dean had said something about that the night before. She blinked at the ceiling, idly fantasizing about stealing Tyler's clothes, just to see what he would do when he stepped out of the stall.

As tempting as it was to play some kind of prank on Tyler while he was damp and defenseless, a shower of her own was far more appealing. Chase sniffed the ends of her hair experimentally and grimaced at the dank smell of river water that wafted off of her. They would reach New York today, which meant it was time to don her last clean change of clothes, which Tyler had grabbed from the Honda when he and Dean went to get the paint rollers. So long as she could convince the gallery owners to give the painting back, this would all have been worth it. It was impossible to think beyond that point—it was as if the future held only the gallery and nothing more.

Chase shuffled off toward the women's bathroom, hoping at the very least they'd have a bar of soap in there. She groaned with relief when she opened the shower stall to discover an industrial-sized bottle of shampoo and a pump-top bottle of body wash—truly a miracle if she'd ever seen one. It took her a long time standing under the hot water to feel truly clean, and the relief of smelling like cheap vanilla and strawberries rather than Topeka mud was enough to make her feel almost drunk with contentment.

There were towels on the rack, the Dollar Store kind that rearranged water more than they absorbed it, but Chase wasn't complaining. It was enough to get her hair mostly dry and keep her fresh clothes from water spotting too badly. Chase grinned at herself in the bathroom mirror and drew a little smiley face in the steam.

Tyler was stripping the sheets off the cots when she stepped back into the sanctuary.

"Never thought you'd be wet and naked in a church, did you?" she asked as she walked up.

"Good morning to you too," he said. He only went a little red around the edges this time. Either she had already peaked when it came to innuendo, or he was getting more comfortable with her sense of humor.

"Have you heard from Dean?" she asked. Without thinking, she reached for her phone to check the time before remembering that it was gone forever.

"He hasn't come by yet," Tyler said, dumping the dirty linens in a pile by the door. "But he said he'd be here early, and we need to get going the minute the car is ready. I think we have another ten hours or so on the road, assuming some idiot doesn't crash the car again." He smiled at her sheepishly.

His damp hair stuck out from his head in every direction, as if he'd run a towel over it and simply left it that way. Chase didn't think before walking over to him and reaching up to form it into a little peak.

"What are you doing?" he asked.

"Trying to give you a mohawk," she replied, "but your hair's too short. It's a shame, too, because I *really* think you could rock that hardcore biker look. All you need is a leather jacket and a tongue piercing."

He laughed, reaching up to pull her hands away. As his fingers closed gently around her wrist, it occurred to her how few times they'd actually *touched* each other. When had they ever been this close, aside from their kiss and the one time she'd nearly drowned?

Now would be a great time to kiss me again, she thought loudly. *It's the perfect opportunity. No witnesses.*

Tyler seemed to realize it, too, but he didn't step away. His hand was still closed around her wrist but loosely now, more as an excuse to keep touching than anything else. "I don't think I could rock a tongue piercing," he told her.

"What about a sick tattoo?" Chase suggested.

Tyler shook his head. "Needles. I hate 'em."

"Oh, I don't know. I bet nobody would mess with you if you got a full back tattoo of a dragon or a really angry bear."

"Xavier would never be able to mock me again," Tyler said thoughtfully.

"Or maybe one on your neck," she said and put her fingers lightly over his pulse. "A barbed wire collar, maybe? Or the Nirvana logo?"

She was only testing the waters, but when he shied away, she let him go. Every time she tried to get closer to him, he put up another wall. At some point, a girl had to take the hint, right?

But Chase had never been very good with hints.

"We made a good team yesterday," she said.

Tyler nodded. "We sure did. I was hoping . . ."

There it was again—the bright expression on his face that she didn't know what to do with. If he'd been someone else, someone bolder, someone who wouldn't fall apart at the gesture, she would have just kissed him herself.

But she wasn't going to keep chasing him. Whatever spark had flared to life between them the other day must have been extinguished by her shitty behavior in the McDonald's parking lot.

And even if he *was* still interested, she wasn't going to force it. Xavier had pressured him into sitting for the portrait. Professor Roberts had, albeit unwittingly, pressured him into getting it back. Chase wasn't going to be the one to pressure him into another kiss, not when he was so obviously ambivalent at best.

"What were you hoping?" she asked, trying not to look too closely at his plush lips as she said it.

Tyler didn't get a chance to respond before the door to the sanctuary swung open and the pastor walked in, looking unfairly chipper and put-together given how early it was.

"Did you two behave?" he asked with an exaggerated fatherly frown.

"Yes, sir," Chase said seriously. "We left plenty of room for the Lord."

Dean grinned and clapped his hands. "Glad to hear it. Well, would you like the good news or the bad news first?"

Chase shrugged and gestured to Tyler.

"Good news," he said.

"All right." Dean rubbed his hands together. "So, I called Earl before I came over, and he was able to get his hands on the part you needed. Your car's all set, except for a couple of dings."

Chase braced herself. "And the bad news?"

"The price changed," Dean informed them. He frowned sympathetically as he said it. "I guess it didn't take the amount of time Earl had estimated at first . . . you know how it goes, an hour here or there, it all adds up. I haggled on your behalf, but I just couldn't get him any lower."

Tyler closed his eyes, looking haggard and brow-beaten. "How much is it going to cost?"

Dean sighed extravagantly, but when his gaze met Chase's, she saw that his eyes were twinkling. "He says he can't go lower than a hundred."

They both gaped at him.

As he took in their expressions, Dean burst into a wicked cackle that didn't befit a man of the cloth. "Oh, goodness, I know I shouldn't mess with people first thing on a Sunday, but y'all's faces are *priceless.*"

"Did you really get him down to a hundred?" asked Chase as the reality of what he'd said sank in. "How?"

"I told him a little bit about your troubles, and he was kind enough to halve his usual hourly fee." Dean held his hands together in an attitude of prayer and lowered his eyes solemnly. "I hold a little moral sway with the good people of this town, and although I would never use it on my own behalf, I know that weary pilgrims deserve a little easement of their burdens."

Tyler stepped in and threw his arms around the pastor, giving him an almost-feet-off-the-floor bear hug. When he stepped back, his eyes were wide and glassy, and he was grinning like an idiot. "We'll be able to afford gas," he said, "and *food.*" Chase got the distinct impression he was fantasizing about a hot breakfast and a decent coffee; she certainly was.

"Make sure to thank Earl. He's a good guy." Dean looked around the sanctuary, his hands on his hips, and rocked back and forth on the balls of his feet. "Well, looks like you kids are all packed up and just about ready to go. Shall we be off?"

Chase hoisted her bag up onto her shoulders, and Tyler grabbed his duffel.

"On to New York," he said.

~

"We can't thank you enough," Chase repeated when Dean dropped them off at Earl's garage. "You've been so kind. And tell Jo Beth that I wish her good luck with the baby."

"We'll need it." Dean chuckled. "Those little monsters have us outnumbered after this. You two take care now. Drive safely. No more accidents!"

"Have fun in church!" she called as the pastor pulled away, and he honked the horn twice to let her know he'd heard.

Chase dumped her bag in the back seat of their Honda, which was currently parked in front of the one-door garage, and went in through the open doorway where Earl was handing Tyler a receipt.

"This is such an incredible help," Tyler said, counting bills onto the counter. "I hope it's not going to set you back too much."

"Aw, heck, I was your age once." Earl leaned forward on the counter, winking at Chase. "Accidents happen. I get plenty of work, so it's not like I'm gonna go hungry, and Dean made it sound like you two are pretty strapped for cash."

"That's putting it mildly," Tyler said.

Earl counted the bills a second time before stuffing them into the till. Their account settled, he handed them the key. "All right, folks, you should be ready to roll. When you get home, I'd take her in to get serviced just to make sure there's nothing else going on with her. For the moment, I *do* recommend praying . . . and staying on pavement. No need to tempt fate again, is there?"

"Thank you again—" Chase started.

Earl waved her off, shooing them out the door with a gap-toothed smile. "Go on, now. I got up early to get you on the road. Dean can be real persuasive when he wants to be, but today's my day off, and I'm going home to pancakes and a morning nap the minute you two are out of my hair."

"That was so generous," Tyler said as they walked back to their car. "I can't believe he agreed to halve the bill like that."

Chase nodded, opening the passenger door. "Makes you wonder, though, what kind of discount he'd have given us if he knew why we were headed to New York in the first place. Or do you think retrieving salacious artwork is allowed on a sacred pilgrimage?"

"I bet they'd have thought it was a riot," Tyler said, shaking his head. "But Dean might not have let me sleep on holy ground if we'd told him."

The engine turned over without a hitch, and Tyler turned the wheel experimentally. "Seems okay." He sighed happily. "I'm glad Earl got it running again. I was sure it was done for."

"Then we should get going," Chase said, buckling herself in. "Quick, before anything else goes wrong."

~

They were on the road by seven, stopping back at the Pilot just long enough to splurge on a hot breakfast and a massive coffee for Chase.

"The McDonald's is just across the street," Tyler said, pointing back at the site of their showdown with Mr. SUV. "Are you sure that you don't want to do a victory lap?"

Chase held up her hands. "No, like Earl said, there's no sense in tempting fate. And remember, when we pull out of the lot, turn *left*," she said. "We don't want to miss the highway again. But if you want to look at the map *before* we start driving . . ."

"You can read the maps from now on," Tyler told her. "After all, you're the Navigator-in-Chief."

Within minutes, they were back on I-70 and headed toward New York. For the first time since they'd left the university on Friday —*God*, Chase thought, *that feels like ages ago*—she felt totally relaxed.

"I don't want to jinx us," Tyler said, "but do you feel like we might have gotten over the hump?"

Chase groaned. "You have to know better than to say stuff like that. Of *course* you've just jinxed us. Now we're going to be arrested on trumped-up drug-smuggling charges or kidnapped by the mafia or ... or abducted by aliens or something."

"Well, if we are, it's going to be your fault."

Chase shook her head seriously. "No way. You're the one who jinxed us. It's all on you."

Tyler clicked his tongue at her. "Yeah, but you're going to be the one who starts a fistfight with some John Wick type. And it's going to be over something ridiculous too."

"Nah." She put her seat back and got comfortable, wriggling around until she found the perfect position. "I respect Mr. Wick. He has a real soft spot for puppies. But you have a point, I'd probably get into it with Theon Greyjoy or whoever the bad guy is in the first movie, most likely as a result of his terrible driving and animal cruelty. So, point taken, it *will* be my fault."

"The final step is acceptance," Tyler intoned.

"Do you want to play a word game?"

Tyler sighed. "As long as it's not Would You Rather."

"Never Have I Ever?" Chase suggested.

"Sounds like a short game, given that it would be the two of us playing." Tyler smirked at her, although his eyes only left the road for a moment. "I haven't done anything, and you have no impulse control."

"I wouldn't say *none*," she argued. "I thought about stealing your clothes from the church bathroom this morning, and I restrained myself *then*."

"What's the point?" he asked. He didn't even blush this time. "You've already seen me naked."

"I've never seen you naked in a church. Besides, maybe I wanted a refresher."

He looked over at her again, his mouth slightly open as if he might be thinking of a response but wasn't sure what to say yet. Chase would have sworn there was some kind of static between them, a charge that might snap at any moment if only Tyler would reach out or open up.

"Never have I ever been skinny-dipping," he said at last.

Chase narrowed her eyes at him. "Tyler. I almost downed *two days ago*. Are you seriously going to bring up water now?"

He flinched. "Sorry, I wasn't thinking."

"But I have gone streaking," she added. "On dry land. Does that count?"

Color flooded his cheeks. "Um."

"Is it that traumatic to think of me naked?"

"No." Tyler glanced over at her, and the way his eyes swept over her left Chase feeling a little too warm. "No, it's not that. I already know that you vandalize your furniture. I was just wondering, does running around naked in an art room count as streaking?"

"You didn't run," Chase argued.

"Then I guess I've never gone streaking, either."

"You should try it sometime. It's liberating." Chase settled back in her seat and took a sip of her coffee. "Let me see . . . never have I ever done drunk karaoke."

"Really?" Tyler asked. "You seem like you would."

"What about you?" Chase asked.

Tyler grinned. "I blame Xavier. It was only one beer, but it turns out that I do a mean Keith Urban cover."

"Country music," Chase groaned. "Of course." She shook her head, letting her eyes slide to Tyler's profile.

For a self-proclaimed boring guy, he still had a few surprises up his sleeve.

They stopped for lunch at a Cracker Barrel when they finally left I-70, and again for a bathroom break near Harrisburg.

"Do you think we'll need a map to get us to New York City?" Chase asked the middle-aged gas station attendant.

He shook his head emphatically. "Maybe once you hit the city to help you figure out where you're going, but it's a straight shot on I-78 now."

"How much longer do you think we have?" Tyler set a bag of chips on the counter and pulled out his wallet. "Sorry, we don't have GPS."

"Three hours, give or take," the attendant said with a shrug. "I guarantee you're going to get stuck in traffic once you hit the city limits, but my wife and I go up there every few weekends. You'll survive."

"We have so far!" Chase told him cheerily. The thought that they could be in the city by dinnertime left her feeling giddy.

Tyler was almost as punchy as she was, and when they crossed into New Jersey, they both cheered. Tyler even laid on the horn for a few seconds while he whooped in celebration.

"Nobody in American history has ever been this excited about reaching New Jersey," Chase said confidently. She was starting to get cramped, and she would have done just about anything to get out of the car.

The attendant had been right—traffic was a nightmare, but when they finally pulled into the Holland Tunnel, Chase was practically clawing at the windows in excitement.

"Where are we headed?" Tyler asked.

"It's near Central Park, I think," Chase said. "On the Upper West Side. If you can find parking there, you'll be fine."

The sun had set by the time they found parking, and the nighttime city was awakening from its business slumber, opening its arms to those who wanted to celebrate the completion of another successful day. Burnt-orange safety lights illuminated the parking sign, and Tyler scowled at the twenty-dollar-a-day fee. "At this rate, we won't be able to afford to get home," he grumbled.

"We were never going to be able to get back on what we have," Chase said gently. "As long as we get the painting, the pressure's off, right? Tomorrow's a business day. We'll call someone from a bank or something . . . There has to be a way for them to authorize a transfer. Or maybe I can do another caricature stand in the city. I bet people would pay more here. We'll figure it out, Tyler." She put a reassuring hand on his knee and felt him relax a little. When they got out of the car, she brought her bag of art supplies with her. If nothing else, she might be able to use it to convince the gallery that she really was an art student there to retrieve her painting. Even if nobody was at the gallery today, they could camp out in the car. Their journey was over. They had finally arrived.

Chase planned to stop and ask someone for directions once they got out of the parking deck, but they'd barely walked a block when she noticed a banner hanging from one of the lampposts beside the park. It featured an acrylic portrait of a nude woman.

"Come on," she said, taking Tyler's hand and dragging him closer. "I think this is it."

Once they were close enough to read the sign, Chase squinted up at the banner. *"Monday night opening,"* she read aloud. *"National Art Display: The Body at Rest.* Huh, well of *course* they would use a nude woman to advertise it. Classic sexist advertising."

Mine was better, she thought smugly, examining the painting. This one was technically good, but it was impersonal; the woman's face was cropped off by the top of the banner, and the artist had put far more detail into her breasts than the rest of her. Typical.

Tyler mouthed the address, apparently committing it to memory, then looked for a street sign. "I think it's close."

They jogged a block along the edge of the park. The smell of something frying wafted from one of the nearby restaurants, and Chase's stomach rumbled; her last bite of Cracker Barrel's all-she-could-eat biscuits had been a long, long time ago.

"All right," Tyler said when they reached a crosswalk. "It should be somewhere close by on the other side of the . . ."

He fell silent, his jaw falling slack and his eyes slowly expanding in undisguised horror.

"Tyler?" she asked. "Are you okay?"

He lifted a trembling hand to point across the road. A passing pedestrian couple shot him dirty looks when they had to walk behind him to avoid being clotheslined by his arm.

"I don't . . ." Chase began, but when she turned to look, she trailed off into silence.

She had been confident her painting of Tyler was good, maybe better than good, and she'd privately wondered what the judges would think. Not that she was going to be able to compete once they withdrew her painting, but it would be nice to know what her chances had been, if Tyler had agreed to let her keep it in the show.

Well, *someone* had certainly approved, because there Chase and Tyler stood, faced with an eight-foot-tall window, the whole of which was taken up by an enormous banner, like the kind they put up in Abercrombie or Victoria's Secret.

Only, instead of a shirtless teenager or an underwear model, this picture was of Tyler.

Maybe it was the low lighting of the city street, but the portrait looked even better than Chase remembered. She'd done a good job capturing Tyler's expression. It looked just like him.

Which, come to think of it, was probably the reason he was whimpering right now.

The crosswalk light changed. They crossed the street in silence and stood looking up at the banner. Tyler's face had gone pale, and he looked like he was on the verge of passing out, a stark contrast to his shy smile in the portrait.

"At least the gallery's logo is positioned over your ass," Chase said at last. "That was thoughtful. Although it's probably a marketing gimmick to get people to come in and see what they're missing."

It was fairly forward-thinking of them, at least, to advertise with a nude male model on the building itself. Maybe the gallery owners wanted to prove that the show had something for everyone.

But Tyler seemed incapable of speech, and Chase had a feeling that calming mental exercises weren't going to cut it this time. Despite her bright, encouraging words, all Chase could think was, *Well, crap.*

TYLER

In all his years of worrying, Tyler had developed some extremely detailed fears. He had imagined hundreds, if not thousands, of terrible outcomes to almost every possible event.

Having his leg bitten off by a shark while taking a dip in the ocean? Check.

Accidentally leaving his door unlocked on the night that a deranged serial killer decided to roam the dorms armed with a butcher knife? Check.

Taking a vacation to Hawaii, only to have the plane drop out of the sky over the Pacific with no warning, leaving no survivors? Check.

Xavier had mocked his oddly specific anxieties, but now Tyler realized he hadn't been specific *enough.* When he'd responded to Chase's flyer, it hadn't occurred to him that the whole endeavor might end with him standing on a dimly lit street corner in New York City looking up at his own naked body, three times larger than life.

"Tyler?" Chase said gently. "Earth to Tyler? Are you okay?"

He closed his eyes and counted down from ten. When that didn't help, he tried the breathing exercise Chase had suggested after the car accident. He could smell something warm and decaying wafting out of the grates nearby; he could hear honking and yelling in the street and a faint pulse of music from somewhere above them; he felt light-headed and queasy but already calmer. Then, when he opened his eyes, all he could see was the painting, and his panic came rushing back.

"The gallery's closed," Chase said as she cupped her hand around her eyes and peered through the windows. "I don't see anyone in there. It's pretty late, and it's a Sunday night . . . I bet someone will be here in the morning to finish setting up. We can come back then."

"You mean we're just going to *leave* it?" Tyler demanded. "No. No way." He backed up, eyes fixed on the banner, slowly shaking his head. "We're going to do something about it *now.*"

"Be reasonable," Chase said, touching his arm. Usually, it would have calmed him down, but now the point of contact only heightened Tyler's anxiety. He looked down at his arm, which at least was better than staring at the portrait, and his gaze fell on the blue length of yarn Chase had tied around his wrist back in Cawker City. He'd called her reckless for vandalizing the monument.

Vandalism.

Never Have I Ever.

He turned back toward the garage as the idea ripped through his mind, his feet chewing up the pavement as a walk turned into a jog, which turned into a near sprint. He couldn't wait for tomorrow. The streets were full of people—surely at least a few of them had snapped a picture of the banner, and then posted it to their socials. It might go viral . . . And if that happened, they might be able to pull the painting from the show in time to keep it from being printed on a magazine cover, but the result would be the same.

No, he had to do something about the painting *tonight* before anyone else had a chance to see it.

"Tyler!" Chase called. He didn't slow down. Maybe they couldn't have the banner removed until someone came in tomorrow, but they could cover it up so that no one would see it in the meantime.

He found the Honda among the rows of parked cars and popped the trunk. His supplies were all in order, and there was plenty of paint left over from the baby's room the night before. Mint green would do, as long as he rolled it on thick enough. It was mixed with a white base, which meant it would be more opaque than a dark purple or deep red, so even one coat should be enough to obscure anything beneath . . .

"Tyler," Chase said, panting when she finally caught up with him. "What are you doing?"

"I'm handling it," he snapped. "I'm going to make sure that nobody else sees that painting."

She looked from him to the paint buckets, then shook her head. "Tyler, if you're about to do what I think you are . . ."

"What's a little vandalism to you?" he demanded, tucking the paint tray under one arm and slamming the trunk closed. He held the rollers in one hand and picked up the bucket of mint-green paint in the other before striding back the way he'd come.

Chase jogged alongside him. "What's that supposed to mean?"

"You talked about it before. In Cawker City. Remember when we ran for our lives from literally nothing? When you pulled your little stunt with the scissors?"

"You mean when I played a *prank* on you and didn't actually cut the twine?" she demanded. "You might have freaked out, but I didn't actually do anything. Tyler, *look at me*—this is going to end badly. The gallery could sue us."

"Or maybe I'll sue them," Tyler said belligerently, "for displaying my body without my permission."

They left the garage, and she followed him down the street, trying to snatch the bucket out of his hand or knock the paint tray aside. He could hear what she was saying, even acknowledge the validity of it, but the moment the banner came back into view, Tyler had no choice. If he could have torn it down and ripped it to shreds, he'd have done it with his bare hands.

He set his supplies down on the sidewalk and began to pry open the paint can. When it wouldn't open, he resorted to using his keys. When Chase grabbed his arm, he shook her off without so much as looking at her. She didn't understand. She never had.

"Tyler," Chase said, squatting down next to him, "I get that you're upset, but you need to stop and think for a minute. Remember what happened with the map? This is the same thing—you've got something to prove here, but there are going to be *consequences*. This is serious."

"*Serious?*" His voice came out louder than he meant it to, and Chase recoiled. "I know that. Don't you think my feelings are *serious?* How would you feel if I . . . if I found a nude photo of you from some streaking adventure or an old boyfriend or something, and I posted it on a wall where anyone could see? Would it make a difference that people didn't recognize you? That you're not a celebrity? Or would you be pissed that your privacy was violated?"

Chase took a deep breath. "Tyler . . ."

He wasn't finished. She was still trying to convince him to calm down. She still didn't understand. "I've never even *been* with a girl, Chase. I don't show off my body to entertain strangers—I trusted you, and I was vulnerable with you, and now you've put me on display in front of the whole *city*." He pointed a shaking finger up at the painting, then to the strangers walking behind, slowing and eavesdropping on the snippets before the flow of traffic carried them away. "Maybe you really wouldn't mind if I was the one who'd painted you. Maybe if it was you up there, you'd be able to own it. But that's not me, Chase. This isn't my choice. You *did* this to me." He shoved the second paint roller into her hands. "And you need to help me fix it."

Chase squatted there, staring down at the paint roller as though she'd never seen anything like it in her life.

So she'd decided not to help him. Fine. That didn't mean Tyler was going to stand around waiting for her to change her mind.

He tipped some of the paint into the pan, then ran his roller through it. When he stood up, he saw that the flow of people had come to a stop, prepared to witness another dramatic New York City story.

Before he could talk himself out of it, Tyler swiped the paint roller across the window, marking a green stripe right down the center of his chest. He wouldn't be able to reach high enough to cover his face, but that was okay; as long as he covered up his body, that would be good enough.

Once he got started, it was easier to keep going. He'd been right about the paint: a single coat was enough to obscure the colorful rendition of his shoulders and torso. He started at the top out of habit, working his way down to the edge of the window the way he would if he was painting a wall and wanted to avoid any unsightly drips. It was such a natural motion, one that came easily to him even under these circumstances, that he could feel his whole body relaxing. This was nothing more than another job, something he had to do. A survival strategy.

He was about to dip the roller again when he felt a heavy hand on his shoulder. "Excuse me, young man," said a deep voice, "I'm going to have to ask you to put that down."

Tyler turned slowly and found himself face-to-face with two police officers.

The younger of the two, a Latina woman who looked not much older than they were, shook her head. "Do I *want* to know what's going on here?"

"Well," Chase said brightly, "it's actually a funny story . . ."

"You can tell the folks at the precinct," her partner, an older Black gentleman, said. "You two are coming with us."

Chase's shoulders slumped, but Tyler kept his chin up. They might be in trouble, but the painting was covered up.

It was worth it.

CHASE

"So you see," Chase finished her explanation, "it's not really *vandalism* so much as protection of privacy. The gallery is at fault."

"Uh-huh," their booking officer said. Her name tag read *Florence,* and she did not seem impressed. "Well, as much as I'd *love* to just be able to take your word for it, you're still looking at vandalism charges and a possible burglary attempt. I'm going to have to go through your things, because if it turns out there are drugs involved—and it's not going to surprise me if there are—it's not gonna be good news for either of you."

"We're not on *drugs,*" Chase retorted. "I told you: it's a mission of justice."

"Mm-hmm." Judging by her expression, Florence wasn't convinced. "We'll see about that."

Chase flopped back into the uncomfortable chair and turned to Tyler. "Remember when you said that *I* was going to be the one that got us arrested?" she griped. "Well, congratulations."

Florence lifted on eyebrow. "You *thought* you were going to get arrested? Should I be recording this?"

"He told me I was impulsive," Chase explained. "And he's not wrong—but I'm a prankster, not a vandal."

"This is still technically your fault," Tyler reminded her grumpily. He was still on edge, and he patently refused to admit he was in the wrong. He had a right to his feelings; Chase wasn't going to argue that, but feeling upset was one thing, and getting them charged with a misdemeanor was another.

"Oh-ho, the blame game starts." Florence shook her head. "Can I get some ID?"

Tyler handed over his wallet, but Chase shook her head.

"I lost mine in the river," she said.

"Mm-hmm." The officer rolled her eyes, as if this was the kind of story she heard every day, and it was getting old. "Hand over the bag, young lady."

"It's just art supplies," Chase said. "Can you make sure not to be too rough with the paper? If it gets crinkled, I can't do a thing with it."

Florence pursed her lips. "Wouldn't want me vandalizing *your* property now, would you?"

"I wasn't vandalizing anything," Chase insisted. "That was all him."

"You were holding a paint roller at the scene of the crime," the officer said. "Which, I'll admit, isn't a sentence I find myself saying every day, but it's fairly damning in context. So maybe instead of trying to place all the blame on your boyfriend, you could own up to your role in the incident."

"Good luck," Tyler muttered, crossing his arms. "I've been saying the same thing for days, and look where it's got me."

"He's not my boyfriend," Chase said.

"Right." The officer nodded. "You just painted his nude portrait and then submitted it to a national gallery without his permission *in a friendly way*. My mistake." She unzipped Chase's backpack and began removing sketchbooks.

"Careful with those," Chase pleaded, trying to keep the desperation out of her voice. "I need some of those for my portfolio, since *someone* won't let me display my best work."

"Well, *technically* you've had your best work displayed in a gallery already," Tyler snapped, crossing his arms and scowling at the table. He had barely looked at her since they reached the gallery, except when he was accusing her of doing all this deliberately. "Or *on* a gallery, anyway. Was that not enough exposure for you? Because I'm feeling pretty exposed, it turns out."

Chase glared daggers at him. "Right, I forgot, I orchestrated all this. It turns out, this is going to help me land future work. I'm definitely *not* going to get a reputation as someone who sabotages galleries that display my paintings." She had to look away when Florence upended the whole box of markers and sent them rolling across the table. "Oh, please, not the Prismacolors. Those cost a fortune . . ."

"You know, my daughter takes art classes, and it's amazing how much they'll charge for even a pencil," Florence said, scooping up the markers and shoving them haphazardly back into their box. Chase couldn't help the way her eye twitched; she'd had them organized by color and shade, and now they were all going to have to be sorted out again. "When I was a kid, if I'd tried to get my momma to buy me anything other than a yellow No. 2, she'd have sent me to bed hungry. It's a scam."

"Artists love a good scam," Tyler said bitterly. "I know this one artist who said that privacy matters, but when push comes to shove . . ."

"Are you implying I wasn't helping?" Chase rounded on him. "Are we talking about the same artist who almost drowned on this little adventure? The one who you almost killed in a car crash because you were trying to show off how *competent* and *assertive* you could be? The one who's currently being booked for *your* poor decision-making, even though she told you breaking out the rollers was a terrible idea? *That* artist? Because that artist has just about had enough of you playing the victim here."

Tyler scoffed and scuffed the heels of his boots against the floor. "I'm also talking about the artist who lost our stuff in the river because she can't stop to think for two seconds. The same one, let me remind you, who tried to start a turf war in a McDonald's parking lot. You're not exactly unimpeachable, Chase."

"You sure you two aren't sleeping together?" Florence asked. She had dumped out the tubes of oil paints and was shoving them back into the tin—once again, in the wrong order.

"I think I'd have noticed," Chase said.

"I don't understand what's so different about this situation anyway," Tyler said, turning his chair slightly to face Chase. "You've spent the last few days telling me to be brave, to stick up for myself, to take risks . . . That's all I did. You wanted me to fight that guy at the McDonald's. How is this different?"

"I was telling you to be crazy-*bold*, not crazy-*crazy*," Chase argued.

"What's the difference?" Tyler demanded. "It sounds like you get final say in what's allowed and what's not."

"There are degrees here," Chase argued.

"Degrees of legality," the officer answered, upending Chase's deflated bag and digging through the pile of yarn, craft scissors, and broken pencils that tumbled out. "Something that wouldn't get you arrested, I'm guessing."

Chase turned to Tyler triumphantly and gestured toward the booking officer in a *this is exactly what I meant* sort of way.

"I wasn't asking you to challenge the SUV guy to a duel to defend my honor," she said. "I was thinking you might, I don't know, tell him to be more respectful? Back me up? Being assertive isn't the same thing as breaking the law, you know."

"You want me to do things your way," Tyler said. "But every time I've tried to take the lead on something, it's backfired."

"No, it hasn't. What about the farmers' market?"

Tyler paused to consider this.

"What about jumping off the bridge to save me?"

"What's this about a bridge, now?" asked Florence.

"We got robbed back in Kansas," Chase explained. "When I lost my ID and almost drowned. Long story."

"You've had quite the weekend, haven't you?" The booking officer shoved Chase's bag across the table, along with the pile of art supplies.

"I saw you giving me side-eye, young lady, so I'll leave you to put everything back. The good news is that there's nothing in there that shouldn't be, and no evidence of intent to commit burglary, so given that you only managed to get a couple of lines of paint on a window-pane, you might be eligible for a DAT . . . That's a voluntary discharge with no bail."

"Thank you," Chase told her earnestly. "You're right, we *have* had quite a weekend. I appreciate your patience."

"In fact, I expect that you'll be released, Miss Zalinski. Now, you"—she pointed to Tyler—"you're going to wait." Florence started to stand up, then dropped back into her chair. "I see what's going on here. Lord knows my ex-husband and I played the blame game better than anyone. So while I handle your paperwork, why don't the two of you take a couple of minutes to *think* before you talk, m'kay?" She patted her hand on the table twice, as if to signal that the conversation was over, then got up and made her way out of the little room.

Chase stared down at the pile of jumbled supplies. Her head was pounding, and when Florence opened the door to leave, she caught the half-burned scent of coffee left too long in the pot.

Tyler was silent, and when she glanced over, he'd pulled his brows together the way he often did when he was thinking. There was a little wrinkle in between them, and she felt a strong compulsion to rub her thumb over it and smooth it away.

Except for the fact that he still hadn't apologized. The car crash had been an accident, and Chase could forgive accidents—but he'd done this *intentionally,* and he refused to own up to it.

"Sometimes it feels like you want me to be a different person," Tyler said suddenly. "Which sucks. I mean, it feels pretty terrible. Because it would be nice . . ."

"Yeah?" she urged when he didn't continue.

His reply was pitched so low that she almost couldn't hear it. "It would be nice if you liked me as I am."

She looked over sharply. He was picking at a spot on his jeans, a little blob of mint green that had splattered against his pant leg when they were being brought in.

"I do like you," she said. "Of course I like you. Are you really that dense?"

"Then why do you act like everything I do is wrong? Even before we left campus. It's because you've tried to get me to be something I'm not."

She scooted her chair closer, abandoning the art supplies. "Maybe when we're arguing, yeah. But I'm not trying to change you. I'm trying to convince you that the person you *are* is great, and that you don't need to be so afraid of what other people think."

"That's sure as hell not what it feels like," he muttered

God forbid he apologize, Chase thought grimly as she began the process of stuffing her art supplies back into the bag. She didn't even attempt to organize everything. She was too upset to bother with it now. *I've messed up, but I've apologized every time. Why is he so stubborn?*

The door opened, and Florence stepped back into the room. She was holding up a stack of papers.

"Miss Zalinski, it sounds to me as if you were merely present at the crime scene, and since your paint roller was dry and there was no contraband in that absurd backpack of yours, we're not charging you." She shook her head solemnly. "Lord, if my mother knew I joined the NYPD to be dealing with this sort of foolishness, she'd be turning over in her grave. Anyway, you're free to go. I'm afraid that Mr. Wilson is going to be here for a while until we can get some more information."

"You're going?" Tyler asked. His face suddenly lit up. "You're *going!* You can get the painting back from the gallery! What time is it? They'll be open in a few hours, right?"

Chase got to her feet and shoved her chair back toward the desk. "Sure, Tyler, don't worry. I'll get the painting back." Once their mission was complete, however, it might be time to part ways.

TYLER

Should I have apologized? Tyler had thought that Chase was mad at him after the showdown in the parking lot, but she'd gotten over that relatively quickly. This time, she'd actually seemed . . .

Well. *Hurt.*

"Do you want your phone call?" Florence asked.

Tyler looked up. It hadn't even occurred to him to ask for one. On impulse, he started to shake his head, but then he thought again. "Actually, yeah. There's someone I'd like to talk to."

"Come with me, then." Florence waved for him to follow and led him out through the hall to another small room with a telephone waiting on a desk. There were tall windows on the side of the room facing the hall. "I'll be waiting out here. Don't do anything too foolish, now."

Wise words, Florence, but it's a little late for that. Tyler nodded obediently and went in. He dialed Xavier's number from memory; it was one of only four numbers he knew by heart, and that included 911.

The phone rang four times before it occurred to Tyler that he still didn't know what time it was, but it was almost certainly an indecent hour. Xavier was probably asleep.

Abruptly, the line clicked, and his friend's sleepy voice answered. "If this is a telemarketing scam, I *swear to God . . .*"

"Xavier!" Tyler exclaimed. "Please don't hang up. I only get the one phone call."

"Huh? Tyler? Why are you calling me at "—there was a rustle of sheets, presumably as Xavier flailed around in his bed in search of a clock—"six a.m.?"

"I need to ask you something," Tyler said.

"Can't it wait?" Xavier asked. "You *know* I need my beauty sleep."

Tyler shook his head, clutching the receiver to his ear. "I don't think that the booking officer is going to be thrilled about letting me try again later. She's not as scary as she looks, but I'm guessing that even *she* has her limits."

Xavier was quiet, so quiet that Tyler was momentarily afraid he'd fallen asleep. Then, in halting tones, he repeated, "Booking officer?"

"Yeah," Tyler said. "Long story, but I'm being held at the NYPD booking station."

"Dude, are you pranking me?" Xavier grumbled. "Because if so, this is a really weird prank."

"No," Tyler assured him. "I am one hundred percent arrested." A nervous giggle bubbled up from his throat at the sentence. "You know, out of the three of us, I would have thought I'd be the *last* one to be charged with anything, but here we are . . ."

Xavier's voice became firmer. "Okay, man, okay. Are you all right? What happened? Did someone hurt you? What do you need from me?"

It was nice to know that when it came down to it, Xavier had his back. He might jerk Tyler around the rest of the time, but when the going got tough, he could count on Xav.

"I actually don't know if I'll need bail." Tyler sighed. "I guess I should have asked. But yes, I'm fine, and no, I'm not hurt. Not physically. Xavier, can you tell me something?"

"Anything," Xavier replied.

Tyler debated where to start. "So, Chase kissed me."

"She did *what?*" Xavier shrieked. It was a little insulting that Xavier could just accept that Tyler had been arrested, but be totally blind-sided by the fact that he actually had something approximating game, even if it had only lasted a grand total of about two seconds. "Does this have something to do with you getting arrested? Did one of you spontaneously combust? Dude, when did this *happen*?"

"After she almost drowned, but before I crashed the car." Tyler pinched the bridge of his nose. "So, let's see, that would have been Friday night? Or technically early Saturday morning? I'm losing track of time."

"Dude," Xavier mumbled. "I don't . . . Okay. I have a lot of questions, but let's get to yours first."

"I'm becoming a regular raconteur, aren't I?" Tyler said flatly. "I guess that makes me worth keeping around for a little while longer. So Chase kissed me, but it seems like we've been fighting constantly since then."

"And your question is . . . ?" Xavier prompted. "Because so far, I can't help you with anything."

Tyler forced the words out. "Why does everyone in my life want me to change?"

Silence. The only evidence that Xavier was still on the line was the lack of dial tone.

"I know that I'm boring," Tyler went on. "And I know that I'm so full of nerves and anxieties and irrational fears that I pretty much hamstring myself rather than making the first move. Not just on dating but on *anything*. But you're my best friend, and I would *never* ditch you just because you don't live your life the way I do. And Chase? It feels like Chase constantly wants me to be someone else, someone assertive and confident and . . . and morally sound. Why does everyone want me to change?"

He fell silent, breathing heavily, and prayed that Florence wouldn't come kick him out of the room before he got answers.

"I don't want you to be different," Xavier said in a small voice.

"You threatened to stop being friends with me if I didn't become more interesting!" Tyler snapped. "Is that not the literal definition of trying to make someone change?"

He expected Xavier to deny it, but his friend only sighed again. "Yeah, I did. But only because I'm an asshole."

Tyler snorted. "You can be."

"I know it's not an excuse," Xavier went on. "You know how you get caught up in your own head? Well, I'm the opposite. You get stuck in a loop sometimes, while my fat mouth makes me say stupid crap without thinking. But that's why we make such a good team, isn't it? Or at least, I thought it was. I push, and you pull, and instead of being one reclusive loner and one reckless dipstick, we average out to two fairly normal people. So yeah, sometimes I push too hard. And sometimes you dig your heels in more than is healthy. I call you on it, and I count on you calling me out too."

Tyler stared at the window into the hall, focusing on his own reflection in the glass. He looked pale and shell-shocked. "Oh."

"I was just messing about finding new friends," Xavier said. "I thought I was doing the mama bird push-my-baby-out-of-the-nest move. I was wrong, and I'm sorry."

Tyler's voice came out thick. "Oh. Okay. Thank you, that means a lot." If he ended up crying because Xavier said something too sweet, it would surely be a sign of the end times.

"Did Chase say you were boring?" Xavier asked gently.

Tyler wrapped his finger in the coiled cord of the phone. "Not in so many words. But she keeps telling me to stand up for myself."

Xavier made a sucking sound with his lips. "Ah. That sucks, bro. Am I allowed to give advice?"

Tyler chuckled. "That's kind of why I called."

"Pick and choose," Xavier said. "If she pushes you, and you realize that you *need* that push? Be bold, my dude. But when she pushes too far, stand up for yourself. To *her*. If she's worth having in your life, you'll figure out a balance. And if she's not, then you're better off without her. Honestly, I'd *like* to see you with someone who can coax you out of your shell a little, but don't let anyone walk all over you, man. Not Chase. Not me. Not anybody. You deserve better than that, Tyler."

Tyler smiled at his world-weary reflection. "Thanks, Xavier."

"Right." Xavier yawned loudly. "Now, can the rest of this wait? I'm whipped. Hit me up if you need bail, huh? I can squeeze some emergency money out of my old man if you swear on your life to pay me back ASAP. I can't imagine that this is a conversation you'd want to have with your parents."

Florence strolled up to the window and tapped on the glass.

"Thanks again," Tyler said. "I'll let you know."

"Night, dude." Xavier's line clicked, and a dial tone droned out of the receiver. Tyler placed it back in the cradle and made his way out into the hall.

"You need some breakfast?" Florence asked. "I'm not going to starve you, but I can't let you go until we can get in touch with someone from the gallery you vandalized."

It occurred to Tyler that he hadn't given Chase any of their money, and that he still had the car keys, so she wouldn't be able to access their snacks—she was going to be stuck walking all the way to the gallery without anything to eat.

She's going to hate me for this.

"I'm okay," Tyler told her. Joining Chase's accidental fast felt a little bit like penance. It might not help her, but at least they'd be suffering together.

"If you say so." Florence shrugged, then led him back to the room where he'd already been waiting for hours. He slumped back into his chair, closing his eyes as Florence left him once more.

He was tired, but he wasn't ready to sleep. The conversation with Xavier had given him a lot to think about.

CHASE

Chase was practically dead on her feet. How could a city as tightly packed as this one be so *vast?* It had taken her almost two hours of weary walking to get from Manhattan Central Booking back past the northernmost corner of Central Park, and she was still a few blocks from the parking garage.

All Chase wanted was to get the painting, climb back in the car, and collapse. She'd pass out right there in the garage if she had to, as long as the attendants didn't mind. Heck, she could probably get comfortable on the sidewalk if it came down to it, as long as nobody tripped over her. The cot in the church basement felt like a distant, heavenly memory.

How can Tyler be so stubborn? Chase hiked her backpack up higher on her shoulders and frowned at the concrete. *Doesn't he see that we're on the same side? Of course I don't want to change him. I just want . . . more. Every time I've pushed him, something good has come out of it. He just needs to realize when to rein it in.*

She really didn't mind when Tyler made mistakes. Chase had certainly made enough of her own in the past. What drove her crazy was how he pushed things too far: he felt emasculated by their fight at the Pilot, so he pulled that macho crap with the map and crashed the car. He didn't want the painting to be displayed, so he vandalized a building, got them arrested, and then had the gall to blame *her* for it. He was so worried about people seeing the painting because he didn't want to be made fun of—but he couldn't see that people *liked* it. Why couldn't he understand that when they looked at the portrait, they weren't criticizing him but admiring him?

And, sure, they were admiring Chase's artistic talents in the process. But that was beside the point.

Plus, she'd taken his side from the beginning. If he'd done a painting of *her*, she'd have let him enter it wherever he liked, but she could respect boundaries. Heck, she'd spent the last four days doing nothing *but* respect his boundaries! Why did he keep blaming her for things she had no control over?

The more Chase thought about it, the angrier she got. He made it sound like everything was her fault. Really, the worst thing she'd done was end up in the river, and she hadn't done that on purpose. He was being absurd.

The gallery was still closed, but that made sense. It was early, and the show wasn't scheduled until tonight. Chase backtracked toward the park with the vague hope that she could at least find a bench and sit down on it for a while, just to give her back a rest from the weight of the art bag.

She passed a small bakery-café, one that advertised itself as a purveyor of fine tea and coffee. The thought of coffee perked Chase up a little. A pastry would be even better. Her stomach grumbled, and Chase grumbled back. She'd been so annoyed in the precinct that she hadn't thought to ask Tyler for any money, and now she was *starving*.

She paused outside the door, taking a deep breath and allowing herself to savor the sweet, sweet aroma of caffeine. A sign on the window informed her that they offered Nutella-stuffed croissants for under five dollars, which would have sounded like heaven if she hadn't been flat broke.

Five dollars. Chase stared at the sign, the wheels in her weary head slowly creaking to life. She swung the pack off her back and rummaged through the pockets; Florence had made a mess of her art supplies, but sure enough, she found a now-rumpled five-dollar bill on one of them: Jo Beth's payment for the portrait of Virtue. Chase had forgotten all about it.

Chase stepped inside and breathed deeply, making her way to the counter. The barista who greeted her was in her mid-forties. She sported burnt-orange highlights and a septum ring, giving off the distinct aura of a woman who'd spent her night at a thrasher concert before coming directly to her early-bird shift. Her shredded T-shirt advertised something called *Duck Duck Goose* in the spiky lettering that Chase usually associated with hair metal bands.

Chase had never gone for that look, but she could appreciate the woman's commitment to the aesthetic.

"What can I get you?" the barista asked in a raspy voice. The smile she offered Chase was nothing short of congenial.

"How much is a small coffee?" Chase asked, flattening her bill against the counter.

The barista leaned her elbows against the counter. "Three."

Chase's heart sank. "And your cheapest pastry?"

"Three and a half."

Chase nibbled her lip. Food was important, but if she didn't get a hit of coffee, she might not be able to stay awake until the gallery opened. She had to get in there the moment someone unlocked the doors.

Aw, screw it.

"I'll take a small coffee, please." She held out the bill.

The barista looked from Chase to the money and back again. Her lips, which sported a heavy layer of black lipstick, quirked up at the corners.

"Is that all you've got?" she asked.

Chase nodded glumly.

The woman waved to encompass the small café, where a few other diners sat scattered around the room. "Take a seat." She plucked the bill out of Chase's hands and waved her away.

Chase obediently staked out a two-top by the front window, where she had a decent view of the gallery door. She let out an audible sigh of relief as she dropped her art bag heavily to the floor. Tyler was right: she could do permanent damage to her spine if she kept dragging this thing around.

Tyler.

Just thinking about him made Chase irritable. He was probably still in booking. If he was lucky, they'd let him get some sleep. They might even offer him a few cups of that burnt-smelling coffee. Maybe a night in holding would give him a chance to think about what he'd done and who was *really* responsible for it.

Chase was lost in a Tyler-induced funk when the barista returned, plopping a cup of coffee down in front of her. To Chase's surprise, it was accompanied by a muffin.

"No nuts," the barista said. "I wasn't sure if you're allergic. I forgot to mention our two-for-five daily special on a coffee and our cheapest pastry. Good thing I remembered, huh?" She winked at Chase before sailing back off to the counter.

"Thank you!" she called. The barista waved over her shoulder.

Chase ate her small breakfast in contented silence, watching the door of the gallery the whole while. She was still exhausted, but her foul mood lifted slightly as the food hit her system. When she was finished eating, she pushed the dirty dishes off to one side and pulled out her small sketchpad.

It was easy to get lost in her sketching. Another layer of weariness lifted from her as she got to work, looking up ever thirty seconds or so to either check the gallery or sneak a glance at the barista. When Chase looked at the woman in person, she was vividly aware of the color contrast in the woman's accessories: her bright hair, her dark lips, the magenta gauges in her ears. But in pencil, she revealed herself to be a sea of textures. As Chase sat there, her rough sketch developed into something beautiful and almost alive beneath her hands.

"Whoa."

Chase jumped and looked up guiltily. "Uh. Hi again."

"Is that me?" The barista leaned over Chase's shoulder. "Damn, I look rad."

Chase sheepishly pulled the page out of the book. "That's what I thought. Do you want it?"

"For real?" The barista accepted the page and squinted down at it. "Wow. You're *good.*"

"Thanks." Chase brightened. The barista could appreciate her art—why couldn't Tyler do the same?

Chase stared out across the street. Tyler had managed to paint over the poster's chest, but his eyes were still staring out at her, that small smile on his face. He'd looked at her like that in person when they were alone in a room together on more than one occasion. Chase was better with images than words, but one popped into her mind as she glanced at the poster: conspiratorial.

Seeing that expression now made her slightly uncomfortable. His accusations still stung.

But maybe—and this was probably the coffee talking—Chase was in the wrong here?

As she stared at the poster, a light in the gallery window flicked on. Someone was moving around inside.

"Thanks for giving me this," the barista said, still focused on her own portrait. "It's pretty cool."

"Thanks for, uh, *remembering* the daily deal," Chase replied. She stuffed her everyday sketchbook haphazardly into her backpack, not bothering with the zipper. "Excuse me. I have to go."

The barista stepped back, and Chase swept toward the door. Her feet were killing her, and her spine was on the verge of snapping in two, but that didn't stop her from sprinting across the street and pounding her fist on the glass.

A slim, older woman in bifocals came out to the doors and peered at Chase curiously. She shook her head, but Chase just smiled and knocked again. She probably looked a little manic. She certainly *felt* manic. After a few moments, the woman came out and opened the door.

"We're closed," she said, pointing toward a sign on the window as if corroborating her own evidence. "You'll have to come back later."

"I'm afraid it's an emergency," Chase said. "I'm one of the artists.

Chase Zalinski?" She pointed awkwardly toward the window, which was still covered in paint. "This one's mine."

The woman's smile immediately warmed. "Oh, you're *Chase?* Of course. Come in." She stepped back and ushered Chase into the room. "I'm sure Marcel would love to meet you. He adores your piece." The woman's smile slipped slightly. "I'm not sure *what* happened to the window, but we'll get that sorted out."

Chase smiled woodenly. "Uh, yeah. Shame about that . . ."

It was a relief to have the noise of the city disappear the moment that the doors closed behind her. There was string music piping through the sound system, and the room smelled faintly of lavender and patchouli.

"There are only fifty paintings in the show," the woman told Chase as she led her through the gallery. "And only the top four will win scholarships. People get to vote on the final results—by QR code, so the results are tallied automatically—and I know that we shouldn't play favorites, but *really* . . . Marcel and I both love your piece. I'm Patricia, by the way. I've been helping Marcel with the show."

"Nice to meet you," Chase said, but her eyes were wandering around the room, checking out the competition.

Not that she was competing, but still. A girl could be curious.

The other paintings were good—good but not great. Chase was a harsh critic, and she was harshest with herself most of all. Still, she found herself picking apart every other painting she passed. The one of the man lying naked on the couch had some issues with the perspective. The composition of the woman reclining on a picnic blanket was a little too clumsy to be intentionally postmodern. That painting of the couple feeding each other grapes was nice, except for the fact that the artist clearly had an issue with hands.

And then, she passed the portrait of Tyler. Patricia was right. It was the best of the bunch.

"Marcel?" Patricia stuck her head through the door of the little office. "Marcel, darling, there's someone here to see you."

A sleek-looking gentleman in a periwinkle paisley-patterned suit glanced up from his computer screen. "Who's this, Patti? We aren't open yet."

"This," Patricia said indulgently, "is Chase Zalinski."

Marcel's lips parted in delight. "How marvelous! For the record, Miss Zalinski, I'll be voting for your piece. Like Patti says, I'm Marcel, the co-owner of the gallery. I do most of the PR, and I want you to know that we've gotten a lot of positive feedback on your piece already. Everyone *loves* the window display." He reached out to shake her hand. "Have a seat. I hope you don't mind me saying so, but you look positively *dead on your feet.*"

Chase settled into the plush chair across from Marcel's desk, warmed to the core by their praise. "Yeah, it's been a long couple of days. Not that it matters. Do you really think the piece is that good?"

Marcel sighed dreamily. "Some of these other works are much more sensual, but there's an intimacy to yours that makes me feel as though I already know your subject. He's *resplendent.* Demure, but coquettish. Why, my dear, he's simply *chock full of personality.*"

Patricia nodded her agreement. "Radiant, I might add. I think your odds are good."

Chase forced a smile. "I appreciate your feedback. The thing is, there's been kind of a mix-up. This painting wasn't supposed to be here."

Marcel pursed his lips and exchanged a surprised glance with Patricia. "Pardon?"

"It wasn't supposed to be entered into the show at all." Saying the words aloud almost killed her in light of their effusive praise, but this was what they had come for, after all, wasn't it? Everything they had gone through had led to this moment, and Tyler had been clear—this painting getting out was his worst nightmare. Chase folded her hands in her lap and forced herself to continue. "A different painting was supposed to be sent in. I want to withdraw this one from the competition."

"Are you sure?" Marcel asked, looking to Chase for confirmation. "If you take it now, you won't have a chance to win the scholarship money. If you place anywhere in the top four, you'll be walking away with at least four thousand dollars. Honestly, I think you have a shot at first. Ten grand, my dear." He raised his eyebrows. "That's nothing to sneeze at."

Chase's mouth fell open. "Ten *grand?*" she repeated.

Marcel nodded and spun his computer screen around so that she could see the email he was drafting. "I was just about the send out the day-of reminder featuring all of our contestants. I put yours right at the top."

Chase sat up a little straighter. "What do you mean, 'just about'?"

"If you'd walked in the door ten seconds later, I would have hit send." Marcel smiled sympathetically. "Is it imposter syndrome, Miss Zalinski? I do know how it feels when you doubt your own work, but I *really* think that you have something special here."

"I was an art student once," Patricia added. "I know what ten thousand dollars would have meant to *me*, back in the day."

"Yeah," Chase said feebly. "I could certainly use the money . . ."

It was only by chance that she'd spotted Patricia in the gallery when she had. How hard would it be, really, to pretend she'd arrived only thirty seconds too late, and the newsletter had already gone out? *I'm sorry, Tyler, but I couldn't stop it. He'd already hit send. And now that it's out online, well, there's no point in pulling it from the competition, right?*

It would be the work of a moment, a single impulsive answer, and her life might very well change forever. Tyler would get over it eventually. It might even be good for him, wouldn't it? Chase could definitely *prove* that the sky wouldn't fall if the guy took a risk or two.

Looking up into Marcel and Patricia's eager faces, Chase took a deep, steadying breath and gave her answer. It was impulsive, she knew. Reckless. She hadn't thought her way through the consequences yet. But if a lifetime of squabbling with her mother had taught Chase anything, it was that she was impulsive by nature.

And really, who could blame her for being what she was?

TYLER

Tyler was dozing in his chair when the door of the holding cell opened. He was startled so badly he nearly tumbled out of his chair. Florence shook her head at his reaction, leveling an almost fond smile at him.

"Good news, Mr. Wilson," she announced, brandishing a clipboard and a pen at him. "I don't know what sort of magic strings your girl-friend pulled, but the gallery has decided not to press charges. I trust you can manage to stay out of trouble for the rest of the time you're in the city?"

"Yes, ma'am." Tyler nodded earnestly. The thought of Chase winning over the gallery owners made the tight knot in his chest ease. She was looking out for him, even though she was probably still mad at him. Maybe, like Xavier, he could count on her to be there when he needed her most, no matter *how* she felt about him at any given moment. So far, it certainly seemed like it.

"I hope so." Florence narrowed her eyes at him critically. "Well, your information is all on the paperwork, so off you go. That had better be the last I see of you. Go on, then, out you go." Florence shooed Tyler toward the door as if he were a stray cat that had wandered into the wrong house.

"Thank you again," Tyler said, dipping his head toward her. "Have a nice Monday, Florence."

She half-smiled at him. "No such thing, I'm afraid."

It was mid-afternoon by the time Tyler stepped out into the streets of New York, and he squinted in the sunlight. After yet another restless night, Tyler was exhausted. Only the thought of Chase, locked out of the car and left without food, kept him moving. He made sure his ID and his keys were still in his pocket, and set out in search of a map.

Tyler briefly considered using what was left of their cash to catch a cab, but instead of wasting the money Chase had earned by hand, he spent a painfully long time trying to navigate the Metro system. He thought it might be easier if he just asked someone, but he couldn't quite work up the nerve. Besides, everyone was moving around him so fast—it wasn't like they were going to stop, anyway.

Chase would tell him he was being ridiculous. If she were here, she would flag someone down and ask them for directions. How would she do it? Probably walk up to the first person who didn't look like they were in a terrible mood and say . . .

"Excuse me?"

The guy that Tyler had hailed looked up from his phone, frowning. "Yo, man? What's your problem?"

Tyler swallowed hard. "Uh . . . any chance you can tell me how to get to the Manhattan Student Gallery?"

The guy narrowed his eyes. "You lost or something?"

"Um," Tyler squeaked. "Sorry?"

The man returned to his phone, but he kept looking up at Tyler warily. *Is he calling the police to accost me again? Or is he taking out a hit out on me?* Tyler's eyes drifted down to the man's neck tattoo, and he shivered. Only yesterday, Chase had commented how badass a neck tattoo could be. If Tyler had spotted it earlier, he never would have messed with this particular passerby.

"Cathedral Parkway," the stranger barked.

Tyler flinched. "What?"

"Cathedral Parkway, man. We're at Canal now, so if you go *that* way"—the tatted stranger pointed down one of the underground

walkways—"then you can catch the red line, and if you go *that* way"—
he hooked his thumb in the other direction—"you can catch the blue.
They're both a straight shot to Cathedral, which is gonna be your
stop, okay?"

"Oh." Tyler nodded. "Right. Cathedral Parkway, red or blue. Thank
you!"

The man nodded, his frown never wavering, and spun away. Tyler
put a hand to his chest; his heart pounded beneath his palm, but he'd
survived his first free-range encounter with an actual New Yorker.
Better yet, he actually knew where he was going now.

He'd have to thank Chase for that later.

Navigating the Metro was akin to passing through Purgatory, but
when Tyler finally emerged from the underworld onto Cathedral
Parkway, he couldn't help but feel a little pride in the accomplish-
ment. He could be brave, when his survival depended on it. Maybe
even brave enough to ask Chase out when he saw her next.

Assuming she wasn't still angry.

He followed signs for Central Park, and before long he spotted
familiar posters advertising the art show. Eventually, he came upon
the cross street where the gallery waited on the corner. The sight of
the still-green window made Tyler smile ruefully, but he paused when
he realized that the larger-than-life copy of the dreaded portrait—
now censored by his own handiwork—was still hanging in the
window. A few paces later, he saw the sandwich board propped
outside. *National Student Competition Opens Tonight! $10,000 Grand
Prize Winner to be Decided by Your Votes! Voting Commences at 5:00 p.m.*

Tyler's mouth went dry. Ten thousand dollars? Chase had
mentioned that there was money involved, but she'd never hinted just
how much was on the line.

An ugly suspicion settled in his mind. What if she'd known the
whole time, and she'd kept it to herself? What if every nice thing she'd
done in the last few days had been in an attempt to change his mind?
If they'd walked through the gallery door together, would she have
suddenly pleaded to leave the piece in the show?

What if she'd only tried to get him to like her so that he'd feel like he owed her a favor?

That's why she only kissed him once. It had been so awful that she couldn't bring herself to do it again, but she must have thought it would give her leverage. In fact, it was probably the reason she'd agreed to come on this trip in the first place.

Tyler did his best to push the paranoid thoughts aside, but they kept clawing their way back in. What other explanation could there be?

People were already walking into the gallery—it must be even later than Tyler had realized. If Chase really *had* sabotaged their mission, maybe there was still time to do damage control.

He hustled inside, looking around frantically, either for some sign of Chase or for the nearest available employee. Panic was settling in, worse than any Tyler had experienced before. If Chase had betrayed him . . .

A willowy man in a purple paisley suit smiled vaguely at Tyler, then did a double-take. He excused himself from a group of visitors and hurried over.

"My goodness," he murmured, his eyes sweeping over Tyler's face. "I'd know you anywhere. It really is a magnificent likeness, isn't it?"

Tyler bit down hard on the insides of his cheeks, holding back a sob. Whoever this man was, he must have recognized Tyler from the painting. Which meant he had *seen* the painting. Which meant . . .

Tyler followed that train of thought to its inevitable conclusion, and a little part of him died.

"I hope you aren't *too* upset by the window," the man went on, ignorant of Tyler's internal collapse. "I convinced her to leave it up— consider it penance for what you did to my otherwise *impeccable* image." He lifted a perfectly manicured eyebrow at Tyler. "I'd also like to *gently insist* that you stop by tomorrow and scrape all the paint off the glass."

Tyler nodded weakly. What did it matter if his face hung in a gallery window, when people would be staring at his nude all night? It was a good painting too. No doubt Chase would win.

Ten thousand dollars. Tyler would probably kick himself to the curb for a cool ten grand.

"You might have convinced Miss Zalinski to withdraw from the show, but I still think it's a terrible shame," the man said. "Art like that is meant to be seen."

Tyler nodded absently, then froze. "Withdraw?"

The man's second eyebrow joined the first. "Indeed. Is that a surprise? Because she made it sound as though that was rather the point of the whole affair."

"She withdrew from the show?" Tyler repeated.

The man sighed, fluttering his eyelids as if Tyler was trying his patience to an unreasonable degree. "I understand that you've had quite a day, young man, so I'll forgive you for being a tad slow on the uptake. Yes, Miss Zalinski's piece is out of the show. Would you like me to show you where she is?"

Tyler nodded, following the man through the gallery, back to the offices. His glazed eyes wandered unseeingly over the patrons, only pausing once or twice on the other pieces that lined the walls. Nude after nude after nude—and all these people had come to examine them. Strange, how something as everyday as the human body could be seen as high art under the right circumstances.

The other paintings were okay, as far as he could tell, but they were nothing to write home about.

Chase was standing inside a small, glass-fronted office, a telephone receiver pressed to her ear. As Tyler approached, she dropped it back into the cradle and clutched her forehead in frustration.

When they entered the room, Chase turned her head. "Oh, hey, Marcel."

"Look what the cat dragged in." The man chuckled, stepping aside so that Chase could see Tyler as well. "I'm sorry that you had to come all this way just to get in touch with me. We *really* should get around to hiring a secretary. Now, if you two will excuse me, I have a show to run. Take all the time you need with the phone, Miss Zalinski, and *you* . . ." He wagged his index finger at Tyler. "I expect to see *you* bright and early tomorrow. I'll provide the razor, but I want you to personally scrape every speck of paint off that window. I won't sign off on it until it's spotless." With that, he turned on his heel and was gone.

Tyler stood there, not quite sure of what to say. The silence was painful, and Chase stood there rigidly, clearly in no mood to put him at his ease.

"Hey," he said at last. "You made it."

Chase crossed her arms and leaned her hip against the desk. "So did you."

"Thanks for convincing him to drop the charges," Tyler said, pointing out the window to where Marcel now milled freely among the other guests. There was a blank spot on the wall next to him, and when Tyler squinted, he saw a tag still pinned below it. *Chase Zalinski,* it read, *Portrait #86.*

The actual painting sat on the floor of the office, leaning against Chase's art bag. Tyler had to stop himself from rushing over and turning it around, lest someone spot it through the window. That didn't matter, not really. In here, there was no risk of it going viral.

"I was afraid that you might change your mind and leave it in the show," he admitted, pointing to the portrait.

"Yeah, well." Chase shrugged one shoulder, and her stiff posture relaxed slightly. "Not gonna lie, I thought about it. Ten grand. *Whew.* But the stuff you said to me the other night? You were kind of a jerk about it, but you were basically right. It's your likeness, and you should get to decide who sees it. I'm impulsive, but I'm not an asshole."

Tyler let out a sigh of relief. "Thanks. I really . . . I don't know what else to say."

"It's fine," Chase said. "And while I don't think that I'd feel the same way if I were in your shoes, you're entitled to your feelings, and I'm not going to force you to do anything you're uncomfortable with. Not now, and not ever." She slapped her palms together as if dusting them off. "So that's it. Mission accomplished."

Tyler nodded, letting himself go limp with relief. "What do we do now?"

"I'm trying to call my sister." Chase hooked her thumb at the telephone. "Ideally, she'll be able to send us some money—if I can ever reach her. Whatever cash we have left isn't going to be enough to get us home." She snorted. "Especially since you have to stick around until morning to work off your debt to society."

"Want me to take your stuff to the car?" Tyler offered. He wouldn't truly relax until the painting was safe in the back seat, hidden from prying eyes.

"Honestly? It would be a relief not to have to carry that monstrosity anymore." Chase tipped her chin toward her bag.

"I'll take it out and come right back." Tyler tried to hoist the bag up onto one shoulder and gasped. "How much does this thing *weigh?*"

"You don't look like a guy who skips arm day," Chase observed. "If a helpless little thing like me can carry it, I'm sure you can too."

Chase was a lot of things, but Tyler would never have called her *helpless.*

On the second attempt, Tyler managed to get the bag up onto his back, then squatted down for the portrait. He clutched it to his chest so that it faced inward. It now sported a thick frame, which made it even more unwieldy. "I'll be right back, okay? And if you can't reach your sister, we'll call someone else. Now that the crisis has been averted, we've got time."

Chase reached for the phone again without responding.

She was a little frosty, but Tyler could understand that. If her delicate nerves had cost *him* ten grand, he'd probably have some feelings about that. Perhaps she didn't appreciate the fact that he'd referred to her artwork as a "crisis," but that was how it felt to Tyler.

He'd find a way to make it up to her. Not the money, probably, but the sense of disappointment.

Tyler maneuvered his way through the office door, then out through the gallery. Curious onlookers stepped aside, making way for the real Tyler, the fake Tyler, and Chase's impossibly large backpack. He smiled at everyone, buoyed by their success. It suddenly occurred to him that his irrational spiraling earlier had been way off the mark —Chase hadn't come along on this road trip to use him, and she had never tried to hold their kiss over his head. She hadn't even been visibly angry just now. Which meant, presumably, that she hadn't spent this whole trip manipulating him.

Which meant that she might actually . . . like him?

Even with the weight of the bag on his shoulders, Tyler practically skipped down the street toward the parking deck. Even if Chase couldn't reach her sister, he could always call his parents. He jogged back up the stairs of the garage, then dashed to the safety of his car. In spite of the odds, it had all worked out.

Tyler set the painting down against the side of the car so that his doppelgänger smiled up at him. He dipped one hand into his pocket, fishing out the car keys, but in his haste to unlock the door, they slipped from his fingers and landed with a metallic jingle on the concrete. Tyler bent down to pick them up, almost overbalancing as he did so, thanks to the heavy pack.

Out of nowhere, something smacked Tyler in the back of the head. He yelped, convinced that someone had slapped him on purpose—was he being mugged? An object fell to the ground next to him, and Tyler froze.

Nobody had slapped him. It was Chase's everyday sketchbook, the one she was always drawing in. It had landed on the pavement with the cover open.

His own face smiled awkwardly up at him.

Tyler snatched his keys off the ground and closed the sketchbook with a snap. Whatever he'd seen was clearly private. Chase hadn't *meant* to show him, and she had respected his privacy. He should do the same.

Then again, that *had* been his face, hadn't it?

Tyler stood up with creaking knees and held the sketchbook at arm's length. Chase had never made a secret of her art, and he really didn't think she would mind if he flipped through it. Besides, the idea that she'd drawn him again was . . . intriguing.

He'd take a quick look. Just a peek. He'd come clean when he saw her again, but there was no way he could just *walk away* after seeing something like that.

Gingerly, Tyler opened the cover of the sketchbook.

The first sketches were of random people, probably for a class, or maybe interesting strangers she'd noticed walking by, all seen with various parts of their campus in the backgrounds. Even the loosest sketches were good—not detailed but somehow *true*. They were like little windows into other minds. Tyler found himself smiling as he flipped through the first dozen pages. Chase had such a good eye for detail. She could capture a wry smile in only a few strokes of charcoal, or preserve heartbreak in graphite like an insect caught in amber. One whole page was dedicated to a cartoon of an old man walking hand-in-hand with what must be his granddaughter. Tyler could feel the affection radiating between them, frozen on the paper along with the distinct sense of motion. The compositional balance on that one was perfect. There was probably a fancy name for the yin-and-yang of the old man's cane reaching for the ground, while the little girl's balloon reached for the sky. He could picture how Chase might have smiled as she sketched that, unable to resist.

Tyler flipped the next page and froze.

His own face stared up at him. He'd known he was in there.

But this wasn't the same sketch he'd seen before. Which meant he was in there at least *twice*.

Cautiously, Tyler looked down to examine the painting, comparing it to the sketch. They were similar but not quite the same. She must have doodled this as a study for the portrait. The sketch of Tyler looked shyer, less confident than the end product, but he was still smiling.

It was strange to be surrounded by himself. Creepy. He turned the page, only to find another Tyler there as well.

Chase had drawn him in profile this time, his eyes fixed ahead of him, his mouth set in a thin line, his eyelids drooping. This must have been from their first day in the car, before he agreed to nap and let her drive. This version of himself looked determined despite the odds.

The next page was an illustration of him standing before the twine ball in Cawker City. Chase had captured the object's sheer mass and Tyler's look of undisguised dismay as he stood in its shadow. This was followed by an angry Tyler, presumably sketched during the fallout of their argument in the car as they sped away from the scene of the twine-based crime. This was followed by a desperate-looking Tyler standing on the edge of a bridge, looking down over the railing.

She hadn't just captured his face. She hadn't stopped at conveying his emotions. What she had sketched was a *feeling*, and there was no disappointment there at all. Seen through her eyes, Tyler was a stranger to himself.

Her words came rushing back. *I'm not trying to change you. I'm trying to convince you that the person you are is great, and that you don't need to be so afraid of what other people think.* Chase had spent this whole trip drawing the spark between them. His body, her pencil. His face, her filter. The Tyler on the page wasn't a coward. He wasn't a loser or a disappointment.

When she looked at him, she saw all the bravery, stubbornness, and passion that she'd captured on paper.

He kept turning the pages, finding more and more of his emotions captured on the page: his vulnerable expression from the night in the car when he'd dared her to kiss him; his despair after the car accident; his bravado at the farmers' market; his sleeping form on the cramped cot from their stay in the church; his punchy laughter from the last stretch of the drive into the city.

She had been watching him this whole time. Seeing him, in his entirety.

And she was still there.

Tyler slammed the notebook shut. Very slowly, he lowered his eyes to the painting. The naked, exposed, and almost beatific Tyler on the pavement only smiled. The real Tyler narrowed his eyes. Chase had made him look brave but vulnerable, shy but certain, wary but curious. He wished he could be the man she believed he was.

"What would *you* do?" he asked the painting.

On the phone this morning, Xavier had made a clear distinction between bullying and encouragement: *If she pushes you, and you realize that you need that push? Be bold, my dude.*

Chase could have kept the painting in the show against his will, but she hadn't. She had respected his choice.

Well, a guy was allowed to change his mind, wasn't he?

When they'd played *Would You Rather*, Chase had told him that the fun of the game wasn't about making the easy choice. *Would you rather be the person you're afraid that you are? Or the person you wish you could be?*

After a moment's consideration, Tyler discovered he didn't need advice from the painting. He'd sat for it himself: ten long, chilly hours under Chase's watchful eye. The portrait wasn't just Tyler—it was the man that Chase saw when she looked at him.

A man who was nervous under pressure. A guy who was scared of unknowns, and girls, and asking strangers for directions on the Metro.

A guy who would jump off a bridge without a second thought if he saw his friend floundering in the eddies below.

"You're right," Tyler told the portrait. "We can do this." He unlocked the car, dumped Chase's bag in the back seat, and got to work.

CHASE

The gallery was filling up with chatting people who milled about as they examined the portraits. Chase shot a weary glance toward the bare spot on the wall where her painting had been displayed. The little tag still proudly announced her name alongside a QR code.

Chase was trying her hardest not to care.

It had been so long since she had called Sarah on anything but her cell phone that Chase had to rack her brain to remember the area code for Boulder. After that, it was anybody's guess. There was a six somewhere in there. Or was it a nine? And did the eight come before the three, or after?

Chase tried a handful of wrong numbers—all of which went to voicemail, thank God—before she finally reached Sarah's phone. It rang through to voicemail too; of course, Sarah would probably see an unknown number and assume it was spam.

At the sound of the tone, Chase sighed. What was she supposed to say about the last few days? There was no easy way to summarize everything that had happened since the last time they'd spoken.

She settled on being direct. "Hey, sis, it's Chase. I'm stranded in

NYC with no phone, no ID, and no credit card. Hoping you can help. Call me back at this number. Love you."

She hung up and stared down at the phone. If Sarah had left the house without her cell on her, or if something was wrong with one of the boys, it could be hours before she replied. Maybe Tyler would have better luck. Chase should reach out to someone else in the meantime, but she drew a total blank on who that could be. She dreaded calling her mother, but if it came down to it . . .

Well, she'd bitten the bullet once today. A second time couldn't hurt.

She was still mad at Tyler—mostly for the way he'd blamed all their troubles on her—but at this point, she was just tired. They could probably make it back to Denver without killing each other. Maybe they'd even stop and visit Dean and Jo Beth on the way.

And in a few months, the magazine would come out, and Chase would get to read about the lucky artist who'd won the ten-thousand-dollar grand prize.

Mercifully, the ringing phone knocked her out of her internal funk, and Chase snatched it up. "Sarah?"

"What are you doing in New York?" Sarah demanded. "Are you okay? Are you hurt? Where's your wallet?"

"Long story," Chase began. "Okay? Yes. Hurt? No. And the last I saw, my wallet was in my handbag floating down the Kansas River." She pinched the bridge of her nose. Sarah's familiar voice left her feeling homesick and more vulnerable than ever. "I'm really sorry to ask, but is there any way you can lend me some money?"

"Oh, no," Sarah said in that brusque big-sister voice that she employed when Chase had done something irresponsible. "You're going to have to let me in on a *little* more detail than that. What *happened?*"

"Long story," Chase mumbled.

Sarah snorted. "I've got time."

Chase filled her in on the broad strokes of their adventure, ignoring her sister's little sounds of shock as each new detail was revealed.

" . . . and that, long story short, is how I nearly died several times in the attempt to make sure that I wasn't awarded a boatload of money," Chase finished.

Sarah whistled. "So, let me get this straight. You could have kept your piece in the show, blamed it on someone else, and still been in line for that cash . . . and you just . . . *didn't?*"

"Yeah." Chase laughed. "I know, right? But I didn't think I could live with myself if I did something crappy like that. Not to anybody, but *especially* not to Tyler." If she'd ever doubted that, the look of relief on his face when he'd stumbled into the office put her mind at ease.

"Hell, yes," Sarah said. "You did the right thing, sis."

"For Tyler," Chase agreed. She flicked her finger against the corner of the desk.

"And for you," Sarah said. "Chase, honey, I'm really proud of you."

"Well, tell that to my student loans," Chase said, but for the first time since she'd insisted that Marcel pull the portrait from the newsletter, she felt something other than sick to her stomach.

"Sooo . . ." Sarah's voice took on a softer, gossipy lilt. "This Tyler guy . . . It sounds as if you really like him?"

"Yeah. I guess I do. He's quiet and super shy, but . . . well, we'll see. I was mad at him earlier, but the more I think about it, we're both hot messes." Chase pressed her palm to her forehead, willing herself not to cry. "You want to know the really stupid part? I didn't bring the other painting."

"Which painting?" Sarah asked, confused.

"The one I meant to enter—the one I thought Roberts was sending in." Chase groaned at the thought. "I could have switched them. Marcel could have put the *other* one in the show. Then I would still have had something on offer, even if it wasn't as good. I guess that's what I get for not planning ahead."

"You'll learn," Sarah assured her.

"So I'm told. All the same, I wish I'd never taken this stupid life-drawing class."

There was a collective gasp from the main gallery, and the chatter abruptly ceased. Chase peered out into the main part of the room through the office window, and the rest of her words evaporated.

Tyler stood in the entrance to the gallery, his eyes narrowed and his jaw set. He was paler than Chase had ever seen him. The knuckles of his hands, still spattered with mint-green paint from his onslaught against the gallery window, were clenched tightly around the frame held in front of him just below his chest, from which his portrait smiled out at the audience. The bottom edge of the frame banged into his knees with each step.

He was breathing hard, covered in sweat, trembling with boldness. And he was naked.

"Chase?" Sarah asked from the receiver as it slipped through her fingers. She fumbled for it, catching it just before it hit the floor.

"Call-you-back-gotta-go-bye," Chase blurted before thrusting the phone back onto its cradle and darting out into the gallery proper.

"My goodness," Marcel murmured to Chase as she approached. "Your model seems to have taken matters into his own hands, hasn't he?"

"He's going to get arrested again," Chase said in wonder, not sure what else to say. "Sorry about this."

"Are you kidding?" Marcel asked, clearly delighted. "This is more fun than I've had in *years*."

Tyler stepped farther into the room. His legs poked out beneath the gilded frame, which was large enough to cover him from his neck to his knees. He was still wearing his paint-stained work boots and socks. As he walked toward her, a few of the other guests turned to sneak a glance at his backside. An older woman in a sheath dress pulled out her phone and snapped a picture, grinning gleefully. She immediately began typing something up. Others followed suit, and the swell of chatter rose again, all focused on Tyler this time.

Poor Tyler, Chase thought, before realizing he had chosen this particular course of action. Chase would never have asked anything like this of him.

Tyler's brown eyes were fixed on her face, and as he approached, his stride became more confident. She could feel something crackling in the air between them—the same bright, electric energy that filled the portrait, the same sharp pop of chemistry that she'd felt when she kissed him.

"Tyler?" she asked.

Marcel leaned toward her ear, not looking away from Tyler. "Don't let this one get away."

Tyler finally reached the easel where the painting had rested and lifted it back into place. Chase braced herself as he adjusted his grip on the frame, and let out a little relieved sigh when she realized he was still wearing boxers. Maybe they wouldn't have round two with Florence after all.

Once the portrait was safely settled on the wall, Tyler stepped back and turned toward the crowd.

"Sorry about removing this earlier," he told the room. "My mistake. This piece definitely belongs in the show."

The older woman who'd taken the first photo whistled, and Marcel let out an enthusiastic burst of applause. Other people joined in, some of them laughing. Tyler glanced between Chase and the crowd as his ears began to turn pink, which only egged people on. She could see his hands shaking, but he dipped into a low bow, channeling a little of the showmanship that he'd exhibited at the farmers' market.

As for Chase, she couldn't take her eyes off him. She'd spent hours staring at him, both dressed and undressed. Her eyes had traveled over his planes and angles dozens, if not hundreds, of times. Every other time she'd seen him this close to naked, however, she'd made sure she was *observing*.

This time, she was definitely *ogling*.

Marcel, who clearly had a lot more experience with this sort of crowd, stepped up and put his arm around Tyler.

"Welcome, ladies and gentlemen!" he exclaimed. "I hope you've enjoyed the entertainment. And with that, the judging for this year's competition will commence!" He slapped Tyler on the back, then turned to Chase and widened his eyes significantly. *Now this is art!* he mouthed with a wink before meandering off to mingle with the crowd once more.

Apparently, New Yorkers didn't find a mostly naked man all that shocking. Within moments, people went right back to chatting amongst themselves, pointing at the various paintings in turn.

"They must really have liked this one," said a nearby gentleman to his friend, gesturing to Chase's piece. "The banner, and now this little stunt . . ."

"Well, it *is* a remarkable piece, isn't it?" his friend replied.

Chase hadn't moved from her spot, and Tyler was still standing by the portrait, each of them stationary islands amidst the tide of people milling around them. At last, Tyler abandoned his post, weaving through the press of art enthusiasts to reach her side.

"Hey," he said. "Listen, Chase, I—"

Chase didn't wait for him to continue. Instead, she dragged Tyler back into the unlocked office. The tall window didn't offer them much privacy, but at least they'd be able to talk without being overheard.

"What was that?" she asked, gesturing to his mostly naked body. "What is *this*?"

Tyler was breathing hard. She could see the unsteady rise and fall of his well-defined chest, and she wanted to comfort him, to talk him down. *Name five things you hear*, she almost said.

"I wanted people to see," Tyler mumbled.

Chase crossed her arms and smirked. "You wanted people to see your *boxers*?"

Tyler shook his head and laughed self-consciously, but he stood his ground. "No. I wanted people to see what a freaking fantastic artist you are. And I wanted you to know that I didn't just chicken out, or do what I thought would make you happy. I could have just told Marcel to put the painting back in the show, but I guess I also wanted to show you that I'm not just reckless when I'm scared." He lifted his eyebrows hopefully, running his paint-stained fingers through his rumpled hair.

Chase couldn't stop her mouth from twitching. "Some cougar snapped a picture of your ass."

Tyler coughed into his fist. "I saw that."

"At least it was covered."

Tyler nodded down at himself. "I would have gone the full monty, but I was afraid I'd be in cuffs before I made the front door."

"I'm pretty sure that Marcel considers the portrait open for judging now."

"I know." His eyes met hers, and for once he didn't look away. "That's the point."

"And someone's probably going to write a viral Twitter thread about this," Chase added. "Possibly the same woman who was so eagerly snapping photos of your . . . *assets.*"

"I know that too," Tyler said. He finally managed to meet her eyes again, and when he did, he sighed deeply. His shoulders relaxed. "But I really don't care what the audience thinks, or even what Twitter thinks. What about *you?*"

"What do *I* think?" Chase finally let her grin overtake her face. "I think I could kiss you all over."

The color rose in Tyler's face and neck, but he smiled too. He was only a pastel pink this time; apparently, the idea of kissing Chase had grown on him with time. "I don't know. I'm mostly naked, and there's a whole gallery of people on the other side of a glass door."

Chase relented. "If it makes you uncomfortable, I . . ."

She didn't get to finish the sentence. Tyler reached for her, pulling her into his arms and pressing his lips to hers. Chase's hands landed on his chest, and she startled at the warm press of his skin. Looking was great, she discovered, but touching him was better. One of Tyler's hands settled in her hair, and the other pressed to the small of her back. Chase let out a breathy sigh against his lips.

Given that this was only his second kiss of all time, Tyler was shaping up to be a prodigy.

When they finally broke apart, Tyler nearly toppled over. "Sorry," he gasped. "Low blood sugar. I haven't eaten in *ages.*"

"Mm-hmm," Chase replied, letting her fingertips rest against her mouth as she swayed on her tired feet. *That wasn't low blood sugar, Tyler. That was life-altering chemistry.*

Chase caught a flash of movement through the window. The older woman who had been scoping out Tyler gave Chase a thumbs up and blew a kiss through the window before sailing off into the crowd.

"We should do that more often," Tyler said.

"For sure." Chase laughed. "I mean, Xavier did have the foresight to pack us fifty-six condoms."

Tyler choked.

"Kidding," she said, patting his back. His skin was hot to the touch, as if he'd been set on fire with that kiss.

Relatable.

Tyler leaned toward her until their shoulders brushed. "I know. I'm still getting used to your sense of humor."

"Oh, honey, I've *really* been toning it down for you until now," she said, batting her eyelashes. "But you've raised the bar with your apology-exhibitionism. I'm *definitely* not going to hold back on the innuendos now."

"Maybe you can amp your jokes up gradually," he suggested. "You know, over time."

His expression was so hopeful that Chase couldn't stop herself from throwing her arm around his neck and pulling him down so she could kiss his cheek.

"Of course," she said. "We can take things slow. I'm in no rush. After all, I think you're going to have a hard time getting rid of me now."

Tyler put one hand on her cheek. "I hate to ask you for a favor, but I really need you to do something for me, if that's okay?"

"Anything," she said.

Tyler winced. "Could you, um, go back and grab my pants from the car? I was in kind of a rush, and I just tossed them in the back seat without thinking."

Chase laughed so hard she snorted. "You don't want to walk around like this for the rest of the day?" she asked, looking down at his boxers. She'd been keeping her eyes north of the equator so she didn't embarrass him further, but now she gave into temptation. His boxers were navy blue with a Baby Yoda print.

"These were a gag gift from Xavier," he groaned, covering his eyes.

"Twitter is going to love it," she assured him. "Do you want to stay back here until I can get your clothes from the car?"

"Actually," Tyler said, "I was hoping to find out who won."

Sure enough, the cluster of visitors faced one wall of the gallery, their eyes fixed on Marcel. He seemed to be gearing up for an important announcement.

"Shall I relay the final tally?" Chase asked.

"Nah." Tyler looked down at himself. "The folks in here have already seen everything, and the walls are glass. I might as well go out with you."

Chase took one of his hands in hers. "Come on, then, my knight in shining Yodas. Let's go see what the results say."

TYLER

"You weren't kidding—your girlfriend *is* good at this." Dalton Young strolled up beside Tyler and crossed his arms, watching as Chase put the finishing touches on the side of the big rig.

Tyler nodded, smiling up dreamily at Chase. *My girlfriend.* They'd only been official for a couple of days, but he had a feeling the glow wouldn't wear off anytime soon.

They'd taken an alternate route home, just to mix things up, and Chase had happened to spot a flyer on their way through Davenport, Iowa. She'd insisted on staying in town that night for the show. To Tyler's delight, he'd recognized the ringmaster as a fellow exile to the singletons table at the disastrous Cartwright wedding. Dalton had exchanged his cheap suit for a sumptuous velvet coat decorated to look like the night sky, and capped it with a black silk top hat that gleamed against his onyx skin.

"I like her version of the logo better than the one *I* designed," Dalton said. "What happened to you not being able to talk to girls?"

"I made an exception," Tyler said.

Dalton shook his head knowingly. "You're going to break that vow in a hot minute, aren't you?"

That night in the church, Chase had bad-mouthed the idea of

rushing into marriage at the earliest possible opportunity—but when it came to Chase, Tyler wasn't ruling anything out.

"Maybe," he said shyly. "I guess we'll see."

A burly bald man in gold shorts came lumbering across the fairway toward Dalton. "Boss? We've got a bit of a problem."

"Don't we always?" Dalton replied. His tone suggested that chaos was as plentiful as circus acts around there. "Who's unhappy now?"

"The clowns." The big man rubbed his hands together nervously. "It sounds like there's a problem with the makeup? I didn't really understand."

"What did I tell you?" Dalton asked, winking at Tyler and tipping his oversized hat. "Managing these clowns is a full-time job." He swept away, and the big man followed in his wake.

Tyler turned back to Chase, who had climbed back down the ladder and was in the process of capping her paints.

"What do you think?" she asked proudly. "Is this adequate payment for your friend's hospitality last night?"

"I think it's amazing." Tyler beamed up at the side of the big rig, where the words *Second Galaxy Big Top* stood out amidst a scattering of stars, planets, and whirling galaxies. It was breathtaking.

As they stood there admiring her work, Tyler wrapped one arm around her shoulders. It was becoming easier to touch her casually, and Tyler had stopped worrying that she'd get upset over little displays of public affection. In fact, she seemed to like them.

Chase leaned in to kiss his cheek. "We should get going, then, don't you think? We're still three hundred miles from home, and one of these days, your boss is going to follow through on the threat to fire you."

They walked back to the car, pointing out the various little tents as they passed.

"We should have gotten our palms read." Chase sighed. "Or at least our tarot cards."

Tyler shook his head firmly. "No way. If something terrible is going to happen, I'd rather not know ahead of time."

Chase elbowed him. "What if there's something good on the horizon?"

"Then it will have to be a pleasant surprise." Honestly, though, Tyler was pretty sure the good surprise was already happening.

They said goodbye to Dalton, waved to the rest of the circus troupe, and got back into the car. It was Tyler's turn to drive this time, and Chase leaned the passenger seat all the way back with a contented sigh.

Just to mess with her, Tyler turned on the radio, flipping through the frequencies until he found the local country station. Chase groaned and covered her face with her sweatshirt. "*Nooo!*"

"I can change it," Tyler offered.

"You might as well leave it," Chase said, her voice muffled by the sweatshirt. "Just keep in mind that when it's my turn to drive, *I* pick the tunes."

They left the circus behind and drove until nightfall. *Never Have I Ever* and *Would You Rather* gave way to an unexpectedly heartfelt game of twenty questions. When they stopped to refill the tank, Chase stole the keys and got behind the wheel. She then subjected Tyler to almost an hour of pop songs belted at maximum volume and accompanied by as much dancing as was possible for the driver of a compact car. Tyler laughed so hard that tears filled his eyes.

They stopped for dinner at a diner outside of Omaha. Tyler happened to look down at the local map that was printed on their placemats and broke into a grin.

"If you want, we can leave I-80 and head south on I-29," he suggested. "Visit Topeka again."

"Keep talking like that and I'm gonna steal the car while you're in the restroom," Chase replied.

"You couldn't leave me," Tyler informed her. "You like me too much."

Chase sighed dramatically. "Unfortunately, that is correct."

That night, they parked the car in the lot of a small park overlooking the Missouri River and settled down into the back seat together.

"Did you see a ranger station?" Tyler asked, looking around suspiciously. "I don't want to get kicked out of another park."

"Why?" Chase pulled him closer. "Are you planning on disturbing the peace?"

He kissed her, laughing against her lips. "No, but I don't think you can help yourself. You're a menace to decent society."

Chase snorted and settled down beside him. "And don't you forget it."

When he'd even bothered to imagine what it would be like to fall asleep beside someone he liked, Tyler had pictured himself in a big bed with heavy covers and at least one comfortable pillow. He hadn't imagined his future girlfriend would smell slightly of paint fumes and diner cuisine, or that her elbows would be *quite* so sharp. There wasn't enough room for them both to lie side-by-side, so Tyler rolled onto his side the way he had on the night of their first kiss. Chase fidgeted around for a while, flopping this way and that, until she seemed to decide that she'd be happiest as the little spoon. Her long, loose hair stuck to Tyler's face, tickling his nose.

"This can't be comfortable for you," she said. "Maybe we should find a hotel."

The seatbelt holder stabbed Tyler's lower back, and his legs had already begun to cramp. "It's perfect," he said, reaching for the sleeping bag. He tucked its unzipped ends around them, then maneuvered his right arm so both he and Chase could use it as a pillow.

Even contorted into an unfortunate pretzel, it didn't take him long to fall asleep.

Three Months Later . . .

Tyler dropped his tray onto the table and slid into the chair across from Xavier.

"Did you give Chase the slip?" Xavier asked, pretending to look around.

"She's still getting her food. She told me not to wait." Tyler peeled the plastic wrapper off his fork. "Good week?"

"Having a girlfriend has made you so chipper," Xavier grumbled. "Just because you're obnoxiously happy all the time doesn't mean the rest of us are."

"Aww, are you sulking?" Chase asked as she pulled out the chair next to Tyler. "Why are you such a grump today?" As she sat down, she leaned in and lowered her voice. "It wouldn't happen to have anything to do with that rude girl running the cash register, would it?"

Xavier ducked his head. "Jenna? Yeah, we went out on one awful date, and now I have to avoid her line forever."

"At least she didn't take out an actual restraining order on you," Tyler said cheerfully. "Although I *do* think that she whispered a hex when you walked by."

"Dude." Xavier held out his hands in a gesture of betrayed dismay. "Low blow. Don't mock the singletons. We deserve your compassion."

"If I'm going to feel sorry for anyone, it's definitely Jenna," Tyler teased.

Xavier narrowed his eyes. "It's one thing when you make fun of me, but when you make fun of me *in front of your girlfriend*, it's a violation of bro code. I could have you reported."

"Well, maybe this will cheer you up, Xav." Chase dug through her backpack and produced a pamphlet with a shiny laminated cover. She held it up with the cover facing her chest and winked at Tyler. "I just got my copy today."

Tyler's cheeks heated up in spite of himself. "Put that away."

Xavier picked up on Tyler's tone and immediately brightened. "Ooh, what's this? Blackmail material?"

"Don't sound so hopeful," Tyler groaned.

"It's not blackmail material," Chase said defensively. "It's *art*."

Xavier's eyes widened in glee. "No . . . dude, is this your nudie? Are you a cover girl now? I kept hoping I'd see you go viral on the Twittersphere, but no such luck."

Tyler groaned and hid his face in his hands as Chase began jabbing him with her elbow.

"Can I show him?" she begged.

"Why would you do this to me?" he moaned.

"Bro, you gotta show me," Xavier said. "This whole nudie thing is the reason you two got together! And who was responsible for that?" He gestured furiously at himself with both thumbs. "Who was that handsome, charismatic fellow to whom you two both owe your disgustingly happy relationship?"

Tyler sighed in defeat.

"I want to hear you say it!" Xavier insisted.

"It was you, Xav," Chase said, fluttering her eyelashes. "You are that handsome, charismatic, *genius* friend. We are in your debt. We are not worthy." She mimed a low bow, still clutching the magazine to her chest with one hand.

"See? The lady gets it." Xavier nodded to Chase, like a king accepting his rightful tribute.

Tyler had known from the beginning that putting Chase and Xavier in a room together would spell trouble, but there wasn't much he could do about it now.

"Fine," he said, still blushing. "Show him. But I swear to God, Xavier, if you make fun of me . . ."

Xavier rubbed his hands together, grinning wickedly. "Oh ho ho, I can't wait. I'm *never* going to let you live this down. Show me his butt, Chase! I want to see his butt!"

Two girls at the neighboring table looked over in surprise. They muttered something to each other and hid their smiles behind their hands. Xavier turned and winked at them, not the least bit ashamed. Last spring, Tyler would have all but died of embarrassment, but now he only waved, shaking his head and shrugging as if to ask, *What can you do?*

"Please let me show him," Chase begged.

Tyler held up his hands. "All right, Xavier, you win. I can't deny the pleading of a tragic singleton."

Xavier made a rude gesture, using his body to block it from the girls at the next table. "Cold, my dude. Ice cold."

Chase laid the magazine down triumphantly. "Well? What do you think?"

Xavier leaned forward. When he saw the cover, however, he groaned in disappointment. "The magazine's name is printed over the good bits! How am I supposed to blackmail you with *this*? It's just a really flattering ab pic. Lame."

Tyler glanced down at the now-familiar portrait with the words *This Year's First-Place Winner* emblazoned across the top. Xavier was right: his nether regions were tastefully obscured by the layout. "I guess you'll never get to see it."

Xavier looked up. "You should show me the original."

"No way." Chase grinned, looping her arm through Tyler's and resting her head on his shoulder. PDA always pushed Xavier's buttons. "That's private."

"Anyhow, you've got your proof." Tyler waved at the cover. "I hope you're happy."

Xavier shook his head in disgust. "I still can't believe that some art gallery shelled out ten thousand bucks for a picture of your ass. Hey, Chase, you want to paint me? I bet you could get twenty grand for a piece of this." He stood partway up, wiggling suggestively. "I'd even go full-frontal."

Chase released Tyler and reached for her slice of veggie pizza. "Nah, I'm pretty sure I'd have to *pay* people to look at that."

Xavier's eyes twitched, and he turned back to Tyler. "Dude, your girl is *brutal*. She has no idea what a hot commodity I am." He twisted in his seat to look over at the two co-eds who were still sitting at the neighboring table, flashing them a cheeky smile. He swept the magazine up, collected his tray, and got to his feet. "Hello, ladies," he said as he left Tyler and Chase behind. "I need your opinion on something . . ."

Chase nibbled the end of her pizza, watching him go. "Twenty bucks says that they'll give him a fake number when he asks."

Tyler snorted and stabbed his fork into his salad. "No bet. The guy needs to learn when to go for it, and when to rein it in." He saw

Chase's smirk but ignored it. Their trip to New York felt like a life-time ago. Had he ever really been that much of a mess?

To his surprise, the girls were still talking to Xavier, who was waving the magazine in front of them while gesturing to Tyler. The girls burst out laughing.

He's made my portrait his wingman, Tyler thought. Even for Xavier, that was a new one.

"What do you think?" Chase asked, watching as Xavier tried to flirt with two girls at the same time. "Are you going to tell him that the full photo is still posted on the gallery's website?"

Tyler shook his head adamantly. "Not a chance in hell. But I'm really proud of you, Chase. You deserved first place."

"*We* deserved first place." She jostled him with her elbow until he smiled. "And I'm really glad you're taking this all in stride."

Watching his best friend brandish the portrait at a couple of strangers felt weird, but Tyler was surprised at how little it bothered him. Maybe it was the fact that, compared to standing in his under-wear in front of a gathering of New York City socialites, this was nothing much.

Or maybe it was the fact that he had Chase sitting next to him, right where she belonged.

"Are you excited about meeting Sarah next weekend?" she asked as she twisted the top off her water bottle.

"A little nervous, actually," he admitted. "I mean, it's the first time I'll have met any of your family."

Chase waved her slice of pizza dismissively. "Oh, don't worry, my sister's going to love you. If she gets too intimidating, you can always entertain Justin and Tim for half an hour. You'll get major brownie points for any scrap of free time you can provide."

Tyler had never had a girlfriend before, which meant he'd never had to meet his girlfriend's family before. He was pretty sure there was supposed to be some kind of ritual involving a front porch, rocking chairs, and a loaded shotgun, but that wasn't what worried him. He didn't simply want her family to like him; he wanted to fit in.

He kept remembering their dinner with Pastor Dean's family in Ohio and how Chase had looked like his future.

If Tyler was going to break the Unwedding Vow for anyone, Chase was it.

"I'll try not to overthink it," he assured her.

"Good." She took a swig of water. "If you go with your gut, you'll do fine."

He believed her. Sometimes it was better to cling to safety for the sake of knowing where he stood.

Other times, it was worth taking the leap.

EPILOGUE

C hase had spent the last two weeks watching eels and sea turtles swim from one end of the massive saltwater tank to the other, and she was ninety-nine percent sure she could make it through the afternoon without having a panic attack.

"You missed a real opportunity for a beachside ceremony," Sarah said as she finished braiding Chase's hair and began the process of pinning it up around her sister's head.

"Nobody likes a destination wedding," Chase said. "It's too expensive. And besides, what would everyone have done? Sat on the beach while we swam out into the surf? This way, we get to check an item off of our bucket list, people can actually see us during the ceremony, and the kids have something to do afterward."

"Mom's going crazy about the fact that you came up with this whole thing." Sarah chuckled. "She was having a fit about the pictures earlier—I guess the fact that you'll have wet hair in the reception photos is a signifier that the end times are upon us."

Chase bit back a laugh. "Where is Mom, anyway?"

"I asked her to keep an eye on the boys until the ceremony's over, but I'm sure she'll be all over you at the reception. Do you want makeup?"

Chase shook her head. "It'll just wash off." She got to her feet, admiring the soft lilac material of her dress. She'd picked it up at the thrift store; she had another, nicer dress that she would change into before the reception, but she liked the color of this one. "Is it time?"

"Almost." Sarah held out her arm. "Let's get you suited up."

Tyler had been the first one to joke about having an underwater wedding, but it had been Chase's idea to hold the event in the Denver Aquarium. He'd been quietly spiraling with every mention of having to get up in front of everyone and say his vows—but in the dive gear, he *couldn't* talk even if he'd wanted to. In Chase's mind, it didn't quite count as scuba diving, but they'd both had to get certified in order to participate, and it was as close to the ocean as Chase planned to get anytime soon.

Sarah led her out to the edge of the enormous tank where Tyler and Xavier were already waiting. Tyler was sitting next to the wall, his head in his hands, but when he saw Chase, he leaped to his feet.

"Getting cold feet?" she teased, standing up on her toes to kiss him. The rest of their friends and family were on the floor below, no doubt settling into their chairs from where they'd be able to see the ceremony and read the vow placards that Chase and Tyler had designed together.

"Never." He wrapped his arms around her, pulling her close. "Just, you know . . ."

Chase lifted a knowing eyebrow. "Making a list of everything that could go wrong?"

"She's got your number." Xavier chuckled.

"Well, duh." Tyler smiled over his shoulder. "I'm not going to break the Unwedding Vow for just *anyone*."

"Break the what now?" Xavier asked quizzically.

"A silly vow I took with some of the other guests at a wedding a couple of years ago. It's old news now." Tyler turned back to Chase. "I'll introduce you to everyone at the reception."

She brushed a soft kiss against his cheek. "I'll have to apologize to them for making you break your oath."

"Trust me," he assured her, "I don't regret it for a minute."

A neoprene-clad figure stood at the edge of the tank, and he waved to Chase as the couple approached. "I'm going to get settled in," Pastor Dean said, sliding his mask down over his face and making his voice muffled and nasal. "The ceremony starts in ten minutes."

"Thanks for coming all the way out here to do this," Chase said. "I know it's a little odd . . . "

"Jesus was a fisherman. I'm sure he'd approve." Dean winked at Chase, then slapped his regulator into his mouth before shuffling forward and dropping into the water below.

Chase was sure her mother would have preferred a stately walk down the aisle, a tearful exchange of vows, and a chaste but heartfelt kiss at the altar. There was nothing stately about shrugging into a BCD, checking to make sure their tanks were open, and pulling on dive masks, but Chase couldn't help feeling that the awkward shuffling and careful checking and rechecking of each other's gear was probably a much better indication of their partnership, anyway. Besides, finesse had never really been Chase's style. Her mother would have been disappointed either way, so why not do what felt right?

The pair of them shuffled to the edge of the tank, letting the tips of their fins dangle over the water. Chase stared down into the murky blue depths and swallowed hard. There were eels down there. And stingrays. In only a couple of minutes, she'd be under the surface, breathing canned air.

Then Tyler shuffled up beside her and slipped his fingers between hers. "Are you okay?" he asked quietly. "We don't have to do this. We could still make a getaway out the back entrance and have a Vegas wedding."

Chase laughed as the tension instantly drained from her shoulders. "Vegas? That doesn't seem like your kind of place."

Tyler shrugged. "I've always wanted to meet Elvis."

"I'm good. I was only looking."

Tyler squeezed her hand. "You seemed a little scared."

"A little," Chase admitted. "But I think I'm supposed to be."

"It's time," said Sarah. Sure enough, Dean was waving up at them from the sandy bed of the oceanic display, and the aquarium staff was all in place. If something went wrong, they'd be fine.

"I love you," Chase said, lifting her regulator to her lips.

Tyler squeezed her hand. "I love you, too. See you on the other side."

Chase took a deep breath through her reg and closed her eyes. They stepped off the edge of the tank at the exact same time, and as the cold saltwater of the tank closed over her head, Chase discovered she wasn't as afraid as she thought she would be.

In fact, she was looking forward to whatever happened next.

The authors would like to thank you for reading the first in the Unwedding Vow series. You can get the next book here: Under a Big Top.

Dalton Young—ringmaster of the financially strapped Second

Galaxy Circus—has a lot on his spinning plates. Broken equipment, injured performers, and investors breathing down his neck threaten to crater everything he's built. Still, he continues to do it all on his own. Partnerships, after all, always end with someone broke or broken. And he should know—ten years ago, the love of his life never boarded the bus heading toward their mutual dream of performing in the circus.

Penelope Baker—a tame, methodical accountant for a prestigious investment firm—made the mistake of admitting she almost ran off with the circus in her youth, and now her boss has assigned her the bothersome task of auditing their riskiest investment: The Second Galaxy Circus. Taking the job will only remind her of the chaotic road she almost traveled. She decides to do the work as quickly and efficiently as possible so she can get back to her stable and routine life.

Things unravel the moment Dalton and Penelope come face to face with each other and their connected past. She was the girl who never showed, and he was the boy left waiting. Yet, just like the name of his circus, maybe they have a second chance at love under a big top.

Help us keep the series going by leaving feedback here: InBroadStrokes. Don't want to miss any of our coming titles? Sign up for our newsletter here: JordanRileySwan

ACKNOWLEDGMENTS

From K. C. Norton:

I would like to thank the Allies in Wonderland and the Darling Assassins (especially the Birches) for giving me the writers' community that pressed me to find my own voice. There's nothing like being inserted into a choreographed dance number—with costumes!—within thirty seconds of meeting your tribe.

My advisors at VCFA urged me to extend my boundaries, and I feel special gratitude toward Rigoberto González for encouraging me to divert from my original course. "You belong somewhere but don't belong here" is a sentiment I've been on the receiving end of many times in my life, but in this case you were absolutely right, and I couldn't be more grateful for that nudge to step out of my comfort zone and into the place I belonged.

Getting to know the entire Story Garden team has been a delight, and I can't wait to see where we go from here.

And finally, thank you to my parents, who have provided feedback since I was banging out manuscripts on our original monochrome Macintosh. You made me this way. It's your fault that I have too many houseplants, and you know it.

From Jordan Riley Swan:

I give my thanks to all the usual suspects: Amy and Ami for our long bouts of plotting—I owe them so much; Diane Callahan, Story Garden's lead editor, who always puts a gun to my head and forces me to craft the best stories possible; and my mom for giving birth to me despite knowing this is where I'd end up. My other partner in crime—Bruce—was there to help till the garden since this story seed was planted.

We have an amazing team over here at Story Garden. I couldn't ask for a more creative and reliable co-writer than K. C. Norton, who tackled every challenge with gusto. Many thanks to Angela Traficante of Lambda Editing, whose developmental feedback brought the "rom" to the "com" in our romantic comedy series. We're grateful for Lia Fairchild's thorough copy editing. Our compliments also go out to the book cover chef James T. Egan of Bookfly Design, who can finally add *In Broad Strokes* to his extensive portfolio.

We can't wait to share the rest of the stories in the Unwedding Vow series—our "Marvel Cinematic Universe" of romcoms. And thank you, dear reader, for reading until the very last line.

Made in the USA
Monee, IL
02 August 2023

40272613R00143